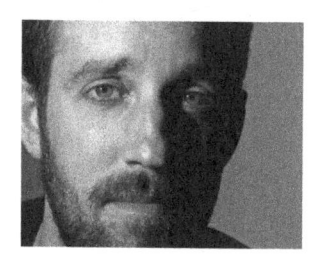

Andrew Blackman is 36 and is the author of *On the Holloway Road*, published by Legend Press in 2009. The book won the Luke Bitmead Writer's Bursary and was shortlisted for the Dundee International Book Prize.

Blackman lives in the UK, but previously spent six years in New York, where he worked as a staff reporter for the *Wall Street Journal*. His work has also been published in *Monthly Review*, the *Cincinnati Post*, *Pittsburgh Post-Gazette*, *Seattle Times*, *Tampa Tribune*, *Toronto's Globe* and *Mail*, *Post Road*, *Carillon*, *Smoke*, and in books by Twenty Stories Publishing, Greenacre Writers and Leaf Books, and he won the 2004 Daniel Singer essay prize. Andrew has a degree in modern history from Oxford University and a Master's in journalism from Columbia University.

Visit Andrew at **www.andrewblackman.net**

Legend Press Ltd, 2 London Wall Buildings,
London EC2M 5UU
info@legend-paperbooks.co.uk
www.legendpress.co.uk

Contents © Andrew Blackman 2013

The right of the above author to be identified as the author of this work has been asserted in accordance with the Copyright, Designs and Patent Act 1988.

British Library Cataloguing in Publication Data available.

Print ISBN 978-1-9090394-5-2

Set in Times
Printed by CPI Group (UK) Ltd, Croydon, CR0 4YY

Cover design by Gudrun Jobst
www.yotedesign.com

All rights reserved. No part of this publication may be reproduced, stored in or introduced into a retrieval system, or transmitted, in any form, or by any means electronic, mechanical, photocopying, recording or otherwise, without the prior permission of the publisher. Any person who commits any unauthorised act in relation to this publication may be liable to criminal prosecution and civil claims for damages.

Legend Press
Independent Book Publisher

a virtual love

Andrew Blackman

Legend Press
Independent Book Publisher

Praise for Andrew's writing

A Virtual Love

'A compelling tale, told from several perspectives, about the identity that people project about themselves in the social media world and the real life identity that we all cannot escape from. A fascinating, modern story that had me gripped.' Award-winning author Alex Wheatle MBE

'A compelling and very entertaining look at the complexities of our hyper-real age, an insightful and witty exploration of the disconnect between image and reality, truth and appearance and whether love and sincere sentiment can overcome the short term thrills of social media.' James Miller

On the Holloway Road

Winner of the 2008 Luke Bitmead Writer's Bursary.
Short-listed for the Dundee International book prize.

'A beautifully written story about friendship and the longing for adventure in an increasingly demystified world, and the eternal question of what life is all about.' Zoë Jenny, best-selling Swiss author of *The Pollen Room*

'Blackman's wonderful book is a modern-day road trip filled with quirky characters and locations. He writes beautifully, making the mundane extraordinary and the everyday fascinating.' Deborah Wright, best-selling author

'There are echoes of Jack Kerouac in this freewheeling adventure down the CCTV-ed, drizzly corridors of modern Britain.' *Daily Mail*

To all those who demand the impossible.

Chapter 1

The clock ticked loudly in the silent front room. We looked at it, so that we didn't have to look at each other. The hands of the clock were all that moved, apart from some fine particles of dust swirling in the still, warm air. I know you always hated that clock, but you watched it anyway. The movement of the hands was imperceptible, but we knew that if we looked long enough, three o'clock would become three fifteen, three fifteen would become three thirty, and then an acceptable time would have arrived for you to make your excuses and leave.

The clock is an old family heirloom, of course, although nobody can remember quite whose family. There's an engraving on the face: Noakes & Sons. At one time I'd planned to track down the company and so, perhaps, to deduce which long-dead person had one day walked into a shop with several months' savings and emerged with a fine, modern timepiece to impress the neighbours. But now it hardly seems to matter.

I still wind the clock every Sunday morning, though, just as I have wound it every Sunday morning for the past fifty years. The sound of the old iron key cranking in the cog soothes me as much now as it did on those faraway Sunday mornings in the old house in Tunbridge Wells, when I snuggled beneath the eiderdown and listened to my father winding the clock out in the hall. Immediately after that, my mother would come in and pull the eiderdown back, exposing my small body to the cold, damp air and say, 'Come on Arthur, get a wriggle on or you'll be late for Sunday school.' Soon bacon would be sizzling in the pan while porridge bubbled on the stove, and my parents would talk softly through the steam rising from their tea, and then it would be the long, cold walk to the big, cold church for hours of listening to things I didn't understand, and home again for lunch and homework and piano practice and dinner and bed, and then back up again in no time for Monday morning and another week of school. I sometimes used to imagine that if one Sunday my father forgot to wind the clock, this strange round of activity would never begin. It would always be Sunday morning, and I would always be an eight year old boy snuggling under the warm eiderdown, listening to the quiet. But my father never forgot.

When he died, the clock passed to me. He never told me where the clock came from or why it was so important to him. All I had was the vague label of 'family heirloom'. Still, for fifty years I have taken care of it with a devotion that, I hope, would have made him proud. Only recently has the memory of those mornings in Tunbridge Wells returned to me, and on some Sunday mornings now I am seized by the puerile urge to stay in bed and see what will happen when the ticking stops. But sense and habit always win, and I get out of bed at the usual time and shuffle downstairs to wind the clock.

'What are you thinking about, Granddad?' you asked.

Your sudden intrusion made me jump. At my age, of course, jumping has long been out of the question, but my body did jerk up a little out of the soft armchair, and I could feel my pulse quickening and my breath becoming momentarily short. Then I saw you sitting across from me, remembered who you were and who I was, and softened my face into a kindly chocolate-box smile. 'Just listening to the clock,' I said.

The only sign of your frustration was a slight tightening of your fingers on your knee, making the rough denim crinkle upwards to reveal a grey sock and an inch of pale, hairy ankle. But I noticed this and knew the cause. You've asked me so many times how I could spend hours just listening to the ticking of a clock. The idea seems to threaten you. I've noticed that, in the silent times between conversations, you often shoot murderous glances at the poor old clock. I could understand such a sentiment in someone my own age: once you've passed eighty, the ticking of a clock can sometimes come to sound like clods of earth dropping steadily onto the lid of your coffin. But you are young. You have all the time in the world, and yet it never seems to be enough for you.

I still blame your mother, God rest her soul. TV would educate you, she said, and video games would develop your reflexes. But she never understood that if only bright colours, flashing lights and noise could hold your attention, then simple pleasures like the ticking of a clock, the flow of a river or the passage of clouds across the sky would always be foreign to you. You would always have to be doing something, even if there was no purpose to it. As a child you could never sit still, and as a teenager it was worse. When your parents died and you came to live with us, you said it was as if you had died as well. Our house was boring. We were boring. There was nothing to do. You buried yourself in your computer, and when you were forced to spend time with us, you just kept looking around, waiting for something to happen. It was the same this afternoon, as you perched on the edge of the sofa, your fingers fidgeting with the fabric, your foot drumming on the carpet, your eyes roving the room for something to grab hold of. I always think it must be rather sad to live that way, unable to exist without either entertaining or being entertained. Once you even turned up on my doorstep attached to earphones, only removing them hurriedly as I started to speak. I asked you somewhat shortly, 'When did you last experience complete silence?' You looked at me as if I were senile.

So now I am always sure to avoid such confrontations. I want you to keep coming. I enjoy your visits, and I know that Daisy does too, despite what the doctors say. Never mind all their degrees and qualifications, they don't know Daisy the way I do. To them she's an object to be studied. When they decided there was no hope of recovery, they lost interest and passed her along from hand to hand like an unwanted complaint letter. There was no upside for them. No miracle cure, no grateful relatives. There was just 'palliative care' as they called it, filling her with pills to dull the pain ('make her more comfortable') until the day, quite soon, when she would die. But I know Daisy. I've known her for fifty years. I know that she's still with me, even if she can't speak or smile. On the days when you're due to visit, I know she gets excited. Then when you're here, sitting across from her sipping tea and chatting, she looks different. To anyone else she'd appear the same, her eyes still gazing unseeing at a point in space, her chin lolling idly on her neck, her swollen legs sprawling inelegantly across the worn threads of the Persian rug. But as I lean over to wipe spilt tea from her chin, I see her mouth trembling slightly and know that she is trying to smile. At the end of the afternoon, as I help her into her wheelchair to go and wave you off, I sometimes feel a slight extra pressure of her fingers on my forearm. These are small, unimportant things to busy doctors and grandsons, but I know they are real. I suppose that, just as silence gradually attunes the ears to distant, small sounds, so my long days of inactivity endow small things with a reality that others may miss. I never speak of these things, of course. I know perfectly well that everyone thinks I'm too old to be looking after her. For Daisy's sake, so that we can stay together a little longer, I keep my knowledge to myself and agree with whatever nonsense the doctors tell me.

'So how's work?' I asked.

You sipped your tea, and glanced again at the clock. 'Fine,' you said. 'I might be promoted.'

'That's good, Jeff. We always knew you'd do well, didn't we, Daisy?'

You put your cup down a little loudly on the saucer and looked around at the old, fading furnishings as I sipped my tea and Daisy stared at the ceiling, her head lolling on the armchair's soft back. 'You sure you're coping okay?' you said finally.

I smiled sadly. The question came every Sunday afternoon, as predictable as the ticking of the clock, and I always had to smile to cover my anger. If I were to say the wrong thing then maybe, one Sunday afternoon, you would not come walking up the path. I wouldn't see the trembling of Daisy's mouth or feel the slight pressure of her fingers. She would have worn her best blue dress and her favourite pearl necklace for nothing. So I smiled and said, 'Yes, fine, thanks.'

'You'll let me know, won't you, if it ever gets too much?' you asked, as always.

I replied, 'Yes, of course. You're a good boy, always worrying about us.' And you smiled and took another sip of tea.

I drained my cup and, knowing that the pot would be empty by now, stood up to put the kettle on, stopping along the way to help Daisy sit a little straighter in her chair. As always, you followed me out to the kitchen and peered anxiously over my shoulder as I tried to light the gas without letting my hands shake too much.

'I can manage,' I insisted. 'I make tea when you're not here, you know. Go back to the living room and keep your grandma company.' When you left me alone, I allowed my shoulders to slump over and leant on the counter to catch my breath. For a moment I felt the panic of suffocation, and then gradually my breaths started to become deeper and more regular. It's not normally that bad, you know. When you follow me, it makes me feel rushed. If you hadn't stood over me like that, I'd have been fine.

When I returned with the teapot and a plate of custard creams, you were sitting on the overstuffed sofa gazing at Daisy who, with her head now propped up on a cushion, appeared to be staring back at you. The low, watery afternoon sun had just meandered round to this side of the house and your profiles were outlined in yellow. Particles of dust hung in the air. For a moment I felt as if I had walked in on a conversation. I stopped in the doorway, waiting for you to continue, but of course you didn't. There were just two vacant gazes and the steady ticking of the clock. I noticed that the clock's oak casing was a little dusty, and that the glass window covering the face could do with a polish. But cleaning it was a job for the first Sunday of the month, and that was not until the following week.

The clock ticked a few more times and you still hadn't noticed me standing in the doorway. I remember feeling pleased. It gave me a chance to observe you without noise and movement. For a moment or two you looked the same as your grandmother somehow. I can't really explain how; physically of course there's no resemblance. But as I looked at the two of you, I found myself remembering Daisy as a young woman, full of energy, and I saw you as an old man slumped in a chair. I saw your past and future self, quite distinct from the flurry of youthful activity in which you're currently embroiled. I saw you as part of something much larger than yourself. I saw your mother and father in you, I saw Daisy, I saw myself, and I saw the unknown man who walked into Noakes & Sons one day long ago and bought a clock. I remembered you as a baby and as a child, and the thought merged with my memories of your father and even of my own childhood, and I thought of you having the eiderdown pulled back on cold Sunday mornings in the old house in Tunbridge Wells and stumbling off to church. I thought of your own future senility and death, and of your sons and grandsons and countless future generations, their lives and deaths seeming to last no longer than a moment. I suddenly felt breathless and a custard cream slid from the edge of the plate. You rushed across to help, fussing over the dropped custard cream as if it were something important, while all I could think about was that brief trance set in motion by a moment of stillness in the low afternoon sun. Yes, I know it was just a fleeting feeling, but somehow it seemed as real as those faraway Sunday mornings when I pictured my father setting the world in motion with the key of a clock.

'I had a letter from that cousin of mine in Canada,' I said after you'd helped me back to my chair, and embarked on a long recitation of family news designed to convince you that my memory was still sound. It seemed to work, for you prompted me with questions and sipped your tea, the concern over the dropped custard cream gradually fading from your face as you relaxed into a familiar pattern of conversation. As I talked, I stole glances at you over the edge of my teacup, searching for signs of what I'd seen before, but of course it was gone. Your flushed, animated face bore no real resemblance to vacant, wrinkled, liverspotted Daisy. Sometimes, to be perfectly honest, you even seemed like a stranger, but I kept talking because I could see that for you the opposite was happening: you were rediscovering the Granddad that you recognised. Your happiness is always more important than mine, because if you are happy you will return next Sunday afternoon, and Daisy will see you walking up the path, and the hint of a smile will cross her old, broken face.

Eventually, though, there was no more family news to draw on. Silence blanketed the room again, interrupted only by the ticking of the clock and the faint, high-pitched shouts and screams of children on a distant field. 'Must be playtime,' I said, and you smiled back absently, not seeming to have understood.

'You know,' you said finally, 'you could at least set it to the right time.'

I looked down at my plate and picked up a few biscuit crumbs. The subject of setting the time was another one that came up regularly on your Sunday afternoon visits. You often managed to hold your tongue, but still the question, or accusation, emerged with the steady, regular rhythm of the clock itself. Sometimes I've tried to answer you honestly, but it's impossible. I can never really describe, even to myself, why I've wound the clock obsessively every Sunday morning for fifty years but still let the old mechanism fall a little further behind every year. I know why, but there are no words for it. Whenever I try to convey the idea to you, a chasm seems to open up between us. So this time, I steered carefully around the topic. I simply said that the gradual slowing of the clock's mechanism over the decades didn't bother me. 'I'm used to it. I translate it automatically to the real time. If I reset it, I'd be confused.'

As usual, you tried to tell me that it confused my guests to have to add five and a quarter hours to get to the real time, and as usual I replied that all my guests have wristwatches, and as usual a frustrated silence ensued.

In the silence, the sudden ringing of the telephone shocked me. I was also a little confused, because the ring didn't sound quite right. In fifty years I have come to know every sound in the house, from the flop of letters on the mat to the creak of each step on the stairs and the nocturnal clanking of the central heating. Although I still think of the telephone as the new one, it must be thirty years old by now. I know its ring just as well as all the other sounds in the house, and something about it sounded a little different. Then I saw you shifting yourself off the sofa and digging in your pocket, and realised that it was your phone, spewing a tinny electronic imitation of a real bell.

Of course, I am accustomed to mobile phones by now, but the idea of them ringing in my own house still bothers me. It diminishes my role as host. I'm used to the idea that in my own house, everything is under my control. If the phone rings while I have company, I can decide whether or not to answer. Now it's out of my hands. You bring your own world into my front room, and I am reduced to the role of a passive observer. I have to watch you flip the phone open with one hand as you hold up the other in half-hearted apology. I have to listen to your voice become artificially slangy, almost American in its slurred consonants and upturned sentences. I have to watch your face become more animated than it ever is with me, your hands making elaborate gestures that your friend will never see. I have to watch your brief transformation into a different person, and ask myself who it is that you perform for. Me, or the person on the other end of the line? Or both of us?

After the conversation was over, you apologised, as you always do. 'No need,' I said. We looked at each other for a while, and then you said you should be heading back, before the traffic got too heavy. We took refuge in the familiar rituals, me fetching your coat, you helping me get Daisy into her wheelchair, me helping you on with your coat and saying that you seem to grow taller every week, you replying that it's me shrinking, and both of us laughing and shaking hands and saying goodbye and smiling and parting and then each of us, you in your car and me in my hallway, letting out a small, secret sigh of relief.

Chapter 2

Being an American in London definitely has its upsides. Every time you open your mouth it's like people think you're some kind of movie star and fawn all over you. One guy even told me I looked like Marilyn Monroe, which is just screwed up. I mean, if you tried to think of someone who looked like the opposite of Marilyn Monroe, you'd come up with something like a picture of me. But it didn't matter to this guy. It was all in his head. And that's where the downsides come in. You get the attention, you get guys coming onto you 24/7, but none of it's real. Or maybe some of it is, but you never know how much. I'm always afraid that some guy would be making love to me and I wouldn't know if it was really me he was seeing or Angelina Jolie or whoever. Being someone's fantasy is not great when it comes down to it. Somewhere along the line the magic dust wears off and he starts to see you as a real woman, and then he moves on.

I guess maybe some of it's my fault. Maybe I like being the centre of attention for once, and maybe I play it up just a little. Maybe I become what people want me to be: an outgoing, glamorous, party-loving American chick. Maybe that's why I only meet guys who want the fantasy, and probably scare off the ones who might want the real me. Who knows? Anyways, the result is that after a couple of years in London I had what everyone thought was a great life – certainly my friends back home sounded pretty jealous whenever I talked about it. I had a job I loved, an apartment in London, and plenty of friends who I hung out with most evenings at the Chestnut Tree Café. Secretly, though, I felt... I don't know, lost maybe. Sometimes I just fell into a funk that took weeks to get out of. Once I burst into tears in the middle of Oxford Street, attracting an awkward crowd of people who lingered close but not too close, hoping I'd stop so that they wouldn't have to say something.

Maybe that was why I started skipping the pub crawls and going home early from the Chestnut Tree Café to curl up in bed with my laptop instead. I started writing a blog, at first just for something to do, but after a while I really started to get into it. On the blog, it was like I could start over and be someone else, someone more like who I really was. There was no judgement about who I was based on external bullshit – it was all about what I had to say. And believe me, I had plenty to say. I wrote furious blog posts on everything from animal rights to climate sanity, and met people from Bangkok to Des Moines who thought the way I thought. And then I met you. At first I never thought too much about you, the real person behind the blog. But as I read your posts in bed every night, I began to feel like you were speaking to me. The more I read, the more I felt like I knew you better than the people I saw every day.

When I told my friends about you, they teased me. 'Find a real man, Marie,' they'd say. 'There's no shortage.' But, of course, you were real. You did exist, I just hadn't met you yet. I'd already visited your blog, though, and left comments on it, and even emailed you. I'd scoured the web for pretty much everything you'd ever written, from the longest blog post – a three-page essay on the folly of the Iraq war – right down to the one-word replies on tech forums. I knew your views on politics, the environment and all the major issues, but I'd also seen you asking for help with your Linux interface and commenting on a recipe for blueberry and apple pie. I felt like I knew you much better than I knew a lot of the friends who denied your existence, and certainly better than a lot of the men who swarmed around me, attracted by my long black hair and my California accent but not really seeing me. You were real to me in every way except the physical, and surely that's the least important. If I loved your mind, then of course I'd love your body too. All that remained was to find a way to meet you in the flesh, and so I kept dreaming at night as if, by dreaming, I could conjure you into what my friends in the Chestnut Tree Café so narrowly defined as reality.

When I did finally meet you, of course, it was way weirder than anything I'd imagined. I was dressed as a clown, and you were in a wetsuit. We were in the middle of a vast concrete plaza in Canary Wharf, surrounded by shiny glass buildings soaring up into the cloudy sky. I think it was a Native American rain dance that we were supposed to be performing. I'd argued against it from the start, by the way, especially when I found out we'd be dressed as clowns, the whole idea struck me as pretty disrespectful. I mean, these are ancient rituals that actually mean something, or meant something, to a lot of people, and I didn't think it was right to make fun of them. But nobody listened to me. So I went along with it and, like everyone else, I wore my clown nose and clown shoes and blew my whistle as loud as I could. Meanwhile you and Marcus circled us in your wetsuits and snorkelling gear, miming the breast stroke. Of course, at that moment, I didn't know it was you. You were just the quieter one of the two guys in wetsuits. If Marcus hadn't broken his wrist like that, I'd probably never have met you.

I'm not sure if any of the office workers got what we were doing. I barely got it myself. Mostly they just scurried past, eating their designer sandwiches wrapped in oceans of planet-killing plastic. A few of them stopped to watch for a while, looking neither approving nor disapproving, neither interested nor bored. Impossible to tell what, if anything, they thought of the whole thing. For them, I think, it was just a show, no different from *Downton Abbey* or *Match of the Day*. It held their attention for a few minutes and then they hurried on, checking their BlackBerrys.

Then it happened. It was hardly surprising, really. All that whisky the two of you had been knocking back on the train. Then the tight wetsuit, the dirty, scratched goggles and the large, ungainly flippers. It was inevitable, really, that eventually you would step on one flipper with the other and go toppling over onto the concrete. Your snorkel came out of your mouth and you just sprawled out on the ground, one flipper on and one off, laughing your ass off. A few of the clowns joined in, but although it was quite comical I didn't laugh. We were there to do a job, not to screw around like amateurs. A bit of fun and laughter was part of street theatre, but it couldn't go too far. I mean, we were trying to save the planet, after all. I tried to start up another chant to keep things on track, but things were going downhill fast. Then Marcus, who had swum ahead of you, noticed the clowns laughing and turned back to see what had happened, and that made him topple over too, and as he fell he put out an arm to break the fall and a sharp crack echoed like a gunshot across the concrete plaza. Even a couple of the security guards winced.

It was lucky, really, not just because it gave me a chance to meet you, but because the security guards had now moved in, and the police had been called. You and Marcus may have been too drunk to notice or care, but the rest of us were scared. We had jobs and futures to think about. I had my immigration process. We didn't want to be arrested. The security guards had suddenly gained some confidence and certainty from whatever their radios had told them, or perhaps it was from seeing that we were just a bunch of young amateurs, falling over our flippers and laughing our asses off.

Whatever the reason, they moved in and formed a tight black circle, forcing us back to huddle together around our makeshift tepee. Then different ones started speaking from different parts of the circle. Canary Wharf was private property, they said. We were trespassing and would be prosecuted. The snorkelling gear made them particularly angry. Covering your face was an offence under the Prevention of Terrorism Act, they said. The clown wigs and red noses could also be grounds for prosecution, one of them added. The others backed him up, although they looked more doubtful on this point. By now, though, Marcus had gone white and vomited on the concrete. He was holding his right arm in his left, the wrist dangling at a strange angle.

'We have to get him to a hospital,' I said, so loudly that the threats briefly stopped. One of the guards started to argue, but I quickly shouted him down. Loud, rude, obnoxious, I was happy to confirm every American stereotype in the book, as long as it kept us out of jail. I'd already pulled out the act from time to time anyway, for lesser causes like getting on the Tube in rush-hour or jumping the line in the Chestnut Tree Café. It wasn't all that different than the act I put on the rest of the time.

As always, it worked. The security guards stood around awkwardly for a while, consulting their radios, and then grudgingly let us leave. One of them said he had video footage of the event. If we returned, he'd have us arrested. We quickly gathered our things and made our way back to the Jubilee Line. Along the way, a little boy pointed at me and tugged at his mother's arm, asking if the clown could make him a dinosaur balloon. We hurried past, smiling our apologies as a siren wailed in the distance. At the station entrance we parted, most of the clowns taking the Jubilee Line back to central London while you and I took Marcus to hospital.

Even then, I didn't really 'meet' you for a long time. We'd been sitting in the waiting room for a couple of hours at least, and I was on the verge of getting up to leave. I didn't even know why the hell I was there in the first place. After I said those words, 'We have to get him to hospital,' it just seemed to be assumed that I would be the one to go, even though he was your friend, not mine, and it was your sorry-ass antics that had gotten him hurt in the first place.

After a couple of hours in that waiting room, though, I was done. You just sat there saying nothing, while Marcus pulled out his cellphone and tweeted with his one good hand. As always in these places, the ceiling was far too low, making the windowless room seem even darker. I felt as if I could reach up out of my plastic chair and touch one of the grimy grey tiles. They looked sticky, somehow, and made me think of all the germs that must have floated up out of diseased larynxes or infected stab wounds over the years and settled up there in the layers of dirt. I must have shuddered, because you asked me if I was cold.

I remember I looked up at you in surprise. It was the first thing you'd said in almost an hour, and I'd almost forgotten you were there. 'You're kidding,' I said. 'It's like a fricking sauna in here.'

'Well, that's the great thing about the NHS,' you replied. 'In America you'd have to pay for the hospital treatment, then pay for the fricking sauna afterwards. Here it's all free.'

Yes, I remember the exact words you used. It made me smile a little bit, although the way you said it was kind of creepy, like a cheap chat-up line. I remember thinking I didn't want to give you any encouragement – I just wanted to get out of that place. So I made my smile as thin and sardonic as it could be, and just said, 'Cute.'

'Look, I probably should be going,' I said. The way you looked at me was weird, kind of like I'd hurt you. It made me feel guilty and so I gave you my mobile number. 'Text me your contact details, we'll stay in touch.'

I was halfway down the hall when your text came through. I stopped suddenly. People swerved around me, tutting. They didn't know my life was changing, right there in that hospital corridor. I ignored them and stared at my phone, reading the name again and again. I turned and went back to the waiting room as fast as my clown shoes would allow.

'I love your blog,' I blurted out as soon as I was within a few feet of you. Hey, the way I was dressed, playing it cool would've been pointless. You didn't say anything, so I tried again, standing in front of you now. 'I can't believe you're really Jeff Brennan. I mean, I read your blog like every day. I mean, you know, it's like I get up, brush my teeth, read your blog.' I laughed too loud. It sounded harsh and shrill in the stagnant air. You looked uncomfortable now, you didn't know what to say. I tried to calm down, to soften my voice. 'I guess you don't like to talk about it, right?'

'He's quite a private person,' Marcus said. You shot him a sharp look, reminding me for a moment of the disapproving receptionist.

'I understand,' I said quickly. 'I mean, that comes across from your blog. You never look for the limelight.'

'He's not like the others,' Marcus said. 'Attention-seekers, most of them.'

'Totally,' I said.

'Totally,' Marcus replied in a mock-California singsong, like he was automatically superior to me because he'd been born in London instead of Beechwood.

I tried not to let myself care about him, though. I was nervous enough at meeting you, and didn't need to feel self-conscious about my accent on top of everything else. For once, my 'gregarious American' act dried up, and I just looked at you, willing you to say something. But you stared at your fingernails, picking at a piece of loose skin. I knew I should leave you alone. You didn't want to talk, that much was clear. I'd blown it. You were a private person. You wanted me to know you as just a guy in a wetsuit. Now that I knew who you were, I'd ruined things. I always ruined good things, and attracted liars and cheats instead. I wanted to cry, and then thought what I would look like. Images rattled around in my head from old movies or TV shows. Smeared makeup, misery beneath the painted smile. Tears of a clown: wasn't that an old song my grandma used to play?

'I'm more into issues,' you said suddenly.

I barely heard you, but I agreed quickly and took the opportunity to sit down next to you. I couldn't believe I was actually sitting next to Jeff Brennan. Your blog had more readers than some newspapers. Your opinions could shift a prime minister's poll ratings, put a company out of business or catapult a nobody to fame. Yet you were so quiet, so modest. I shivered slightly. It was impossible for you to be so perfect. Other bloggers, like myself, dreamed of being you. We vied for the honour of being first to comment on your latest post, and the spike in traffic that it would bring to our own blogs. A link in your sidebar was the ultimate prize, coveted by thousands, achieved only by a select few (you had integrity, sound judgement, it wasn't like you linked to just anybody). I'd been trying for a year now to get you to notice me but with no luck, apart from a couple of polite email replies with a disturbingly generic feel. And now, after all the calculated attempts had failed, after all the late-night dreams had come to nothing, here I was in an East London hospital waiting room with a couple of half-assed eco-anarchists, and one of them turned out to be you. 'Jeff Brennan.' I realised too late that I had uttered those last two words aloud. You smiled slightly, and looked at the floor.

'Sorry,' I said. 'You must hate this.'

'No, it's fine.'

I tried to think of something else to talk about, but all I could think about was the blog. I thought about mentioning the protest, but it seemed so irrelevant now. It failed, what else was there to say? I looked at you, hoping you'd help me out of my misery, but you looked equally tortured. Amazing that it started like that. Marcus, meanwhile, looked like he was stifling a laugh.

'So how long have you been involved in the movement?'

you asked in a quiet, uncertain voice.

This was the moment when I first felt close to you. Somehow, out of all the questions you could have asked, you hit on the right one. Answering it, I was on familiar ground. I could talk about it for hours. 'My whole life, really,' I said. 'I mean, environmentalism runs in the family.' I babbled on about my parents, who were in at the beginning: Greenpeace, Rainbow Warrior and all that. Then my grandparents, who I always include as greens, even though they didn't really have a word for it back then. Flower power, that was the first environmentalism. They started an organic farm way before anybody had a clue what organic farming was. They were just following their instincts. After that I really did start babbling – about the ancient Eastern religions they followed, and how most traditional ways of life have respect for the environment, and after a while I saw your gaze wandering and realised I'd been talking too long. 'Sorry, I'm getting off track. I do that a lot. Point is, I was brought up in this stuff. Never ate meat in my life, never wasted anything that could be re-used.'

'That's great,' you said.

'Yeah, they taught me a lot. I mean, you wanted a milkshake in my family, you didn't just open a pack of Nesquik. We used fruit from hedgerows, milk from soy beans, and mixed it in a blender powered by an exercise bike.'

'Wow, they were... '

'Fruit loops,' Marcus muttered.

'Committed,' you said.

'Should have been,' Marcus said. 'I mean, imagine making a child pedal for her milkshake.'

I felt my defensive hackles rise up. Sure, I could see where the guy was coming from. Believe me, as a teenager in Beechwood, California, the very last thing I wanted to do was pedal for a fucking milkshake. I hated my parents for being different, for being the kind of people that Mrs Roberts and her cronies gossiped about after church. I hated them for throwing out a pair of jeans I'd saved my own money to buy, just because of the 'Made in Indonesia' label. I hated them for dressing me in hand-me-downs and not giving a shit how bad it made me feel, for caring more about people in Indonesia than about their own daughter. I couldn't wait to get out of there. But anyways, if I do still hate them a little bit then as their daughter I guess I'm entitled. But hearing some smug English guy making fun of them is a different thing completely. So I shot him a venomous look that made him recoil a little and draw his arms into his body, like he was afraid I'd snap his other wrist. 'My parents have always lived their beliefs,' I said. 'People have always called them crazy, but what's more sane? To drive an SUV to the gym, pay to use an exercise bike, drive back home and make a milkshake out of powdered chemicals in a blender using electricity from coal-fired power stations? That sounds like crazy to me.'

'I understand,' you said gently. 'I don't think they were crazy.'

You seemed so perfect then. So understanding. I gave you a grateful smile, and went silent for a while as I tried to control the fluttering in my stomach. Instantly, I loved everything about you. Right there in the hospital waiting room. I loved your quiet voice, your polite dismissal of your own work, your understanding of difference. It fit perfectly with the Jeff Brennan I knew already online: always ready to draw attention to others but shunning the spotlight himself, even as his readership rocketed. While other famous bloggers put out books and DVDs and willingly became pundits for the very 'mainstream media' they'd built their fame from criticising, you always stayed true to your roots. You hid in the shadows, watching, thinking, and giving the world your daily perspective on events, just as you had done for almost seven years now. You posted no information about yourself, not even a photo. So reclusive were you that, in my darker moments, I'd wondered if you really existed. You seemed somehow too perfect. Perhaps the secrecy covered a lie, and one day 'Jeff Brennan' would be unmasked as the creation of a corporate guerrilla-marketing department. I'd even searched through your old posts, looking for patterns: a subliminal shoe-buying message woven into the political analysis, or a particular brand of soda mentioned too often. But there was nothing. You were real.

'Do you want a coffee?' you asked.

'No, I'm good, thanks,' I said, smiling and playing with a few strands of hair. You were thoughtful, as well. Too good to be true.

'Marcus?'

'No thanks, mate.'

'Well, I think I'll get one.'

When you started to get up, I panicked suddenly at being left alone with Marcus and grabbed your arm. 'It's okay, I'll go.'

'You sure?'

I got up. 'Yeah, it's fine. You sit with your friend, and I'll get it. I could use a walk anyways. Milk and sugar?'

'No, just black. Espresso if they have it.'

'Sure thing. I'll be right back.'

As I walked off to look for the machine, I remember I glanced over my shoulder. To be honest, I hoped you'd be watching me, but you'd already turned to talk to Marcus. At that moment, I felt a sudden urge to go back. I felt sure that if I walked out, I would never see you again. After all, nobody really *wants* that coffee from a machine in a hospital. People only get it when they've been up all night worrying over a dying relative, and even then it's only to have something warm to hold onto. I was sure this was just a pretext to get rid of me. You hated me, just like all the nice guys hated me. When I returned, you'd be gone, and I'd be left standing in the waiting room, a clown with a cup of coffee.

I searched the long, blank white corridors for a coffee machine, but all the time I was thinking of you. I probably even passed a couple of those stupid machines and didn't even notice. All I could think about was you. It's funny, I'd imagined meeting a thousand times, but never come up with this version of you. On your blog, your voice was older somehow, more serious. It sounded like someone who had seen the world from many different angles and understood them all. In person you were lighter, and so unsure of yourself. It wasn't what I'd expected, but I could get used to this new you. In fact, I felt all warm and fuzzy just thinking about getting used to you.

I found myself standing in front of a machine and pressing a button. Black liquid spurted angrily into a plastic cup. I felt weightless, like that moment when you drive too fast over a hump-backed bridge. Who knew love would feel that way? It was the weirdest thing, but standing in front of that coffee machine, for the first time in my life I knew exactly what I was feeling. I wouldn't have to fake it like I did with the other guys, to convince myself to feel something. This was real. You weren't as funny or as cute or as charming as the guys I normally dated, but what did that matter? The feeling in my stomach and my heart, that strange weightlessness, told me everything. As I tramped loudly down the corridor, I wished I'd brought a change of clothes. A sexy change of clothes, something to make me feel like I had a chance with you. But I hadn't. I was just a clown.

When I entered the waiting room, Marcus was sitting hunched over, one hand still propping up the other. Next to him was an empty plastic chair. In that moment, I got the opposite of that weightless feeling. Everything inside me seemed suddenly to be heavier than lead. My body wanted to sink down to the floor, curl into a ball and never move again. Marcus looked up, sending me a look of bemused innocence. Not my fault, the look said. Don't blame me. The idiot even tried to splay his hands in the kind of shrug he'd copied from the Italian soccer players on TV, but the pain was too much and he hunched over again to nurse his wrist.

For a few moments I stood in the waiting room, doing

nothing. I felt the eyes of every bored spectator fixed on me, waiting for the show to start. I wanted to make a dramatic gesture, to throw the cup of scalding coffee at Marcus, or in the miserable face of the receptionist. That would be something to see. I couldn't do it, though. My body refused to perform. I felt very tired and just wanted to go home. The spectators seemed to sense this and started to look away in disappointment. Nothing would happen. I was just a clown holding a cup of coffee. There was no punch-line.

Chapter 3

Marcus Higgins @marcushig	**3h**
Police brutality at Canary Wharf protest! In hospital w/ broken wrist. Spread teh word!	
Marcus Higgins @marcushig	**3h**
In hospital with broken wrist, BORED!	
Marcus Higgins @marcushig	**2h**
Still bored	
Marcus Higgins @marcushig	**1h**
Where are the doctors???	
Marcus Higgins @marcushig	**1h**
@JeffB u missed an opportunity there m8, she was GORGEOUS!!	
Marcus Higgins @marcushig	**50m**
@Martin2010 No, didnt get photos	
Marcus Higgins @marcushig	**47m**
@Martin2010 No vids either. No time b4 they attacked	
Marcus Higgins @marcushig	**45m**
@Martin2010 u don't believe me? Fine. Ohters will	
Marcus Higgins @marcushig	**25m**
RT Police brutality at Canary Wharf protest! In hospital w/ broken wrist. Spread teh word!	
Marcus Higgins @marcushig	**23m**
Back home from hospital. Why no response???????	

Chapter 4

We went in together. Always done things together, you and me. Not now, of course, but it was different in those days. I was right beside you as you kicked down the door. We waited. Silence inside. A few more seconds and then you gave the signal and we were in there, in the darkness, bullets ripping from the muzzles of our M240 machine guns. Nobody fired back, but for a minute or two we just stood in the doorway with our fingers on the trigger, spraying bullets anywhere and everywhere. Unstoppable.

I ducked behind a pillar, flicked on the lights. The shattered remains of a grocer's shop, broken jars all over the shelves. Dried fruit and beans spilling on the floor. Pools of liquid that looked like blood, but turned out to be milk and fruit juice pouring out of ripped cartons. A clock ticking loudly, but otherwise nothing. Total silence. From behind the counter, a shaky hand waving a white handkerchief. Then a bald man with a moustache and raised hands stepping out, his whole family following behind. Woman in a headscarf, three wide-eyed kids, somewhere between seven and twelve. Their hands trembled as they held each other. Clock ticked. The whole family lined up, staring back at us, pleading for life. Too tempting. With a flick of your finger, you sent bullets ripping from the end of your gun, shooting out sparks of fire. Blood spurted from the chest of the old man and the head of his wife. The bodies of the children were pinned against the back wall for a few seconds by the rounds of bullets you pumped into them. Then they slumped to the floor where their blood mingled with the spilt milk and fruit juice.

I laughed. 'Fucking sadist.'

'Hey, you can talk. You just cluster-bombed a mosque in the middle of evening prayers.'

'True, true.' We took sips of beer as our kills were tallied on screen. Your face was still flushed with adrenalin, or perhaps just from all the beer. Empty cans all over the living room floor. A classic Saturday night. How many did we have like that over the years? Must be hundreds. Later we'd get a curry and watch *Match of the Day*. But for now there was the computer, TV, beer, cigarettes and the new *Burningpilot* album as a soundtrack to the whole thing. Work with all its boredoms and stupidity seemed like it was part of someone else's life. Right now it was just you and me. The haze of yet another beautifully wasted Saturday night.

'Sick game, this,' I said, waving at the screen with my beer can. 'So realistic.'

'Yeah, did you see how the blood came out of those kids? Pure poetry.'

I reached for a cigarette and lit it. Had to squint slightly, so it must be almost ten o'clock. Time for a curry soon. 'You remember those arcade games we used to play when we were kids? All cartoon characters doing crap kung fu moves?'

'Yeah, and when they died they'd just flash a few times on the screen and vanish.'

'And we thought it was so amazing. Imagine if we'd played *Desert Wars* in those days. We'd probably have spooged all over our joysticks.'

The joke caught you in the middle of a sip of beer, and you spurted it over the screen. That was the great thing about our Saturday nights, the way they used to be. You always laughed at my jokes and I laughed at yours, and the two of us had a big enough store of memories that we didn't need to make any effort to make new ones. With other people through the week it was all bullshit, putting on a face. With you I could just have a few beers and pissball around on the web. No need to be someone else.

'Hey, looks like Terry's having a good night,' you said. I jumped to Facebook to check out the latest pics from his mobile phone: Terry with pint, Terry with blonde, Terry singing with a ketchup bottle as a microphone, Terry sticking his tongue out to show how blue it was from whatever lurid shit he'd been drinking.

'They're like the ones he posted last Saturday.'

'Yeah, but it works, doesn't it? Look how many comments he's getting.'

'True,' I said, taking a swig of beer. 'I suppose nobody's going to be impressed with a pic of me playing *Desert Wars* in my living room in Milton Keynes, are they?'

'Not unless you can find someone cuter and blonder than me to sit beside you.'

Silence for a bit while we scrolled through Terry's pages of photos, all from that night. All the same but different.

'We should do something like that soon,' you said. 'Haven't posted any photos for ages. People'll think I have no life.'

'You don't.'

'Yeah but they don't know that, do they? We need something big. Stag night in Amsterdam or something.'

'Yeah, we will.' Truth was, we wouldn't. Not until weeks went by and the new friend requests really started to dry up or, worse, people actually started to de-friend us. Then we might arrange some party and take pictures of each other getting shitfaced in Robert de Niro fancy dress costumes: hair slicked back, sharp suit and 'Whadda you lookin' at?' sneers on our faces. Just something to let people know we hadn't died. When the friend requests started to flow again it would be back to the usual Saturday nights in, you and me, beer and *Desert Wars* and *Match of the Day*. Our guilty little secret.

'I met a girl the other day,' you said, but I'd just clicked on a fucking hilarious Youtube video and had to watch it to the end. It was footage of David Cameron and Nick Clegg spliced together to make it seem like they were singing a duet of *I Got You Babe*. I had to rate it and leave a comment, and then reply to a couple of stupid comments by Tories or Lib Dems who were all offended at it, and then reply to their replies, and then share the link on Twitter and Facebook, and then watch a couple of other videos that people had posted in response to the first one, which were inevitably not as funny as the original.

'What was that you said about a girl?' I asked finally.

'Just someone I met in London.'

'What the fuck were you doing in London?'

You took a swig from your beer can, then shook it like a wino begging for change. 'Time for a refill,' you said, and disappeared. By the time you got back, I was leaving comments on Terry's latest pics – in a nightclub now, sweat pouring down his face, making a comedy moustache out of one of those limes they give you in poncy beers.

'What are you doing?' you said. 'Do you want everyone to know you've got nothing better to do on a Saturday night than stay in and comment on someone else's night out?'

I shrugged. 'The truth, isn't it?' But I deleted the comment anyway. 'So what were you doing in London?'

'Hey, I was thinking about that David Cameron video,' you said. 'Posting it on Youtube is alright, but what you really need to do is get into his website, grab one of those smug photos of him waving to the crowd and Photoshop it to make him do a Nazi salute. You know, sly, underhand shit.'

'Yeah, whatever,' I said. 'Up the fucking revolution.'

'Look, it's not a political thing, it's just a laugh. You know, like the time you hacked into the school computers and changed all Gavin Baxter's lates and absents into a perfect attendance record?'

I laughed. 'Yeah, he ended up winning some school award

for perfect attendance.'

'And that was his credibility gone. Never bothered us again, did he? He was too busy defending himself against all the people taking the piss.'

'True.' I took a sip of beer, savouring the memory.

'So how about it?'

'That was all a long time ago, Jeff. What have I done since then?'

'You've done stuff. You hacked into the library system, deleted all those overdue DVDs I had so that all my fines were wiped off and I could keep them forever.'

You listed a few more things, but I cut you off soon as I could. 'Small shit, Jeff, and you know it. Pissing around, having a few laughs, but what have I really done in the last few years?'

You shrugged. 'Biding your time I guess.'

Another thing I liked about you. Everyone else was always telling me what I should have done with my life, how I should have been in Silicon Valley or wherever. You could have done that as much as the rest of them. More, probably. All that time we spent at lunchbreak talking about being dot-com millionaires and retiring by twenty-five. But you never did, and I was always grateful. I mean, being a salesman for Hertfordshire's leading chain of curtain and blind specialists is not exactly what I'd planned. But you never asked why I just took the first job that came my way, and then spent my weekends doing for free what I should have been doing for a living. You shrugged and said I was biding my time.

'So you think it could be done, that David Cameron thing?'

'Of course. I mean, people have hacked into the fucking Pentagon – I'm sure they could make David Cameron look like a Nazi. The dude wouldn't even need much Photoshopping.'

'I don't mean people, Jon. I mean, could you do it?'

What were you trying to say? If it could be done, then I could do it. Saying the same thing. I mean, it was just code.

Everything on the internet is just code. Go online to check your bank balance and think it's all as real as the branch on the High Street if you want, but it's not. It's code. Some of it cleverer than others, some of it with better or worse security, but still just code. I shot you a look. 'Write new code, work out how to get past the security, and you've got your Nazi pic.'

'So maybe we should do it. You know, for a laugh. For old time's sake.'

Old time's sake. Like we were in it together. Like you could even come close to touching me when it came to stuff like that. When we were eight years old and finding Easter eggs in Sonic the Hedgehog, maybe. But not since then. 'You mean, maybe *I* should do it. Maybe I should give up every weekend and evening for the next few months for some gimmick that two people will see before they take it down and arrest me.'

'They wouldn't arrest you.'

'You kidding? Libraries are one thing. Nobody gives a shit. But where there's real money or power at stake, they'll come after you with everything they've got. Didn't you hear about that guy in California who was giving people free internet? He's looking at a life sentence.'

'He'll probably get off on appeal,' you said. 'Everything you see on TV is exaggerated by a factor of ten. Come on, I'm hungry. Let's order a curry.'

I smiled and reached into my pocket for my mobile. 'Now you're talking. It'll arrive just in time for *Match of the Day*. Usual?'

'Usual.'

Another thing I'd never admit to anyone but you, I had the curry house on speed-dial, and didn't even have to give my name. They just recognised my voice and knew our orders straight away. Two chicken bhunas with basmati rice and nan bread, one delivered to my flat and one to yours. To be honest, this was the only part of the evening where it felt a bit weird not being in the same place. For the rest of the night, it didn't make a difference. We were both hooked up to Skype, so we could see each other and chat just like we were together. I mean, video calls for as long as you want, completely free. That's shit we could only dream about when we were kids, so what the fuck's the point in driving all across town in the middle of the night to meet in person? This way we could still watch the same TV programmes, play the same games, visit the same sites. We could see each other's comments and forum posts and status updates. We had mobiles, emails, instant messaging. How much more communication do you need? In some ways, it was even more real than real life. That little square in the corner of the screen that showed me an image of my face as you saw it on your screen. Watching myself getting more red-faced through the evening. My hair getting fucked up, my gestures more random. All there in front of me. Can't do that in the pub, can you? In the pub you always get that surprise when you stand up at the end of the night and find out you're completely spackered. At home I can see it happening, minute by minute, in real time, on my own computer screen.

But getting two curries delivered to two separate addresses just felt weird. Sometimes they arrived at different times, and one of us had to sit there hungry, watching the other one wolfing down a bhuna. Even when they were both on time, we still had to look away from the screen to eat, and lost a bit of that feeling of being in the same place. Still, it was worth it. Better than one of us having to get dressed and leave home and drive from one flat to the other, then having to stay sober to drive back. Reality's overrated.

'Curry's on its way,' I said as I put my headset back on. 'So anyway, what were you doing in London?'

But on the screen was just an empty sofa, a handwritten sign propped up on it saying 'Gone for a slash.' I chuckled and checked my email while I waited. *Match of the Day* was starting as well, and I watched it out of the corner of my eye as I flicked through the messages.

'That's better,' you said, your head filling my screen for a moment as you eased down into the sofa, before you sat back and cracked open a new can.

'Here, look at this,' I said, forwarding you an email. Can't remember what it was now, just one of those jokes that seems funny at the time. Helped pass the time, anyway, while we waited for the curry. Then I remembered, and asked again, 'So what were you doing in London?'

'Just meeting Marcus.'

From the way you looked away from the camera I knew you'd been helping him with another stupid protest or something. The cunt did nothing else but protest. Don't know what you ever saw in him. He was just like the rest of us, working some dry job – Pret a Manger, making sandwiches for office workers – but always liked to think he was special. Always some agenda or cause, something to protest about. Third world poverty, global warming, AIDS, racism, sexism, whatever. And he always made it my fault because I was born white and male. I know you got sucked into feeling guilty and all that, but not me. Life's too short. It's not like I ever did anything to the oppressed people of the Congo, I'm just living my life. Only met Marcus a couple of times, and both times he tried to make me feel guilty for living. It's good you never tried that with me. Don't need that crap.

'So what happened?'

You shrugged. 'Nothing interesting.'

'I mean with the girl. What's her name, for a start?'

'Marie.'

'Good name. Like her so far, even if she is a friend of that dick Marcus.'

'Yeah. American girl. Long, dark hair, quite tall...'

I knew what was coming next. There was always some woman, and always some reason why she wasn't interested in you, or maybe she was but you never found out because you couldn't find a way to ask her. I wasn't much better myself, I've got to admit. Hardly ever went beyond fantasy, and when it did, it didn't last long. We failed, and then we met up on Saturday night and drank away the humiliations. Amazing how after enough beers and *Desert Wars* missions, nothing seems to matter that much.

'So what went wrong?' I asked.

But this time, the script was different. 'Actually, she was crazy about me.'

Just then the doorbell rang. For a moment I couldn't tell whose it was: that's how fucking great my speakers are. But you didn't move, so I knew it must be mine. Went to the door to pay, thinking all the time about what you'd said. She was crazy about you. I started to shake just like that Iraqi dude with the handkerchief. Things were changing. Don't get me wrong, I was happy for you and all that. But, you know, curry for one? Not the same, is it? I got this vision of you living miles away in sunny suburbia, laughing with your perfect American wife as your beautiful daughter played on the lawn. The sun, the green grass, the blue sky and the three happy faces filled the screen. No room for anyone else. My dark, cramped, manky little flat was like a bad dream. I walked back with my curry and felt the dirty carpet crunching under my feet, saw the burn marks and fag-ash all over the sofa. Fucking rank. That was my life. Rank. Not surprising you wanted to move on. 'Maybe you got it wrong,' I said when I got back. 'You're not good at that sort of thing, you know.'

'I'm sure. She was all over me. But there is a problem. Oh, wait, here's mine. Back in a minute.'

As you disappeared again I tried to eat my curry, but I had no appetite. I was a mess, to tell you the truth. I was relieved when you said there was a problem, but then I felt guilty for feeling that. It was like that fantasy role-playing game we were so into back in Year Eight. You got so much more power than me that I began to hold you back. In the end you went head-to-head against the most powerful player in the game, Valkyra, and the only way you could win was to kill me and take my powers for yourself. I knew you had to do it, and I let you do it, and I still rooted for you when you fought Valkyra. But in the end I was secretly happy when you got your arse handed to you and had to quit the game.

Soon you were back, and shovelling chicken bhuna into your mouth. I waited until you came up for air, then asked what the problem was.

You shoved in a bit of nan bread and wiped your lips with the back of your hand. 'She thinks I'm Jeff Brennan.'

'And?'

'No, I mean, *the* Jeff Brennan.'

I laughed out loud. 'The blogger? She thinks you're that wishy-washy liberal bullshit-merchant?' I laughed even harder, almost choking on my curry.

'It's not funny. I really liked her.'

I tried to stop myself, I really did, but the beer and maybe the relief just kept me laughing. Guess I shouldn't have laughed – maybe that's what made you do what you did. But no point looking back now. What's done is done. 'Sorry, mate,' I said. 'It's just the idea of anyone falling for that twat.'

'She fell for me.'

'Yeah, 'cos she thought you were him.'

'Still.'

'Should have played along, then.'

'I did. Well, Marcus did. Thought he could suck her into his 'movement."

I spooned up the last of my rice, and mopped up the sauce with a piece of naan bread. 'For once, I agree with Marcus,' I said. 'Not about his shitty one-man movement to save the world, but about playing along. You did go along with it, didn't you?'

You sighed, and looked at the screen with tired eyes. 'For a while. But then it just felt wrong.'

Would have been so easy for me just to say you did the right thing. Forget about her, move on, she's not worth it, and all that. It was all I had to do, and I'd still have my Saturday nights with you. The one part of the week I could actually look forward to. We'd console ourselves over our latest failures, and watch football and eat curry and burn Iraqi villages to the ground. Nothing would have had to change. I wanted so much to tell you to forget her. But I couldn't say it. I saw the look in your eyes as you talked about Marie. It wasn't the usual stupid fantasy, you really were hooked. You'd've got over it of course, but I couldn't let you do that. I wanted you to win for once. Even if I couldn't, maybe you could.

'Look, don't be so squeamish,' I said. 'Everybody lies a little bit these days.'

'Don't think my granddad's told a lie in his life.'

Sometimes there's no arguing with you. Look, I like your granddad, but he's from a different world. I mean, you were always telling me yourself how out of touch he was. And now you were setting him up as an example of how to live in the modern world, like that was even possible. What were you going to do, rip out your internet connection and throw away your mobile? Spend your days listening to the wireless in front of a coal fire?

'You remember when we were kids?' I said. 'We spent our whole fucking childhoods on Planet Doom. You were Avalon and I was Anwyn.'

'The demon and the warlock,' you said with a dreamy smile.

'We racked up more skills points than anyone else.'

'Except Wrath. We could never go up against him. He must have been plugged into the game since birth to get so much power.'

'You're right, except Wrath.'

For a few minutes we were both silent, thinking about the epic battles on the world of Toth, the Sargassian Wars and all the honours we won together, the friends we made, the younger players who looked on us like ancient heroes.

'Why did we ever stop playing?' you asked.

'They changed the rules, remember? Two hit points per attack – it was supposed to even things out, help the newer players.'

'By betraying the older ones.'

'Right. Totally ruined it. We had to leave.'

'You could have just hacked into it, like you did with Starport. Given us more powers, so many powers that we'd have been invincible even under the new rules.'

I thought about it for a moment. 'You're right, I probably could have. I remember I looked at the code once and it was fairly simplistic. But it was a point of principle. We were Avalon and Anwyn, the heroes of the Sargassian Wars, and they screwed us over for the sake of getting new people to join.'

'You're right. It was a stupid game. Why did you bring it up?'

'Oh yeah. My point was, you were Avalon in that game, right? Then in Centurions you were Khan, a completely different character.'

'The peacemaker.'

'Right. You used to make potions to heal people. Buy swords and sell shields. You had this idea that if you could buy up all the attack weapons in the game, you could create peace.'

You laughed. 'Yeah. Never worked, though. Game was too big. New players joining all the time, all issued with a sword and dagger when they started. Besides, nobody wanted peace. They just wanted to kill people.'

'Then later on we got into chatrooms, remember? You were a hippy on one site, a Young Tory on another.'

'Don't forget F@tB@st@rd,' you said, laughing. 'F@tB@st@rd used to get people so angry they wouldn't be able to type any more. I just disagreed with everything, took the piss out of anything anyone said. F@tB@st@rd was fantastic.'

'He was, he was. Now you're on, what, Facebook, Twitter, Myspace and whatever else. That IT site where you have a nice clean-cut photo and you're all polite and help people solve problems and hope that one day somebody'll give you a job. The music one where you pretend to be a stoned-out rocker. All those blogs you started up a while back. Last.fm, Flickr, Flixster. When you add it all up, over the years you must have had, what, fifty different online identities?'

'More, probably.'

'Well, you don't think of them as being lies, do you? They're just different parts of you.'

You shot me this accusing look. 'So there was a point to all the fond remembering, then.'

Like I said, sometimes there's no arguing with you. You didn't want to shut up and play *Desert Wars*, but you didn't want me to help you either. You tried to make me feel like I'd tricked you, just because I was making a serious point for once. 'All I'm saying is it's no different with this Marie. You're doing the same thing you always do. Playing a part. Difference is, the stakes are higher. When it falls apart, you can't just remake the character, or delete it. You're stuck with it, and the fallout will be messy. It's the fallout you're scared of.'

You winced and looked doubtful, but only because you didn't want to believe it. 'So what do I do?'

'Make sure you don't get caught out. Make sure there is no fallout.'

'She's out of my league, mate. Sooner or later she'll see what a wanker I am and wonder what she was thinking.'

'Yeah, well, sooner or later the sun will explode and we'll all be dead. In the meantime, get some pleasure and enjoy it while it lasts. Besides, you're not a wanker.' There was an awkward silence after that, and I cut it by saying, 'Look, let's kick some jihadist butt, alright? Too much fucking seriousness for a Saturday night.'

You grinned. 'Now you're talking.'

We both joined up to our old network game again, so we could continue from where we'd left off. I got a pang as the familiar series of screens flashed up. Thought of you moving on, leaving me behind. 'Hey, you said Marie was cute, right?'

'Yeah, really beautiful.'

'So maybe we won't need to do this Amsterdam stag night after all. A few photos with her on your arm, and you'll be drowning in friend requests.'

You laughed. 'Yeah, true. Better than yet another photo with just you and me in it, people'll start to think we're an item.'

I laughed and turned my M240 on you, pumping a few rounds into your chest until you were pinned against a wall, blood spurting out everywhere, your body disintegrating in front of me. Then I lobbed a grenade onto your corpse, scattering body parts all over the camp.

'Alright, alright,' you said, laughing at the mess I'd made of you. 'Shit, I was only joking.'

'Yeah, very funny.' I quit without saving, and we went back to where we were before, side by side, fully armed and ready to lay waste to another village. Another advantage of computers: there's always an undo option.

Chapter 5

| Marcus Higgins @marcushig | 7h |

Flashmob! Back to Canary Wharf, Apr 9th, double the numbers this time!

| Marcus Higgins @marcushig | 6h |

@JulieGemmill Why cant you make it?

| Marcus Higgins @marcushig | 6h |

@JulieGemmill U think MLK cared abt arrest?

| Marcus Higgins @marcushig | 6h |

@JulieGemmill Cant get permit, only massive NGOs get those. Dont need one NEway

| Marcus Higgins @marcushig | 6h |

@IrishDan Cant u get a babysitter??

| Marcus Higgins @marcushig | 6h |

@IrishDan Icecaps are melting but cant do anythg cos yr babysitter has exams? WTF????

| Marcus Higgins @marcushig | 6h |

Need to take some risks to get sthg done! U dont need government's permission to protest against govt!!!

| Marcus Higgins @marcushig | 6h |

@Jane4evr You as well??

| Marcus Higgins @marcushig | 5h |

RT Flashmob! Back to Canary Wharf, Apr 29th, double the numbers this time!

| Marcus Higgins @marcushig | 5h |

Anyone?

| Marcus Higgins @marcushig | 5h |

@JeffB Thx m8, glad someone's got some balls

| Marcus Higgins @marcushig | 2m |

@JeffB Forget it, nobody else up for it. we'll do sthg else

Chapter 6

Dust hung in the air, falling slowly. Daisy was sitting in her usual spot, gazing blankly out of the window. I was perched – rather uncomfortably, I have to admit – on the arm of the chair, with my hand on her shoulder. In the sun-streaked glass I could see our faint reflection, an old couple in an awkward pose, staring stiffly forward. It reminded me for a moment of a painting I'd seen once in a museum in Europe, but for the life of me I can't remember which one. All I have is a vague image of a big gold frame, heavy, dark oils and an old couple staring stiffly forward. Daisy and I would have been young then. Probably one of those little holidays we took before your mother was born. I suppose we would have looked at the painting and moved on, chattering about something from the guide book, never imagining that eventually we too would be painted into a canvas, sealed in with varnish and left fixed, immobile, staring stiffly forward. The thought made me want to move, suddenly, but I didn't want to upset Daisy. I know she likes the feeling of my hand on her shoulder. So I stayed with her, and tried to ignore the cramp spreading up my right calf.

Since it was the first Sunday of the month, I'd spent the morning cleaning. As usual, I started with the toughest task. It's an old, unbreakable habit, instilled by my father from an early age. 'Face up to the devil, and the rest is child's play,' he used to say. He would constantly ask me my worst fear and make me confront it immediately, whether it was a spider, a girl, a history essay or a bully at school. The old man wouldn't let me rest for a second until the toughest thing in my life at that particular time had been accomplished. In cricket practice, he used to rip out two of the stumps, leaving only one to bowl at. 'It'll be easy when you come to matches,' he'd say. 'Having three to aim at will feel like child's play.'

He was right, of course, and I would later thank him when I became, for a time, one of the most feared medium-pacers in the north London leagues. But somehow, no matter how many tough tasks I faced, there were always more awaiting me. The golden age where everything was finally child's play always remained my father's broken promise. After the bullies and the girls and the history essays came work, tax returns, marriage, a baby, a mortgage and a thousand other tough tasks. I threw myself at all of them, patiently waiting for everything to seem like child's play, but the easy life always remained tantalisingly just around the corner. Finally I focused all my hopes on retirement, feeling sure that then I could finally 'put my feet up', as everyone said. But after a brief respite, I found myself once again paying bills, worrying about my pension, filling my life with tasks. And then Daisy got ill, and my arthritis got worse, and our only child died, and tough tasks seemed to take up the majority of my life once more. Now I am well aware that life will never seem like child's play. But a habit is a habit, and so I still handle the toughest tasks first.

For many years that meant tackling the kitchen before anything else. Scraping burnt lard off the stove and scouring gravy stains from the counter top. But one Sunday a few years ago, I started doing the bathroom first; such are the small indignities with which one measures the descent into old age. From the bathroom I move swiftly to the living room, which also serves as Daisy's bedroom these days. Then it's my own bedroom upstairs, then the hall, the dining room, and finally the kitchen. These days there's no lard, or gravy, to scrub at. It's just mopping patches of spilt tea and combing up toast crumbs.

It doesn't take long.

Finally I move to the clock. Technically it's a difficult task and should be tackled earlier, but the clock is the one exception to the rule. After the hard scrubbing on arthritic knees, it feels like a treat to spread out the old oilcloth on the coffee table, lift the clock carefully down from the mantelpiece, sit on the sofa and begin to dismantle it. Daisy used to ask why I had to clean the inside of a clock when nobody would ever see it. But these days she understands. Anybody who saw the inside of the clock, the elegant machinery of springs and weights, wheel trains and escapements all intersecting in perfect harmony, would understand why I could never let it be sullied by dirt from the outside world. When I am cleaning it, I slip into a trance. Time stops, my thoughts fly away, the world around me fades, and all that exists is the familiarity of the movements. My hands seem to act from memories of their own, without the need for conscious thought. I always remove the parts in the same order, squirt on the same cleaning fluid to remove solidified oil, use the same cloth to wipe the metal clean, and apply the same amount of fresh oil in the same places, before slipping everything firmly back together in the reverse order. There's a neat circularity to it, progress of a kind. The metal gleams brighter than before, the parts have been checked, and the possibility of a catastrophic failure averted. That's about the only kind of progress I can believe in these days.

On this particular morning I became so absorbed in the glint of sun on the oiled cogs that I forgot myself completely, and realised with a start that time was moving on. With a shade more haste than usual, I reassembled the parts, replaced the clock carefully on the mantelpiece and stepped back to admire my work. I almost drifted off again, but the ticking brought me back to reality and I glanced anxiously at the driveway. You'd be here any minute. I looked at Daisy, resplendent in her best blue dress and favourite pearls, and smiled at her. 'You look lovely today,' I said, and went to perch next to her on the arm of the chair, the pose that now, half an hour later, was becoming increasingly uncomfortable.

'I don't understand where all the dust comes from,' I told Daisy. I watched it swirl and dance in the sunlight, mocking my earlier attempts to capture it and confine it to the kitchen bin. 'Oh, I know, I know. But surely we can't shed that much skin, can we? I only cleaned this morning.' The dust was making beautiful patterns now, and it occurred to me that perhaps my words had created those majestic spinning and twirling shapes. The air forced through my throat into a static room, stirring up the status quo and creating something new. Feeling a little foolish, I waved a hand through the air. The thousands of tiny dust particles responded, billowing sharply to one side and then the other, like a flock of starlings at sunset. I looked at my hand and wondered if some of them had settled there, the dead mingling with the living. I shivered and glanced at Daisy.

Her face looked different somehow. The change was almost imperceptible, like the momentary shift in light quality as a wisp of cloud passes over the sun on a bright summer afternoon. But I know that face well, have known all the incarnations of it over the past fifty years. I have charted the progress of every wrinkle and blemish, and the gradual fading of its complexion from vibrant pink to something soft and sallow, like candle wax. Nothing is lost on me. In that moment I knew for certain that when I looked out of the window, I'd see your jeep backing into the driveway.

'You always spot him first,' I said, squeezing Daisy's hand and getting up rigidly from the arm of the chair. By the time I'd shuffled into the hallway, you had already bounded up the front path and rung the doorbell twice. Then you pushed the letterbox open and started peering into the gloom, probably looking for a body. 'Coming!' I called. One day I won't answer, and you'll have to force the door open and search for the two bodies, Arthur and Daisy, asleep forever in each other's arms. I've talked to Daisy about this. It's the only way that makes sense, when things get too bad. But for now things are not too bad.

The sunlight was harsh after the gloom of the hallway. It blinded me momentarily to all but the dark outline of your body filling the doorframe. You were saying something, but I couldn't concentrate on it. I stepped back and smiled, hoping you'd come in. You did, and I closed the door, leaning on it for a second to catch my breath and adjust my eyes.

'Are you okay, Granddad?'

'I'm fine. Happy to see you. Daisy's been looking forward to it all week. Have some tea?'

From there, all progressed as it should. We had tea and biscuits, and the ceremony filled up the spaces between our conversation. After a couple of hours, though, there was a lull. I tried to think of something to say, but the ticking clock and the falling dust mesmerised me and I couldn't seem to focus my mind.

'Are you sure you're coping okay?' you asked.

'Fine, thanks,' I replied. 'You're a good boy, always worrying about us. How's work?'

'Fine.'

There was more silence. I felt time slowing and stretching out like putty. A cloud passed over the sun. Your heel drummed loudly on the thin carpet. You kept shifting in your seat and looking around the room as if expecting something to change.

'Have you been using the computer?' you asked.

I hesitated, feeling that chasm opening up again. To say I had tried to use the machine would open me to your exasperation when you switched it on and I didn't know what to do. To say I had not tried made me feel guilty. The machine looked more complex and expensive than anything I'd ever owned, even though you insisted it was old and worthless. I felt ungrateful to leave it sitting in the dining room under an old, faded brown tablecloth, only exposed to the light every few weeks on a Sunday afternoon.

'No,' I said finally. 'I haven't used it.'

You sighed, clenching and unclenching your fingers on the rough denim crinkles in your jeans. 'I just wish you'd at least try,' you said. 'The internet is perfect for someone like you. You can order your food, meet people, interact with the whole world without leaving your house.'

I put the china cup to my mouth and let the hot tea still my tongue. I didn't know how to start explaining it. I've tried before, and the words didn't make sense to you. I have no interest in ordering my food from a warehouse in Newcastle. I like to go to the greengrocer, squeeze the peaches and choose the ones where I can feel the juice just beneath the skin. I like to hand over real money and get back real change from a real person whose skin I can feel briefly skimming mine as the coins trickle into my hand. I don't feel a need to 'interact' with the rest of the world. I'm happy here, with Daisy, in this house. The world is too big to understand anyway. In this house I can grasp everything, notice all the small changes in Daisy's appearance or the state of the garden. I can walk down the same pavements, pushing Daisy's wheelchair carefully over the same bumps and cracks. The roots of the cherry tree in the garden of number 45 have been extending out to the road, pushing up the paving stones; if it gets much worse, I'll have to write to the Council. Closer to the High Street, the crisp packets and Styrofoam fast-food boxes have been multiplying. A couple of times I even saw gnawed chicken bones discarded in the gutter, and wrote a letter to the local paper. These things may seem small and petty to you, but they're on the right scale for me at this time of my life. I'm like the aging household pet who, tired of scampering about after mice and balls of string, now chooses to curl up in his warm basket next to the radiator, reacting to passing events with nothing more than a half-cocked ear.

'I'll teach you again,' you said.

'It's fine.'

'No, really. Come on, it's ridiculous that you can't learn it.

Plenty of people your age and older have their own blogs.' You got up and started walking towards the dining room.

I glanced at the clock. Only two thirty. I stood up slowly and followed you. I remembered how you were as a little boy, always wanting to play some game or other. I used to humour you then, too, and it never felt like a strain. 'Back in a minute, dear,' I said, giving Daisy a pat on the hand. By the time I arrived in the dining room, you had already fired up the machine. Messages were flashing up too fast for me to read. I sat down, pulled my reading glasses from my top pocket, put them on and looked at the bright screen, my eyes already starting to hurt. 'It's like staring at a light-bulb,' I complained.

'You get used to it,' you said, staring unblinking into the centre of the screen. 'Remember when I made it less bright? You complained you couldn't read the text.'

'Yes, yes,' I grumbled. 'I never have that problem with books, you know.'

'Well, with books you can't travel around the world at the click of a mouse.'

'Yes, all right.'

You passed me the mouse. I remembered my piano lessons in the draughty school annex, the teacher breathing cough sweets over me and telling me to play a scale. My eyes would see the right keys to play, but my fingers would fall on the wrong ones. 'You haven't practised, boy!' the teacher would say, and with the sickly wave of cough sweets would come the sharp thwack of a ruler on my chapped knuckles.

'You remember how to start?' you asked softly.

'Of course,' I said, and tried to manoeuvre the arrow onto the 'Start' button. It headed off in the wrong direction, though. I tried to correct myself, but now the arrow disappeared off the screen altogether. I jerked the infernal thing around desperately, but couldn't see the little arrow anywhere. It was just how it used to be: the keys were merging into a mess of black and white and I couldn't remember which scale I was supposed to play.

'Here,' you said gently, taking the mouse from my fumbling hand. 'To start, you press 'Start', remember?'

'I was trying to, but the arrow went the wrong way.'

'You moved the mouse the wrong way,' you said, a note of impatience creeping into your voice. 'You always do.'

'It's not easy. The screen is vertical and the table is horizontal. I have to translate.'

'That's why you have to practise,' you said tightly.

I stared out of the window at the garden. The roses had gone a little wild lately with the combination of warm days and plentiful rain: perhaps they needed pruning. Weeds were showing through the cracks in the path again; my knees ached in anticipation. I felt stifled in this room, learning something that was supposed to liberate me. I just wanted to be in my garden, feeling the damp soil in my fingernails and smelling the fragrance of rosebuds and wet leaves. For a moment I closed my eyes and let my mind fill with a miasma of memories and sensations: the smell of cut grass in the summer, the sharp chill of a crisp winter afternoon, damp air rising from cracked paving-stones, the distant, distorted sounds of shouting children and radios.

'Granddad? You weren't even watching, were you?'

'The screen was hurting my eyes.'

'We've only just started.'

'Sorry. I'll try. So we're on the net now?'

'Yes, Granddad.'

'Good. So we have the world at our fingertips. What shall we do?'

'Anything you feel like. Anything at all, Granddad.'

'Can we eat a peach?'

'No.'

'Climb a tree?'

'No, but... '

'Bake a cake?'

'Stop being silly, Granddad.'

I sighed, and adjusted my reading glasses. 'You said I could do anything,' I said sulkily.

'I meant anything realistic.'

'You meant that I could read, type or buy something. The very things I spent a lifetime doing before these machines were invented.'

You let your head hang down, and ran a hand through your hair. 'I can't teach you if you won't at least try, Granddad.'

I felt sorry for you suddenly. You were like a child, so eager to show off your latest game, and I was being an old curmudgeon. 'I'm sorry. Go on. Show me what you like to do. Interact with somebody.'

'Okay.' Your fingers hammered the keys, you clicked the mouse, and the screen erupted in a blizzard of colours and words. I must admit that I did feel a certain admiration for your mastery of the machine. What to me is foreign is, to you, as easy as writing or talking. Perhaps, even easier. How long, I wonder, before writing is no longer taught, and how much longer after that before speech itself becomes obsolete?

'See?' you said, and I realised I had drifted off again.

'Sorry, it was all too fast,' I said. 'Show me again.'

Your lips tightened. 'It doesn't matter,' you said. 'Let's just go from here. You see where we are?'

I saw a lot, but didn't know where to start reading. There was the coloured strip across the top of the page, the text underneath, the words down the left, the pictures on the right advertising products I'd never heard of. You helped me out by pointing to a small image: a young man with a long fringe, his eyes staring up at the camera, his chin and body chopped off. 'That's you,' I said.

'Right.'

'And that's your name at the top.'

'Right. It's my online profile.'

I sighed. 'Meaning what?'

'It's my identity. It's what I show to the world.'

Something screamed inside my chest. This is not what identity is formed of, I wanted to say. I wanted to tell you all the things I have learned in my long, long decades on this Earth. I wanted to stop you from making the same mistakes as everyone else. I wanted to help you to be wise instead of clever. I wanted all this, but knew it would never happen. You'd never listen, or if you did you'd never understand. 'That's nice,' I said.

'My friends have profiles too, and I can see what they're doing and they can see what I'm doing.'

'Can they see me, too?' I asked.

You laughed, as if I were an endearing child. 'No, Granddad. This thing is too old to have a webcam. I just meant that I can tell them what I'm doing.' Your fingers clattered across the keyboard again, typing out the sentence, 'I am visiting my granddad.'

I smiled. 'That's nice,' I said. 'Like writing a postcard. Here, let me give you a better photograph, though. I have lots of them in that shoebox on the shelf there. Pass it to me, there's a good lad. There's that nice one from last Christmas, you could use that.'

You laughed again. 'It's okay, Granddad. I chose this one.'

'But it's distorted. Your eyes are stretched and your chin is cut off. I hardly recognised you.'

'Yeah, I know. It's the way people do it. Nobody wants just a bog-standard snapshot.'

'Oh. It's part of your identity.'

'Right.'

'You want to distort yourself.'

'Right.'

'What about the information? Is that distorted, too?'

'No. Well, it's what I want to put up. It's not everything, of course.'

'You say 'Politics: very liberal.' I didn't know that.'

You emitted a little cough. 'Well, as I said, it's just what I choose to put up.'

'What you want to show the world.'

'Right.'

I stared at the screen, but my eyes hurt again, and I pushed my glasses up onto my forehead and looked out of the window. The sun had gone, now, and the garden looked colder and more wintry. I felt glad to be inside.

'Why liberal?' I asked. 'I mean, they haven't been a serious force since David Steel, and even then they didn't have much chance. Now with that what's-his-name in charge, they're a joke.'

'It's liberal in the American sense, Granddad.'

'Oh. You mean free markets?'

'That's neoliberal.'

'Oh. Old liberalism, then: John Stuart Mill. Freedom from constraint.'

'No. It just means sort of left-wing.'

'Oh.' The cursor blinked on the screen for a few moments. I listened for any sounds from the living room but could hear nothing other than the faint gurgling of pipes in the attic.

'Like I said, Granddad, it's just an identity, just how I choose to portray myself.'

'And how you choose to portray yourself with me, the dutiful grandson, drinking tea and chatting politely and asking if we're doing okay, is that your real identity?'

'Of course, Granddad.'

'So it's just on the net that you're not real.'

Your response was a weary sigh. 'It's not that, it's just that I have different identities for different places. I experiment.' You started to stand up. 'Look, let's forget about it. It doesn't matter.'

'No, no,' I said. 'This is interesting. Teach me some more.' I put my glasses back on my nose, took the mouse and haltingly moved it across the screen.

You smiled and told me I was doing well. 'Click there,' you said, pointing somewhere at the top. With great difficulty and a few false starts, I managed to get the arrow positioned on top of the box. I clicked, but nothing happened. 'A bit to the left,' you said.

'They make it hard for you.'

'You get used to it.'

I moved the mouse the wrong way, then got it back into position and clicked. Suddenly the screen went white. 'Oh dear,' I said, thinking I'd broken it.

'It's okay, just a new page loading.'

'Oh,' I said, not wanting to ask what loading meant in this context. Soon enough, to my relief, the screen was filled again. Nothing made sense, though. In the jumble of text, I could make out a woman's face, her dark hair covering her forehead, large eyes staring up into the camera lens, chin cut off. 'Who's that?'

'Her name's Marie. I met her a couple of days ago.'

'On the computer, or in real life?'

'In real life, Granddad.'

I smiled. You never talk about women you meet. Perhaps I should make more effort with this computer. 'That's nice. She looks nice. Why is she on here?'

'She wants to be friends with me.'

'But you said you were already friends.'

'In real life, yes. But not online.'

'Oh.' I pushed my glasses up again and looked away from the screen, my eyes smarting and my head now beginning to throb a little. 'So she knows the real you, and now she wants to know the fake you?'

'Not fake, Granddad.'

'All right, the identity that you choose to show the world, is that correct?'

'Yes.'

I stood up. 'I think I need another cup of tea. All of this is too confusing.'

You looked up at me, hurt, and once again I was reminded of you as a little boy, playing games incessantly, never satisfied, always ending up with that same hurt expression whenever I said it was time to stop. 'I was going to sign you up on here too,' you said. 'It'll only take a minute.'

I smiled. 'I think one identity is enough for me to be going on with, Jeff. But you carry on. I'll be back in a minute and you can show me more. I just need a break, that's all. I'll be back.'

'Okay, Granddad,' you said, and you seemed to have forgotten me already, as your eyes locked into the screen and your fingers flew effortlessly across the keys. I went to the kitchen. My trembling hands turned on the gas, fumbled with the match and eventually got it lit. The blue circle of flames jumped up, and I filled the kettle and put it on. I looked around the room, my tired eyes drawing comfort from the scratched wooden table, the rickety chairs, the torn lino. I remember thinking how each item in the room is completely known to me. I can chart the history of every scratch in the table. I remember the exact day when the cold tap began to stick a little on the second twist. I could quite easily fill the kettle and light the gas with my eyes closed. If I lost my hearing and my sight, I would still be able to turn the gas off at the right time, spoon the correct amount of tea into the pot, and let it brew for just long enough before pouring it out. Not like your world, where everything is instant, leaving no time for opinions to be fully formed, friendships to be solid, beliefs to be firmly held. Everything as changeable as the weather. I prefer my tattered old kitchen, where things are scratched and soiled but nevertheless solid; they feel the same from day to day and from year to year. Even after I am gone, they will still be here and will still look the same, at least until you sell the house and the new owners gut it.

The brief thought of death sent a panic through my heart, and I rushed to the living room. 'Are you all right, love?' I asked softly. Daisy gazed out of the window. 'Good,' I said. 'I was worried.' I pulled a tissue from my pocket and surreptitiously wiped something from her chin, then patted her hand. 'Don't worry, we'll be back in a minute. I'd bring you in there, but you wouldn't be interested. Besides, it's always colder in that back room. You stay here, make yourself comfortable, and we'll be back soon.'

When I returned to the dining room, you had stopped typing and were just clicking every few seconds, making the screen change from one lurid colour to another. Videos popped up, started to play and were abruptly cut off. Advertisements flashed and disappeared, long stories were digested in a few seconds and dispatched with a click. I lost my balance for a moment, and put my cup down hastily so that I could grab the table for support.

The clank of china disturbed you, and you looked up sharply. 'Are you okay? You should have called me. I would have helped.' You started to get up, but I waved you away impatiently. Really, it's too much.

'It's fine. I can manage. It's only a cup of tea.' I sank heavily into the chair, picked up my cup again and sipped from it. 'There we are. So, where are we now?'

You smiled. 'I was just catching up on the news.'

'Really? What's happened?'

'Nothing.'

'Oh. Are you friends with Mary now?'

'Marie. No, I'm not.'

'Why not? She seemed like a nice young girl.'

You shrugged. 'It was a misunderstanding, really. She thought I was someone else.'

'Who?'

'You wouldn't understand, Granddad. Someone online.'

'Oh. But this is not you either, is it? This very liberal football fan with a floppy fringe and big eyes.'

You laughed, and for a moment you looked like a boy again. 'No, I suppose it's not. You're learning fast, Granddad.'

'Well, it's not so hard.' I thought for a moment. 'So if this Marie thinks you're somebody else, then it really doesn't matter, because this *you* is somebody else anyway. It's just what you choose to show the world. And if it tires you, you can change it, or delete it and start all over again. Correct?'

You laughed again, and looked at me with something like respect. 'I think you really understand it today. All this time I thought you weren't interested.'

I smiled sadly and looked at my roses. 'I'm just not ready for it,' I said. 'I prefer things the way they are. Simpler.'

'Life is complex, though, Granddad.'

'I suppose so. I always thought maybe one day it wouldn't be, but I suppose it is. Anyway, show me how you make friends with Mary.'

With a few clicks, it was done. It was all too fast for me to understand or remember, but it didn't matter. After you'd gone, I would dust down the large screen, empty out the crumbs from the keyboard, unfold the faded old brown tablecloth and spread it over the machine for another week. I was indulging you, as years ago I indulged you in a game of Snakes and Ladders. 'Good,' I said. 'So now you're friends. What happens now?'

You shrugged. 'We can write to each other, chat, see photos.'

I looked at the screen. 'Interesting.' I let you click and clatter for some time, and then suggested that we return to the living room. 'Grandma will be missing us.' You looked up at me, disappointed, but acquiesced. You tried to teach me once more how to shut down, but I can never remember that I have to click on 'Start.' 'Show me one more time,' I said. For once, you seemed not frustrated but amused at my forgetfulness. Perhaps, even in your world of constant change, it is still comforting to have some things remain the same. Perhaps you don't really want your granddad to understand fully, because then you would not be able to teach him. I led the way into the living room, offered you a Bourbon biscuit and, glancing at the clock, suggested that the traffic on the M1 would soon be getting heavy.

Chapter 7

When I saw that empty seat, I thought it was all over. I dumped the coffee, ran out of the hospital and kept running, as fast as my stupid clown shoes would let me run, until I got home. I felt so embarrassed, so ashamed. My dream had come true, I'd finally met the great Jeff Brennan, and I'd completely screwed it up. I decided to put you out of my head. Of course you weren't interested in me, I'd been stupid to think you ever could have been. To go from two-bit losers with Marilyn Monroe fantasies straight to Britain's number one political blogger was always going to be a stretch. Stupid to aim so high, and then be disappointed when my fantasy bubble burst. I decided to put you out of my head, and get back to real life. I wrote a blog post and a few tweets about the protest without even mentioning you. I was done with you.

Then something changed. Mrs Roberts and the church folk back home would have said that the devil got into me. Without meaning to, without consciously deciding to do it, I found myself looking at your Facebook profile. I'd seen it before, of course. My obsession with Jeff Brennan had taken me to all corners of the web. But this profile never seemed to fit, somehow. It made no mention of politics, apart from the stock response 'Very liberal.' It never referred to the blog, and the blog never referred to the profile. The friends of this Jeff Brennan didn't seem likely friends for Jeff Brennan the blogger. They were average twenty-somethings, doing average jobs in average places and going on vacations to Spain. The photo, too, didn't match my vision of Jeff Brennan. It was a photo of a younger, more fun-loving person than the Jeff Brennan I knew from his blog. A blurred, distorted mobile phone shot taken in a dark pub, not at all the sort of smooth glamour shot you'd associate with a celebrity. Besides, if you were so publicity-shy on your blog, surely you wouldn't set up a Facebook profile. You might exist in some more exclusive corner of the web, but not on Facebook. It was too easy. Friending this Jeff Brennan seemed too desperate even for me. I'd always dismissed it.

Now, though, I looked at the profile with new eyes, and understood it. You had the blog to express your politics, and this was the more private you. Of course the two identities never referred to each other: to do so would be to encourage every desperate fame-seeking blogger to friend you. This was your respite, your day off, the place where you posted holiday photos, kept in touch with old friends and filled in questionnaires about which Star Wars character you most resembled. It seemed to fit, now, and I began to experience the warm feeling I'd had sitting next to you in the hospital waiting room. I smiled, remembering that feeling, remembering your kind talk about my parents, and it seemed impossible that you wouldn't want to know me. I'd put a new profile picture up recently, and everyone said it was sexy. If you saw it, you'd see me as more than a clown. I hit 'Add as Friend', typed a few different messages and then settled on the shortest, lightest, least stalker-like version: 'You left suddenly. Something I said?'

After I'd sent the message, I felt a surge of relief. I'd done all I could, it was in your hands now. If you didn't reply, I really would forget you. I'd delete your blog from my favourites, cancel the RSS subscription, delete the cookie. It would be easy, because there would be no doubt: you really didn't want to know me. For a few hours I heard nothing. I tweeted about my hospital humiliation, leaving out your name of course, and my followers all said I should just move on, turn the page, forget about you. For a while I did just that. I read, I blogged, I commented and I bookmarked, all with no thought of trying to impress you. I felt liberated. It was all out of my hands. If you hadn't replied, I would never have thought of you again.

But, of course, you did. You accepted the friend request at three twenty-six on Sunday afternoon, saying 'Thx 4 teh add. At grandad's, wll write more later.' Then, later that night, you added: 'BTW, definitely not something you said, just had to rush off. Great to hear from you!!'

I remember exactly what you said. Hundreds of messages have passed between us since then, but it's the first two that I remember the most. After the second one, I tweeted the good news, and my followers all said I'd done the right thing. I'd been positive, proactive, had seized the day. The support poured in from all sides. I thought of how my popularity would soar if I revealed the identity of my mystery man, and was tempted for a moment to unleash this power, but I held back. After all that time of being treated like a bit of California fun, I'd finally met someone who liked me for who I was, even if I was dressed as a clown and looking ridiculous. You were the great Jeff Brennan, and you were interested in *me*, you said it was great to hear from *me*. I could never out you just to get a popularity boost. You were more important than momentary fame. You were real, lasting, maybe even permanent.

The excitement of announcing the news carried me through the rest of the day and late into the night. I began to update my profile obsessively, putting up all my best pictures, listing all my most interesting features or experiences. I did the same on all my other presences across the web, hoping to pre-empt your Googling of me. I wanted everything to be perfect: no embarrassing photos, no ill-considered opinions. I purged my blog of all but the best posts, and took down a couple of the links to more radical anarchist sites, just in case. I even deleted an account of a weekend trip to Prague: the sunset photos of the Charles Bridge were truly beautiful, but could not offset my horribly irresponsible carbon consumption. On Flickr I got rid of all the random shots and kept only the best, the most artistic ones, the ones where I looked the thinnest. On Twitter I deleted the stuff I'd written about meeting you, in case it made me sound too desperate. It was probably pointless: you'd no doubt seen it all already, and however many sites I purged there were hundreds more I couldn't get to. But I had to try. I wanted you to see the best of me, because I thought that was my only chance. After all, there must be a reason why all the men I attracted were assholes. You were so different from them, so much better. I had to make myself better if I wanted to have a chance of making it work. I had to show you the best photos, the best opinions, the funniest videos. Only the best would be good enough. Anything less and you'd lose interest, and I'd be back to falling for assholes who dumped me five minutes after getting me in the sack. This was different – I could see it even then – and I put everything into making it work.

I never again felt that calm, free feeling of the Sunday afternoon when I thought you were out of my life. After that day, everything I did was done with you in mind. Every blog post, comment, tweet, Facebook update or friend request was composed with you sitting in the front row of the audience. Whenever I commented on your blog now, I had to be careful to hide our real-life connection: I respected your wish to keep your personal and political lives separate. But sometimes I couldn't resist slipping in secret references, private jokes that only you would understand. After the initial contact on Facebook, we began composing flirtatious tweets on an increasingly regular basis. After a few weeks you gave me your personal email address. Then, a couple of months later, I found the courage to suggest meeting up in person, and after an agonising couple of hours of silence, you replied with your real-life address and phone number and a few tentative dates. And now I was sitting on a train passing through the outskirts of Milton Keynes, where you had promised to be waiting for me at the station.

I felt so nervous, like I was a teenager going out on my first ever date. I'd drunk too much coffee, and my heart was jumping around in my chest like a bird in a cage. I looked out of the window at the housing estates rolling past, and tried to calm down, but it was no use. It was like this was my final chance to break the cycle and actually get together with someone good, someone real. I'd already blown it once, but had been handed a second chance. The last few months of getting to know you online had been like a dream. You were so kind, so self-effacing, so humble. Most guys with a blog as famous as yours would have needed an extension on their garage to have space for their ego. But not you. You were the opposite. You hardly liked to talk about being famous at all. You were more interested in finding out about me and my lame kind of a life in London. You told me how much you admired me for working at a homeless shelter, making me sound like Mother Teresa or something. I said that what you did was way more important, but you insisted it wasn't. You really tried to make me feel good about myself, and although I didn't really believe it, I loved the fact that you tried.

I tried to picture you living in one of these places I was looking at through the dirty train window, but just couldn't. You were Jeff Brennan. You lived in a newer world, where the only currency was popularity. There were no rich blogs, poor blogs, suburban blogs or high-rise blogs. There were only blogs, and their worth depended on numbers of comments, pingbacks, clickthroughs, page views. Some blogs, of course, were better designed than others. But still, an expensively-designed blog with no readers was worthless. I just couldn't place you anywhere in this world of small brick houses and toy-strewn gardens.

In the world I knew you in, the photos were always cropped close. Outside the borders of the image could be a palace or a squat. It didn't matter. The only time any background context was shown would be on a special occasion: a holiday to the Caribbean, a backpacking trip to Latin America. Then, suddenly, the person shrank and the beach or the mountain took over. When the two weeks were over, though, the photos either stopped altogether, or shrank once again in scale, with the background of Bletchley or Hemel Hempstead erased and the blogger's face once again expanding and filling the frame.

In this world nobody took out the garbage or mowed the lawn. People had jobs, but never mentioned them except to rant amusingly about an annoying boss, wacky colleague or stupid management memo. People posted up photos of their cats every Friday, but never fed them or cleaned their litter trays. People had families, but they were always invisible or referred to by pseudonyms. People had houses, but the houses were never shown unless it was to post proud, carefully cropped photos of a new loft conversion. Nobody lived in a housing estate on the edge of Milton Keynes looking out through the rain at a postage-stamp garden next to the railway, covered with cracked plastic toys and rusting laundry poles. Nobody sat on slow commuter trains looking at these sad houses to pass the time. Everybody's life was edited mercilessly. The boredom and humiliation were cropped out, leaving only glamour and excitement. Popularity, after all, was the currency. Housing estates in Bletchley and slow commuter trains on rainy afternoons were the guilty secrets, the shameful inadequacy. They'd bring down a blog's value just as surely as a leaky sewer would erode property values.

The train began to slow down, and a crackly voice announced Milton Keynes Central as the next stop. People started to stand up and gather their bags, but I sat paralysed, staring out of the window and suddenly wishing the housing estates would keep rolling by forever. I was scared, now, to meet the real you, one on one, in your territory. I'd wanted it this way, of course. I'd planned it. I could've just turned up to the next environmental protest and met you there. But I didn't want to meet you again dressed in a ridiculous costume, with Marcus and a dozen other half-hearted, whistle-blowing protesters for company. I wanted us to be alone. I wanted to be dressed well, in my black skinny jeans and a casually low-cut top. I wanted to wear makeup that accentuated my best features, which everyone said were my high cheekbones and big brown eyes. I wanted my long black hair to be tossed casually over my shoulder in a way that framed my face perfectly, and now I glanced at my reflection in the window to make sure for the tenth time that everything was as it should be. Then I stood up, fluffed my hair one last time, slipped my bag over my shoulder and headed for the door.

On the platform, the country wind tossed my hair. It was definitely colder up here. Even though I was in a town, I could smell the fields that the air had passed over. It reminded me for a moment of the summers I'd spent with my grandparents in Iowa, walking across the big open fields and feeling the wind that seemed to have blown for a thousand miles over identical fields stretching to horizon after horizon from coast to coast. I remembered the dust settling in the crevices of my summer dress, the sudden torrential rainstorms that I used to run out into, my grandmother's silhouette against the porch light, her cracked voice shouting at me to 'git back inside', the rain thrumming on the tin roof, the hard-baked mud melting in the rain and flooding my sandals, the sudden quiet when it was all over, the sweet scent that rose from the soil as I squelched back to the house. I was so deep in the memories of Iowa that I was surprised when, as I walked blankly through the ticket gate, an Englishman stopped me and said, 'Hi.'

'Hi,' I said automatically, and then I saw you and remembered to smile. 'Good to see you.'

'You too,' you said uncertainly. 'I've just parked outside.

I'm on a yellow line, so we'd better go. I've been here ten minutes already.'

'Sure, sure, no problem. Sorry to keep you waiting.'

'Not your fault. Bloody trains, eh?'

The two of us chattered on like this all the way to the car. It was horrible. I searched my head for all the interesting things I had planned to say, but they were gone, swept away on the winds over the broad Iowa plains. So instead I talked about train timetables and parking regulations, laughing wildly at each of your feeble jokes and feeling desperation creep up on me with every step. In the car, there was a moment of peace while you closed my door and walked around to the driver's side. I tried to collect my thoughts. I knew from your blog that you were more interesting than this, and I knew I was too. But I just couldn't focus. My thoughts were still scattered. I was thinking about the car now, a dirty old diesel jeep. At the protest in Canary Wharf you'd joined in with everyone else as we blamed those bankers for killing the planet, but you probably did more damage just starting that thing up every morning than any of those people drifting past with their sandwiches and BlackBerrys. As you pulled away from the kerb it roared like a tank, and I could just feel the carbon dioxide pouring out of the tailpipe as we juddered out to the main road. It didn't make any sense. I was sure you'd written something on your blog about the damage caused by old jalopies. And although you'd never discussed your finances on your blog, from hints you had dropped I knew you were rich enough to be able to afford something newer. But I was so nervous that I couldn't remember whether manufacturing a new car caused even more pollution than running an old one, and didn't want to sound like an idiot. You were Jeff Brennan, after all. You must have thought it through more than me. So I kept quiet, and let you break the silence with talk of lunchtime traffic.

The broad avenues of Milton Keynes reminded me of home, or at least a miniature version of it. Most English cities

I'd seen before were dominated by their history, trying to channel cars and buses down medieval cart-tracks. This city, however, was built for cars. The few pedestrians scurrying around in the cold looked lost among the oversized shopping malls, thousand-space parking lots and four-lane avenues. They were either teenagers or geriatrics: everyone in-between seemed to live in the world of convenience, gliding along the slick highways from Debenhams to BHS, from BHS to Pizza Express, from Pizza Express to Costa Coffee, from Costa Coffee to school, from school to home, cheerfully spewing the pollution that will one day put this place underwater.

I started to ask you about all this, expecting an insight, but all I got was defensiveness. 'I need a car, living out here,' you said. 'When they build a biofuel tram to my house I'll be on it, but until then I've got to get from A to B.' You were practical. You saw life the way it was, not the way it could be. I felt as if I didn't know you, and fell silent again.

You parked in front of Pizza Express. I honestly thought it was a joke, that somewhere behind this generic box was a cute little independent vegan café with a table for two laid out ready. I can't remember what I said but I remember the way you looked at me. It was a look I used myself as a child, when I was afraid of having said the wrong thing. 'You don't like pizza?'

'I love pizza,' I said. 'I just don't like chains. You know as well as I do they're destroying our towns, homogenising our culture. You wrote about that earlier this year.'

Again, you got defensive. You told me there was no choice. The town was built like this, on a scale that only the biggest chains could ever afford to inhabit. It was homogenised on the planning board, destroyed before it was created.

'So why do you live here?'

'I was born here. Besides, it's where the jobs are.'

'But you're a blogger. You can blog from anywhere.'

You hesitated. 'I wasn't always full-time. I needed a job at one time, so I came back here. Then I decided to stay anyway.

It's a kind of laboratory for me, a place where the corporate future is being incubated. If you want to argue against it, you have to understand it, right? Can't shy away from it and pretend it doesn't exist.'

It was that reply that saved the day from ruin. It was a reply that showed me the Jeff Brennan I knew. The choices that had seemed contradictory now made perfect sense. As I sat there in the car, staring at the corporate chain restaurant in front of us, I saw that you were right. You have to understand before you can criticise. Suddenly I felt that it was my life that was contradictory: living among artists and activists, eating at organic cafés, cycling everywhere, self-righteously criticising the modern world while the modern world completely ignored me. And why wouldn't it ignore me? I was irrelevant. I had made myself irrelevant in my quest for purity and correctness. I had locked myself away in a guilt-free, carbon-neutral bubble while all around me, in places like Milton Keynes, the real world went on. You were facing it all head on while I, like a child, covered my eyes to make it go away.

I started to cry. I cried for my blog, I cried for all the protests and marches I'd been on, and I cried for all the people living confused, stumbling lives, the people who, until now, I'd just written off as ignorant or uncaring and tried to hector into agreeing with me. I cried for my parents cycling for milkshakes, my grandparents catching rainwater from the farmhouse roof, for all the people around the world who run around and around in a colossal, frenetic attempt to change what will never change. I cried for England, I cried for America which is just the same really, and I cried for all the people around the world who starve and die so that this pointlessness may continue a little longer.

'Look, we don't have to go to Pizza Express,' you said. 'It was just an idea. We can drive out to the country, find a nice little teashop or something.'

I shook my head, trying to blink away the tears. 'It's not that.'

'A country pub, maybe. Most of them are older than your whole nation, you know.'

I let out a little spurt of laughter, but the tears continued. I could feel your panic building. I wanted to reassure you, but I couldn't stop the tears. I did the only thing I could do. I turned away, got out of the car and stood in the cold grey air of the parking lot, letting the chill wind sting my cheeks.

'We can go anywhere you want,' you said quietly, walking around to my side of the car and putting a tentative arm around my shoulder. 'Anywhere.'

I smiled. The cold had calmed me, as always. I felt dwarfed by the huge buildings looming over the broad avenue as far as the eye could see. In that environment it seemed impossible to maintain the illusion that my emotions were important. Whereas my grief had filled the car, it now simply melted into air. I was small, and my emotions were smaller. I saw my sorrow as absurd, my concern for the starving as melodramatic. The tears slowed, my breathing became deeper and more rhythmic. I reminded myself who you were, how much I'd got to know you online, how much I had staked on you being the one. This feeling of not recognising you was just first-date nerves, an awkwardness that would pass. It would work this time. It had to work this time. You pulled me a little closer, and it occurred to me that you probably thought it was your arm that had stemmed my tears. I indulged you, leaning in a little closer and resting my head on your shoulder. The cold wind began to bite. I felt you shiver a little. 'Let's go,' I said.

'Where to?'

'Here. Pizza Express.'

'Are you sure?'

I nodded. 'I'm sure. Right here. This is where I need to be.' I took a deep breath, pulled you closer, and walked with you towards the revolving door.

Chapter 8

Marcus Higgins @marcushig	40m
@JeffB congrats mate. Glad it went well	
Marcus Higgins @marcushig	39m
@CalifM u sure u know what u r doing? :-)	
Marcus Higgins @marcushig	37m
@CalifM seriously tho am happy for you	
Marcus Higgins @marcushig	37m
@LoveLadyGaga Thx 4 the link	
Marcus Higgins @marcushig	36m
@HouseFanLester Ignore the haters!	
Marcus Higgins @marcushig	32m
@JeffB @CalifM Hey, why no reply, whatre you two up to???	
Marcus Higgins @marcushig	30m
@LoveLadyGaga The 1st vid is better IMO :))	
Marcus Higgins @marcushig	27m
Everyone keep the 15th free. BIG protest planned!!	
Marcus Higgins @marcushig	11m
@JeffB @CalifM Fine, going to bed now, catch you in morning	

Chapter 9

First time I met Marie, it was like a dream and a nightmare all rolled into one. The dream was her: the look of her, the smell of her. She'd worn this unbelievable outfit of black calf-length boots, bare legs and a short black skirt, with a loosely-buttoned white blouse and her hair tied up at the back to expose her neck. When I went to kiss her hello, I just got caught up in the scent of her and didn't want to let go. Got to admit, I wanted to find fault. Some reason why she was wrong for you, why it wouldn't work, why you'd come back to me and our Saturday nights. But she was so cheerful and warm in that American kind of a way. True, the political stuff was a bit too much for me, I mean, when she talked about being vegetarian it sounded like she was Jesus Christ preaching on the mountaintop. But she never guilt-tripped me like Marcus did. Just said her crazy piece and left it at that.

The nightmare was me. Knowing she was out of my league and there was nothing I could do about it. She was out of yours, too, or would have been if you'd told her the truth. But you didn't. She made an assumption and you never corrected her, and I hoped for your sake she wouldn't find out, at least not for a while. That night she was all crazy for you, and it didn't matter that it was only because she thought you were famous. You were happy, and I had to swallow it and smile. Knew straight off I couldn't compete with her. Maybe if I'd have met her earlier. Maybe then it would have been different. She'd have been the one who had to be nervous. But by then you'd made your choice.

I was the one on trial, not her. Marie was the new star in your life, and I was demoted to the reserve team, only to be called into action when she was unavailable. That night she was on the form of her life, and I didn't even get a look-in.

It made it worse that I get all nervous around women who look like that anyway. When she smiled at me and blew a strand of that long dark hair off her face, I felt like a teenager again. All my confidence disappeared, and all I could do was smile and go along with her. Even when she asked me the question I hated more than anything else, I couldn't come up with my usual sarcastic reply. You'd been trying to big me up, telling her all about my hacking exploits, and she asked me why I didn't go and work for Google or something.

'Too late,' I said. 'You got in at the beginning at Google, you made a fortune in six months. Now they're like any other company, just a salary and a shitload of pressure.' I could see her looking at me like I was chatting shit, and you had this weird kind of pitying expression that I didn't want to see. I knew how it sounded. Usually it sounded a lot better, like I was this genius who'd just been born at the wrong time, but this time it sounded self-pitying and stupid and I knew it. Still, I carried on to the end. The whole story. Growing up dreaming about the dot-com boom. People making fortunes just from an idea and a basic website. Then there was Google, then Web 2.0, and I'd missed the boat on all of it. 'Programming's a commodity now,' I said. 'Any idiot can learn it. They outsource half of it to India, and what's left is underpaid bullshit. I'd rather make my money doing something else, and do what I enjoy in my spare time.'

Give her credit, Marie didn't let an awkward silence fall. She said straight off how it made sense to her, even though I could see it didn't. I could see her thinking there'd be other new things all the time and if I'd missed one I should just stop whining about it and get on the next one. I mean, that's what I'd have thought if I was her. Like I said, usually it came out better. Still, she flashed me one of those massive American smiles and said she was sure

I'd hit on something big one day in my spare time, and then changed the subject.

I knew things weren't going well, but I stretched it out for as long as I could. Insisted on going out for some food, and since there was nothing much around your place we ended up in Xscape. Drifting around from bar to bar, grabbing some chips here, a donut there. Even went bowling to make the time go faster. Normally you were the most competitive fucker I knew. You'd count the pins yourself, and if the machine had missed one you'd call the staff over to spend ten minutes reprogramming the thing, just to increase your score by one point. But Marie thought bowling was stupid, and so you laughed along with her and threw a couple of balls deliberately into the gutter to make her feel better about her score. And all the time I drank more and more, knowing that I couldn't say anything to you because you would just side with Marie and I wouldn't even be on the reserve team any more. I'd be released from my contract altogether and left to ply my trade in the lower leagues. I just bowled and drank, and a sweet haze settled over me so that I hardly saw you any more, let alone cared what you were saying. I listened to the loud music and saw the bright lights flashing and blurring in front of my eyes, and I bowled and drank, bowled and drank, bowled and drank, until at some point I realised I was bowling alone.

After that, things got all fucked up. Since we were kids I'd always called you up whenever I felt like it, but now you always had some excuse. Sometimes I'd see you online and try to chat to you, but you didn't even reply, and a minute later your status changed to 'Unavailable'. I felt like I had to book an appointment with you, like you had to ask Marie's permission before you said yes. It made me feel shit. I started going out more with Terry and that crowd, and if you looked at the photos I posted you'd say I was having the time of my life. I was always munted, always laughing, always surrounded by groups of people laughing and making faces for the camera. But really all I wanted was our old Saturday nights. A few beers, a few *Desert Wars* missions, a curry and *Match of the Day*.

Even when you did get a Saturday night off, you still spent the whole time talking about Marie. We'd be smashing the shit out of some terrorist stronghold, and you'd just start saying Marie said this or Marie did that. It felt like you didn't give a shit, like you were only going through the motions. You killed and maimed like before, but you didn't savour it. You laughed at Gary Lineker's puns, but you didn't really find them funny. Every time you ducked away to get another beer, I imagined you telling Marie you wouldn't be long, saying you just had to spend a bit more time with me for old time's sake. I mean, I was happy for you that you were all loved up and all that, but it made me feel pretty shit. Only time you came alive was when you talked about Marie. You talked about the lies, and the lies that resulted from the lies, and I told you everything would be alright. Still good for something I suppose.

You quickly found out the hardest lies were the small ones. I mean, the big stuff took care of itself. First one was the easiest of all: Marie made an assumption and you didn't correct her. The lie was told, and not even by you. After that, the other big lies, like making your CV coincide with the real Jeff Brennan's, were a piece of piss. He was some kind of sad recluse, so apart from his blog there wasn't much about him online. If he did drop in a mention of some poncy school he'd gone to, all you had to do was memorise that and treat it as your own story. Those things don't come up very often anyway.

The day-to-day shit was harder. You got it into Marie's head that blogging was like a normal nine-to-five job for you, so when she saw you going off to work every day she didn't think anything of it. Even admired you for it, your dedication and all that. It was simple enough to pretend that you blogged from a rented office space in a big building in the centre of Milton Keynes, the building where, in reality, you went and worked your balls off for someone else. The timing of Jeff Brennan's blog posts gave you problems at first, but you got it all sorted pretty quick. Wasn't one of those blogs that comments on news by the minute anyway. Normally just one post a day, around mid-morning, and mostly on something that had happened a day or two earlier. Seems like his great selling-point was posting well thought-out responses, not knee-jerk reactions. Whatever. It meant you had time to read his posts at work, trawl through all the comments and be able to talk about it to Marie in the evening. When he posted at a weird time, like when you were on your way home or with Marie, you could just tell her you'd written the post at the office and scheduled it to come out later to space them out.

Problem was, you wouldn't know what it was about. Once, it almost killed you. The two of you had gone to bed early, you were all evasive about what you'd been doing, but it was pretty obvious. Anyway, seems Marie got up from the tangled bedsheets and went into the living-room to eat chocolates and surf the web for a while. You were just dozing off to sleep when she came in and jumped on top of you.

'I loved your post!' she said, kissing you hard on the mouth.

'Thanks,' you said. 'I'd wanted to write about Afghanistan for a while now. What's happening there is just horrible.'

'No, I mean your latest one, silly! It was just beautiful. Where did you get the idea to write about that?'

Your mouth went dry. You looked up at Marie's face. All flushed and excited. Almost no difference, though, between excitement and anger. Flip a switch, expose a lie. Let a few little words slip out of your mouth. Suddenly Marie's eyes burn with a different fire. Her knees still pin your arms to your sides, but not playfully any more. Her face is still flushed, her breath still short. She still bends over you, but to do what? Slip her fingers around your throat? Reach across for the scissors on the bedside table and bury the blades into your carotid artery? Just a few small words. You stared up into Marie's wide brown eyes and felt her hair brushing your cheek as if for the last time, and it made you scared. Not guilty, just scared. Scared that it would all end. Scared you'd have to go back to who you were before.

'What are you thinking about, sweetheart? You're miles away.'

The words floated at you from space, like they had nothing to do with the way Marie's lips were moving. Your reply, as well, came from somewhere else. 'I'm thinking I don't want to talk about blogging,' you said, and with a smile you wriggled your arms out from under her and reached for her waist, pulling her down on top of you. She gasped slightly and you rolled her over onto her back and kissed her just as she was about to speak. Kissed her so long and hard that whatever words were about to come out never did. You didn't say any more, but I could imagine the rest. Some time in the night, with Marie deep in sleep, you slipped out of bed and into the living room and caught up on everything you had to know. What it was I can't remember, and who cares anyway, all those posts are the same really. Point is, you survived, but only because of some words that came from outside. If that instinct or whatever it was hadn't kicked in, your relationship was over.

After that I persuaded you to buy an iPhone. Wasn't like you could afford it, but what's a bit more credit card debt if it saves your relationship? You subscribed to Jeff Brennan's RSS feed and got a message whenever he posted, so you could check it out instantly. Still, though, there was a whole heap of shit you had to keep in your head all the time, a whole life you had to make your own. Marie might ask 'How was your day?' and you had to be careful. Your day, all the office politics and stupid user errors, wasn't what she was asking about. You had to stop instead and think what sort of day Jeff Brennan the blogger would have had. Think about the post he wrote, the comments he got and what sort of mood that would have put him in.

Every word counted. Even a passing doubt in Marie's mind could lead to a whole load of places you really didn't want her to go. You had a filter in your head for every thought, every comment, every joke. Made you sound like a politician being interviewed on Sunday morning TV. That little pause before speaking. The smile or furrowed brow or deep breath or some other bullshit to cover it. So fucking transparent. Even did it with me, didn't you? Out of habit, I guess, since you had nothing to hide. Of course I took the piss, but you kept on anyway. Had to try and convince yourself it was really who you were. Best way to lie is to believe you're telling the truth and all that. So you put up with the piss-taking and talked like a politician.

The pressure really began to get to you after a while. Too much to keep up with, too many balls for one person to have to keep in the air all the time. Always that fear that something would happen, no matter how hard you tried to keep things safe. Everything would be fine, and then you'd lose it for a second and a ball would drop. When one drops they all drop. Illusion's over. Had to happen in the end. You knew it, I knew it. Like I said in the beginning, nothing lasts forever. Just getting together with Marie at all was a major fucking achievement. Way better than the handful of drunken snogs I'd managed in the same amount of time. I was rooting for you to keep the balls in the air as long as you could. Trouble was, knowing it has to end one day is one thing. Facing the prospect of it ending today, right now, this minute, is different shit altogether. The uncertainty, that's what killed you more than anything else. The ball-crushing fear every time you opened your mouth. Cacking yourself every time the phone rang. Scouring the web like an OCD motherfucker on speed, looking for that one random photo or comment that would ruin it all. Who can live like that? Sometimes I felt sorry for you, thought maybe you should've just steered clear after all. But then I looked at Marie's profile picture, looked around at my skanky flat with its empty bed and fag-stained carpets, and decided that all the shit you were going through was most definitely worth it.

Chapter 10

Living with the great Jeff Brennan was not at all how I'd imagined it. I'd pictured myself getting all the inside scoops, having these amazing conversations with you about life and politics and how the world really worked. Pretty dumb of me, right? I mean, since you were so modest and self-effacing on your blog, of course you'd be the same way in person. But there's modest and then there's downright secretive. You never told me anything. You went off downtown every day and wrote these unbelievable, beautiful, insightful posts, and came home talking about what was on TV that evening. You introduced me to some of your friends, but only people like Jon who just wanted to get drunk all the time. I knew you must have other friends – serious, intelligent people like you – and decided you were hiding them from me, or me from them. You were probably ashamed of me, this unemployed American girl who hadn't achieved a damn thing in all the years you'd been running Britain's most popular political blog.

When I asked about your blog you just shrugged and told me something I knew already just from reading it. When I pressed, you said you didn't like talking about work, and turned the conversation back to me, like my day of surfing the web and chatting to my friends really mattered or something. I guess you were just trying to be considerate, to make me feel better about my lack of a life, but all it did was make me feel shut out. To find out about your day I had to read your blog, just like anyone else. I'd even leave comments sometimes, and you'd reply as if you didn't know me at all. I know it had to be that way, but it didn't stop it from hurting me. Sometimes that feeling from the Pizza Express parking lot came back, that feeling of not recognising you. But every time it came, I took a deep breath and pushed it away. You were different from all the others. I'd gotten what I wanted, the man of my dreams, and I wasn't about to let myself screw it up.

I really should have been happy, shouldn't I? You were Jeff Brennan, the famous blogger. So kind, thoughtful, eager to make me happy. Maybe that was the problem. Having someone so desperate to make you happy is a lot of pressure. It made me feel like I'd failed you if I had a bad day or a bad month. It's hard to be happy when you're feeling guilty half the time.

No, it's not fair to put it on you. It was me, I guess, and my feelings of not being good enough. I mean, you were this bigshot blogger, and what was I doing? Nothing. Moving in with you in Milton Keynes meant quitting my job at the shelter, and finding new work was tough. The job agency windows were full of ads for finance managers and IT consultants, but nothing I was qualified for or interested in. I retreated to the flat to search online, and ending up spending more time Skypeing my friends in London or tweeting or Facebooking or emailing. But all the contact just made me feel more isolated than ever. Your need for anonymity forced me into lies. I did as you suggested, and told my friends you worked in IT. But then how could I tell them about the excitement I felt when I read your blog, or about the inferiority I felt every day living with a high achiever and achieving nothing myself? You were famous, and I was nobody. How could I tell them that I wanted to share this other part of your life, that I felt so hurt when you shut me out? I couldn't talk to anyone about all that, couldn't even talk about not being able to talk about it. So I said things were fine, and talked about the minutiae of my job search.

Meanwhile my friends talked about exhibitions I wouldn't see, openings I wouldn't attend, parties I hadn't gone to. I could enter their world through my computer screen, but then it was over and I was in an empty flat with nothing to do until you came home. Sometimes, if the loneliness got too bad, I did call you on your mobile and you'd come home and lift my spirits for a while, but you were always looking at your watch and, after the allotted half-hour had passed, you'd make your excuses and leave.

When I finally found a job, I thought things would change. It seemed perfect for me: a charity for the homeless, right in the centre of Milton Keynes. A more senior position than I'd had in London. Better pay, more responsibility. I'd be doing policy work, setting strategy. I could really make a difference. At the shelter in London I'd been on the front lines, dishing out food, helping people to find housing or access benefits or challenge an abusive landlord, which was all very well, but nothing ever really changed in the big scheme of things. No matter how many people I helped, there were always more coming through the door. With this new job, I'd be able to solve problems instead of just applying a Band-Aid. I felt so excited as I filled out the application form, and my excitement must have seeped into the paper because they called me for an interview even though I didn't have all the qualifications and experience they were asking for. At the interview I just bowled them over with my energy and ideas and all that stuff, and a few days later they called and offered me the job. I started the following Monday, and as you drove me to work in the jeep it felt like the first day of school. I felt important again after all the long weeks of nothingness. I felt like we were both driving off to improve the world, you in your way and me in mine. I felt almost equal to you for a while. I burst into the office with the same enthusiasm I'd felt as I filled out the application form.

Gradually, though, my energy and enthusiasm leaked away

like water from a burst pipe. I was left dry and lifeless, needing to visit the coffee machine more and more often before I could face my work. All my ideas were met with cynical smiles and responses like, 'In an ideal world, yes, but you'd never get approval for something like that.' I felt naïve for caring, stupid for sitting up late at night letting the ideas tumble into my notebook and shrugging you off every time you tried to coax me to bed. I felt grandiose for thinking I could change even the organisation's policy, let alone the government's. I slowly realised that my boss talked about wanting out-of-the-box ideas and blue-sky thinking simply because he liked the way the words sounded in his mouth. When I took him at his word and suggested allowing homeless people to sleep in our office while it lay empty at night, he came up with a million reasons why it wasn't practical. Over the weeks and months I slowly adapted, and gradually things became easier as a result. I no longer crashed into limits, but stayed comfortably inside them, producing what was expected of me.

What was expected of me was this: analysis of fundraising efforts. What sort of response rate did we get from one ad versus another? Which one plucked at the heart-strings most effectively? What were the trends? White teenage boys used to be the most effective because they reminded people of their sons, but their stock was down, now they evoked feral hoodies. Black teenagers had always been a no-go zone and remained so. Asian was good, although too Middle Eastern and people started to think terrorism. Old people could be good if they were frail enough, otherwise potential donors started to think about scroungers and benefit cheats. It turned out that the biggest return on advertising spend was generated by an image of a white teenage girl with ethnically diverse friends in the background. And so that's what I wrote in my report, and I included lots of charts and graphs and presented it confidently to my boss, and he was blown away by it. So then I had to produce more reports, digging down in greater detail: the advertising copy, the format, the delivery, the effectiveness of internet versus billboard versus magazine versus direct mail. Which combination of words and images, in which particular place and time, cut most efficiently through people's defences and made them reach for their credit cards? It was a never-ending job.

Some mornings, though, I just couldn't bear to get started. I know it sounds terrible, to have gotten everything I wanted and still be unhappy, but it was how I felt. I remember this one particular Wednesday morning when everything came to a head and I just felt like killing someone. The office was tiny and claustrophobic. It was half a floor of an old sixties building, separated by a thin partition from an accounting firm. Cold air rushed in through the huge windows, and personal heaters were banned due to health and safety. The grey and beige colour scheme was broken only by the family photos and holiday-souvenir bric-a-brac on the desks, and by two large potted plants either side of the door with signs in the soil warning 'DO NOT WATER'. A small room to one side contained a photocopier and rows of empty shelves that, rumour had it, used to contain stationery, and then in a small room opposite there was a fridge, a sink and a coffee machine. Sitting at my desk I was always conscious of the other faces around me. Over the months I had tried various ways of blocking them, to give myself the illusion of privacy, but nothing worked. I could position my head so that I was shielded from Jason by my computer screen and from Julie by a stack of gossip magazines, but that still left Martin. There was no antidote to Martin, who sat diagonally across to my left. More magazines would be too obvious, and most other structures large enough to shield me were prohibited by more health and safety regulations. And then, of course, there was Jerry to my left, a quiet man generally but sitting so close that sometimes, if we both reached for a document at the same time, our hands touched. And there was Shweta to my right, and a whole row of four people behind me who could turn around and look at my screen or call my name at any time, and my boss who sat not far away and simply stood up and called out whenever he wanted me, and all the people who walked past on the way to the kitchen.

The only way to achieve privacy was to go the toilet, to go outside or to retreat into the kitchen or photocopying room. If I took too long, though, there'd be a joke when I got back – 'Thought you'd got lost!' or 'Working part-time, are we?' – and I could never complain because they were, after all, only jokes. But jokes can quickly become reputations, as they did with Valerie, who had two small children and serious sleep deprivation, to compensate for which she would let her eyes close and her chin fall to her chest for a few minutes every morning at around ten thirty. It became a standing joke in the office. The atmosphere of suppressed mirth would start to build at around quarter past, and then the emails flew around as her eyelids began to slide slowly down, defying her sporadic efforts to yank them back up. As soon as she woke up and went to the kitchen to get another cup of coffee from the machine, the stifled giggles would be released and the jokes would bounce around from desk to desk. Everyone was sad when, one morning, Valerie's name plate was gone and a security guard came to pack her photos and coffee mug into a small cardboard box.

So even though I wanted to get away from my desk on that Wednesday morning, I didn't dare. I just sat there with eyes on me from all angles, clicking in circles from email to 'to do' list, to a report I had no interest in writing, to the internet but not for too long, and back to my email. Years could pass in this way, I felt. For an hour or two each day the feeling of futility seemed to subside just long enough for me to make progress on my report, and one day it would be finished, and my boss would praise it, and I would be called a success, and would start to write another report. Nobody seemed to know exactly what my reports involved or how long they should take, so nobody questioned all the hours spent just waiting for time to pass. In any case, I'm sure they were all guiltily sheltering their own lost hours, too.

I began to play with the cord of my phone, twining it absent-mindedly with my fingers and then untangling it again. The fingers of my right hand started to brush the buttons: '0', '7', '7', '5', '8'... Of course I wouldn't actually call you. This was your prime writing time. While I played with a phone cord, you would be immersed in the latest intricacies of Westminster politics, formulating an argument that would put the whole thing in a new light. I couldn't actually call you. Besides, what could I say to you, with Jason and Julie and Martin and Jerry and Shweta listening to every word? They didn't know about you. I could never tell them, or anyone else. If you were a different kind of person, I might have been featured in those gossip magazines stacked on the desk. A grainy shot of me going to the newsagent's, with a sidebar speculating over whether I'd had a boob job. But that wasn't your style, and I respected you for it. You wanted to remain anonymous, and I couldn't let your secret out. So I didn't tell them a thing. I went along with the office banter and pretended I was just an ordinary person like them.

My fingers brushed over the phone's buttons again, and again, and again, and then they began to press harder, toying with actually dialling the number, depressing the keys not quite enough to make a connection. Then suddenly the phone sprang into life: the screen light came on, and the numbers flashed across the screen as the tones rang out from the speaker across the silent office. In a panic I picked up the handset and turned off the speakerphone.

'Hello,' I heard you say. 'Hello?'

I longed to say something, to tell you I loved you, but it would have sounded stupid. You hated being interrupted in the middle of your writing time, I knew that. Before you could say anything else I put the phone down with a clatter, my heart racing, thankful only for the fact that the office phone would have been identified to you only as 'Private number'.

'Thought better of it, did you?' Jason said teasingly. I smiled tightly and clicked my mouse.

'Better of what?' Julie asked. And Jason repeated the whole story of my aborted phone call, and then repeated the repetition for a couple of other people who missed the first telling, and five or ten minutes passed with a discussion of my possible motives. Thank God, they never guessed the truth. They decided I was suffering from the post-coffee blues, those terrible doldrums after caffeine has been swallowed but before it has taken effect. Those ten or fifteen minutes, everyone agreed, are the hardest in the day, even tougher to get through than the after-lunch energy crash or the grindingly slow wait for five o'clock. Julie said that while she was waiting for the coffee to kick in, she couldn't even face checking her voicemail, let alone making a phone call. Jason said he felt like a ship with no wind in its sails, a suspiciously pretentious-sounding image that got him a whole load of mockery. They all agreed, though, that it was just when you felt the coffee would never release its power, and you would go through the rest of your life with that blank, empty feeling, that you suddenly felt your eyes pop open and your blood begin to pump again.

At that point I managed to bring the conversation to an end by sitting up with my arms out in front of me and saying, as if I was at an evangelical meeting, 'I can feel it, I can feel it!' Everyone laughed, and went back to their computers. I phoned someone in accounts whose call I'd needed to return for several days, and afterwards everyone congratulated me on surviving the post-coffee blues. I left it a good amount of time, and then walked as casually as I could to the elevator, went down to the ground floor and out into the empty pedestrian walkway and began taking huge gulps of fresh air like a drowning swimmer bursting through the surface.

I needed to see you. That much was clear. I needed to tell you the truth, to stop pretending that everything was alright. I needed to say what I felt so guilty for saying: that although I had you, and I had a good job working for a good charity doing good things, it still wasn't enough. I needed to tell you that I'd taken a wrong turn. I'd taken a wrong turn, and if I didn't turn back now, I'd be lost forever in the undergrowth, thrashing around in the darkness and praying for the weekend. Somehow I'd gone from helping people to figuring out how to exploit their image for money. Perhaps it was a more important thing I was doing now, but I missed the old days at the shelter in London. I thought of the regulars, the old guys who didn't really want help but stopped by every morning for the free tea and biscuits, half an hour in the warmth of an office with the comfort of human contact and a bit of innocent flirtation with the American girl behind the desk. I missed their wrinkled faces, their thick, dirty hands, their masked vulnerability. So what if they came back every day, and never ended up with a job or a house? A cup of tea and half an hour of harmless chit-chat was what they wanted, and I gave it to them. It was more than I'd given to anyone in this new job. Here I would evaluate them as commodities, judging each face on its capacity to generate cash if placed in front of a camera. I'd taken a wrong turn, and I wanted to go back. I looked at my watch and hurried back up to my desk, wondering who would be the first person to smile at me and say they'd been about to send out a search party.

All morning I had my eye on the clock at the bottom-right of my screen, and as soon as it hit twelve I picked up my handbag and coat and went out. 'Early lunch?' Jason inquired with a raised eyebrow.

'Yeah Jason,' I said. 'Better send out a press release: Marie In Early Lunch Shock – Pictures!' My voice must have carried an edge, because he looked hurt until I forced a laugh from my mouth and said 'Joke'.

I paused just long enough to see that I'd fixed the damage, and then I was out of there and into the streets. I remembered the building you'd pointed out to me from the jeep one day, a tall glass building on one side of a square concrete plaza. I even remembered the window you'd pointed to, one of a hundred in that huge glass face. I'd passed by often in my lunchbreak, sometimes even stopping for a bite to eat in Starbucks or Strada and sitting in the plaza gazing up at your window, imagining you behind it tapping inspired words into your computer. Because you never talked about it, the whole thing still seemed unreal to me. So I sat there sometimes in the plaza and imagined you creating your blog, trying to make it real in my mind. I think maybe if you'd let me in just a little bit, I'd've been happy and could have left it alone. But you shut me out so completely that I began to wonder what you really did all day, to imagine all kinds of crazy shit.

So now I would see it for real. I had to. If I could just see it, then perhaps I could stay in that job after all. Maybe I was just being impatient, and if I stuck with it then one day I could be the boss and do things differently. Maybe, but all I knew was that I needed to see you. I hurried across the concrete plaza, through the growing herds of workers grazing for food, and ducked inside the office building.

'Can I help you?' asked the security guard from behind the desk. I thought of the day I'd met you, the guards circling us, you dressed as a diver and me as a clown. The tone now was quite different: my respectable clothing had given me admittance. But still I lacked the ID badge that had taken you straight up to the eighth floor, the one that dangled around my neck was for a different building, and had no currency here. Beneath the pleasant enquiry was the edge of a challenge.

'I'm here to see Jeff Brennan,' I explained. 'The blogger.' As soon as the words were out of my mouth, I felt stupid. You'd gone to so much trouble to protect your anonymity that you would hardly advertise your presence in the lobby of the building. You'd have rented the space under a different name, some corporate entity. I smiled to myself as the guard frowned doubtfully but checked his register out of duty. I knew what he'd find.

'No bloggers here,' he said finally, looking up from his book. 'This building is mostly law firms, we don't really have individuals.' He was warming up a little bit now, perhaps feeling sorry for me and my mistake.

'It's okay,' I said. 'I must have the wrong building. I'll call him. Thanks anyways.' The guard smiled openly now, all suspicion gone as I walked through the revolving doors with my mobile pressed to my ear.

'Hi sweetheart,' you said.

I was caught off guard. When I was calling I thought I could always hang up again if I changed my mind, but I'd forgotten that this time you would recognise the number. I had no choice but to continue. 'Hi,' I said. 'Sorry to interrupt, but... '

'What's wrong?' you asked, your voice full of concern. I knew that if I said I was ill or in trouble, you'd drop everything and come to meet me. Your blog post would remain half-written, your notes in a pile on your desk. You'd abandon it all for me. Whatever great post you'd been writing would be lost forever. When you returned to it the next day, you'd struggle to pick up where you left off, and even if you did finish it, it wouldn't be the same. I'd have ruined your blog for a day. And what if I got into the habit of doing it? What if I started calling you regularly, dragging you away from your work, enjoying the thrill of coming first? What if the lost days piled up, your blog began to suffer, and you began to resent me for it?

'Marie?' you said. 'What's wrong?'

'Nothing,' I said. 'Just missed you.'

I could hear the relief in your voice as you said, 'I miss you too.' Then the pause, then the but. 'But we'll see each other tonight, it's just a few hours.'

'I know, Jeff. I'm just having a bad day, that's all. Wanted to come and see you.'

You said what I knew you would say, about how you were in the middle of something right now, but could maybe get away in another hour or two. I could hear you clicking and typing as you talked, and suddenly I felt selfish to have called you. All you wanted was some time to write your blog, and I couldn't even give you that. I said no problem, I'd see you tonight, blew you a kiss and hung up.

After that I took a long walk, all the way out along Midsummer Boulevard and out to the edge of town, where a promontory overlooked open countryside. I stood there for a long time, looking out at the green hills dotted with sheep, the wind blowing the office staleness off my face, the sun flitting in and out as the sheep moved slowly, steadily across the hillsides. Was I too much of a romantic? Was it too much to expect that the person you're living with should want to share his life with you? I'd done everything I could to get you to open up, but still this huge part of your life was closed off from me. Maybe it was unfair, comparing the real you to the image I'd built up of you over the months of fantasy. Maybe it was bound to end in this weird sense that something didn't fit.

I stared out at the hills, looking for answers, but saw only sheep. I remembered the time I'd asked you about going public. You could have so much more influence, I said, if instead of just blogging you also wrote books, newspaper articles, opinion pieces, maybe even started giving keynote speeches or appearing on TV. You already had the base of support from all your blog followers, and this way you could reach whole new audiences. Plus it would mean we wouldn't have to lie about who we really were. I thought I was being real persuasive, but when I'd finished you looked at me like I'd just tried to kill you or something. You started spluttering about how fame wasn't what you wanted, you couldn't just change overnight into a celebrity, you thought I understood and all that. Okay, maybe I went a bit overboard with the TV thing, but I don't see what was so terrible about the other stuff. It wasn't about fame, it was about getting the word out, raising awareness about the things you cared about. I thought I could support you, that maybe it would bring us closer, having everything out in the open. But it was no use. You wouldn't budge an inch. I kept trying – I'm nothing if not determined – but each time you had that same fear, that same stubbornness, that same wounded look on your face.

I thought about the office, where I knew people would already be looking at the clock and wondering aloud whether I'd gotten lost. As I was about to turn back, the sun came out from behind a cloud and lit up the hillside. I thought of all the trees and sheep and blades of grass that had lived and died on this spot, the ancient landscape staying unchanged for centuries. It had even survived having a big concrete city dumped on its doorstep. I could probably have stood at the same point a thousand years ago and seen sheep meandering slowly up the same curve of green. The thought of it calmed me. Like the city of malls and highways behind me, I was a newcomer to this landscape, bringing with me my own sense of time. Perhaps things here just moved at a slower pace than I was used to. Perhaps I was rushing things too much, expecting instant change when, if I was patient, I would notice that the sheep, which had looked still to me, had in fact progressed almost up to the line of oak trees at the brow of the hill. Things had moved, but just too slowly for me to notice.

I just had to remind myself of what I was doing here. It wasn't about my job. If you'd been doing the same bullshit in some other office, I'd have been suicidal. But you weren't. You were out of the world of office politics and barbed-wire jokes and staplers with someone's name Tippexed on the back. You were thinking higher thoughts, making a real difference instead of just playing at it. And I was part of that, and so I could do whatever it took to make sure I stayed part of it. After all, what was the alternative? Go back to London and all those toxic relationships with men who didn't care about me? You loved me, I knew that, and if you didn't want to share everything then I could live with that. I had the relationship of my dreams, the one I'd spent so much time waiting for. Wanting it to be perfect was being too greedy. I would take it as it was. I would work in this job and live not for me but for you. I looked up at the sky, took a deep breath of the cool wind and turned back towards the city.

Chapter 11

Marcus Higgins @marcushig 4h
Climate Flashmob reminder! Tonite 7pm Shell station Grafton St Milton Keyens MK6 5LY. Fck big oil, save the cliemate!

Marcus Higgins @marcushig 4h
@JeffB alrite c u there mate

Marcus Higgins @marcushig 2h
Cliamte Flashmob FINAL REMINDER!! Tonite 7pm Shell station Grafton St Milton Keyens. Lets make it huge!!!

Marcus Higgins @marcushig 1h
Climate Flashmob reminder! I'm here at Shell Milton Keynes. Bring a placard

Marcus Higgins @marcushig 1h
Where is everyone???? Come to Shell Milton Keynes! MK6 5LY

Marcus Higgins @marcushig 1h
Jeff's here now, we're starting. Guess rest of you'll be here soon

Marcus Higgins @marcushig 58m
We're trying 2 keep it going but NEED MORE PEOPLE!

Marcus Higgins @marcushig 45m
http://tweetphoto.com/23242d22 Like our sign? Honk for Solar!

Marcus Higgins @marcushig 26m
@Jane4evr Its alrite i dont hate u. Shlda cum tho

Marcus Higgins @marcushig 25m
Freezing out here. Shoulda worn my long jons

Marcus Higgins @marcushig 22m
@mellaka LOL dunno wot long jons are eiterh!

Marcus Higgins @marcushig 1m
Too cold, going to pub

Chapter 12

'So when do we get to meet this Marie, then?' I asked. You flinched, as always. It was so easy to torture you. It didn't even make me feel guilty. I mean, you'd brought it on yourself, trying to keep secrets. Besides, the three of us working there in the smallest room in the whole building, we had to do something to pass the time. I decided to keep on with it. 'Come on Jeff. You email her constantly, call her ten times a day, and you can never go for a drink after work any more because you've got to rush off home to your little darling Marie. So why do we never get to meet her?'

'She's very busy. She works late a lot.'

'Then why do you have to rush off so quickly after work?'

'Sounds like he don't want us to meet her,' Dex chipped in. 'Sounds like we're not good enough. Thinks we'll embarrass him.'

'It's not that,' you said, pulling back from the computer screen and running a hand through your hair.

'What then?' I asked. 'You know I'm going to get it out of you sooner or later. What's so hard about bringing her along to the pub one night?'

'She'd be uncomfortable. She wouldn't know anyone.'

'That's a shit argument, mate,' Dex boomed. 'If you never met no-one you didn't already know, you'd never meet no-one. You'd be a hermit.'

'Like you, you mean?'

Dex went back to his computer. 'I'm bored with this shit,' he declared. 'Never goes nowhere. Don't bring it up again, Annie.'

I shook my head. 'Don't know what I did to deserve getting stuck in here with you two.' I put in my headphones and pretended to be listening to internet radio. It was my only escape when things got too much, as they often did in that tiny room. The broom cupboard, people called it. Every available space was filled with computers, monitors, keyboards, circuit boards and a thousand other pieces of junk. There were no windows. It's a miracle we didn't kill each other, the three of us stuck in there together. A bit of piss-taking was probably the safest option.

Meanwhile Dex went back to his computer game. You remember that stupid game he played every day? A simulation of an office, where the idea is to throw a rolled-up piece of paper into the bin. He got points for every successful throw and, as he explained at every opportunity, the real challenge was provided by the office fan which could blow his paper ball off-course if he didn't make the proper adjustments. It was pathetic. For everyone else, the novelty wore off after a couple of games, but Dex played it every day. He had a real bin in the office, of course, and huge stacks of computer paper he could screw up and throw. But after he tried it once and missed, exposing himself to piss-taking for the rest of the day, he stuck to the computer version, racking up immense scores each day and raging at anyone who disturbed him.

Of course, I knew why you couldn't let us meet Marie. You'd told me the whole thing that time at Cristina's leaving party, when I got really drunk and kissed you. I still remember that kiss, as drunk as I was. I remember your hands uncertainly gripping my body just below my ribs, your soft lips responding to mine, the sour taste of alcohol and sweat. Then afterwards, the look on your face as you pulled away from me. I like to think it was regret, but it may have been pity.

'I've got a girlfriend,' you said.

'Fucking liar,' I replied. 'If you don't like me just fucking say it, bastard.' Then I hit you, a stupid, clumsy whack across the chest, and I might even have started crying. I was pretty drunk, like I said. And on top of that, I was humiliated. I mean, you were my fallback. I'd had a shit year with men. At university I could get a date pretty much any time I wanted, but everything was so much harder at work. People were more serious, more married, more afraid of breaking company policy. I'd been knocked back a couple of times, but thought I was safe with you. To see that look of pity in your eyes just made me feel like I was nothing.

You looked around anxiously, but the music was too loud for anyone to have heard, and besides, they were probably having their own drunken gropes, arguments and tears. 'It's true. Her name's Marie.'

'Yeah? Well why've you never mentioned her then?'

And that was when you told me all about meeting her, and the misunderstanding, and how you never corrected it. How you could never tell anybody about Marie, or tell Marie about anybody else. After all, she thought you were a big famous bloke doing great things all day. She'd kill you if she knew you were just a nobody going to work in a stupid office, wasting time like everyone else. You swore me to secrecy, and being drunk I swore with absolute sincerity that I wouldn't tell a soul. Then the next day, I told Dex. Not the whole thing, mind. Not about the lie and everything, but I told him you had a secret girlfriend, and the two of us had been torturing you about it ever since. Hey, you know what that office was like. We had to do something to pass the time.

When I think of those times, I think of long, long stretches of time with nothing happening. I think of the sound of a phone ringing, with nobody picking it up. You'd be typing frenetically, probably composing yet another doting email to your precious Marie, and Dex would be playing his stupid game, while I read a magazine or picked at some dry, plastic-packaged salad from Boots. And the phone just rang and rang and rang. On my very first day at Smith & Jefferson I remember you took me aside and said, 'Go on the web as much as you want. Dex is cool.'

Cool is not the word I'd use for Dex, but I know what you meant. It's not that Dex tolerated us wasting time, he actively encouraged it. 'If you're instantly available, they'll get the idea they can call you every time they want to change the photo on their screensaver,' he said to me at my corporate orientation session. 'We've always got to be too busy to help them. Never answer the phone – let it go to voicemail and delete all the messages. They've got to get the idea they can only contact us by email, and that it'll take a day or two to come out to them. Important things we can fix more quickly, but everyday bullshit they can just live with. Ninety percent of the time they work it out by themselves in the end anyway.'

So the door was always closed, and the phone was always ignored, and the music was always on, and the days went by with Twitter, Facebook, Youtube, email, texting and cups of tea. Nobody ever entered the room, but just in case, Dex had stationed himself right at the back, behind a massive stack of computer paper that never seemed to be used. We could see him and he could see us, but from the door he was invisible. If anyone did come in, they would see you first, a little to the left, then me on the right. Only the truly persistent or desperate would fight their way past the two of us, over a pile of obsolete keyboards and around the tower of paper to discover Dex's hiding place. I worked there for two years and never saw anybody get more than a foot inside the doorway. Dex was safe.

Around three o'clock, when things started to drag a bit, Dex would usually organise a network game of Zombie Attack for office morale. Otherwise he left us alone. It was your job to monitor the inbox and alert Dex to any requests worthy or interesting enough to be investigated. Mostly he rolled his eyes, rattled off the solution and told you to call them in a day or two to see if it had been fixed. But occasionally something penetrated the fog, and he'd grudgingly assign the task to you or me, still muttering that it was 'probably something obvious'. Once a server went down, and the usual fix didn't work, and that time even Dex sat up a little in his seat. You and I were busy all day in the server room, with Dex issuing instructions over the phone, as two hundred lawyers waited impatiently to be able to use their computers again. It was the closest it ever came to feeling like a real job. But apart from occasional crises like that, the days went by in much the same way. Not exactly a dream job, but I suppose there are worse ways of paying the bills.

'Why do you join in with Annie and that whole thing?' you asked. I smiled to myself. The other advantage of having my headphones in was that you and Dex always assumed I couldn't hear what you were saying. I heard Dex sigh and click his mouse, presumably pausing his precious game to avoid jeopardising his high score.

'Passes the time, that's all, mate,' he said. 'Bit of a laugh. I dunno why you don't just bring her to the pub one night. Show her to Annie, put an end to this shit, she can leave after an hour if she wants to and it's done. We can have some fucking peace again.'

'I don't see why I can't have my own life,' you said. 'I don't have to share everything with everybody.'

Dex sniffed. 'Don't have to do nothing if you don't want to, mate. You can keep your little compartments and all that, and put up with Annie interrogating you. Don't bother me – at least it provides some fucking entertainment, which is more than you're normally capable of.'

'This room's too small,' you said sulkily.

'Fine,' Dex said. 'There's an email from Fay Dunwood in the inbox. She wants help changing her desktop wallpaper from a photo of her children to, and I quote, a cute little one

I just took of my dog in a party hat, smiley face, end quote.' I smiled to myself. 'Go and help her out,' he said, an edge to his voice that indicated he was pulling rank.

'Come on, mate, I'm sorry, I won't bother you any more.' You were whining now, like a child. That'd never work with Dex, you should have known that.

'Too late. You can get out of this small room, have your space and your freedom and all that bollocks, and leave me in peace. I've got another one for you afterwards. Some idiot with a memory conflict. All he needs to do is reboot his machine, but you can go up to the tenth floor and walk him through it. And bring me a cup of tea on the way back.'

'Can I at least finish my email?'

'No. Fay and her party-hat dog are waiting anxiously for you. Go on. Fuck off.'

As you left, I looked up from my screen and raised an eyebrow, and you gave the little shake of the head which had come to mean that Dex was in one of his moods. I took my headphones out for a moment and said, 'Tea would be great, thanks. Milk and sugar.' I didn't dare look back, but I could hear Dex give a little snort of laughter and so I knew I was okay. Generally he only picked on one of us at a time. That way he always had the numerical advantage. Clever guy, Dex. Psychopath, but clever. You pulled a face as you walked out, but you couldn't complain, you'd have done the same. Dex always got us to side with him and against each other. It was just the way things were.

Twenty minutes later, Dex and I were halfway through the first set of the Wimbledon final, and hardly noticed when you walked back in.

'You could have waited for me,' you said.

'Fuck off,' Dex answered. 'Break point.' He served with a quick flick of the gamepad, the tip of his tongue slipping out of the side of his mouth and his forehead creased with effort. I could see him out of the corner of my eye and smiled slightly as I fired back the return. Dex always tried too hard. He slammed the ball frenetically to all sides of the court, and I just patted it back to him, letting him tire himself out, waiting for the error. The hollow pop of ball on racket resonated around the room. I prolonged the rally as long as I could, enjoying your mounting frustration and Dex's feverish grunts equally. Eventually Dex went for a massive backhand pass down the line, and the ball smacked into the top of the net. 'Fuck!' he shouted.

'Watch it, Dex,' I said. The walls aren't that thick, you know.'

'Fuck,' Dex replied, but a little more quietly this time. 'It's this fucking gamepad. Don't respond properly no more. Gotta get new ones.'

'Good luck,' you said, walking back to your desk now and stirring your tea. 'I don't even know how you got the firm to pay for these ones. Saitek, top of the line. Must be fifty quid each. You can't get any more, they're watching the budget now.'

Dex curled his lip. 'Watch me.'

'Whatever,' I said in the bored rhythm of the American mall. 'Can we start the next game, please?'

'What about me?' you asked.

You sounded like a child denied an ice cream. I asked Dex what he thought, but he gave a dismissive shake of his head. 'He took too long. It was only a fucking dog with a party hat. Five minute job, tops. Then the reboot was a no-brainer, should have been perfect for him.'

'She didn't have admin rights to change the photo,' you protested, but Dex just sang the words back to you in a mocking, childish whine.

'I know why he took so long,' I said. 'Must have been calling his darling Marie. Spent ten minutes saying, I love you. No, I love *you* more. You hang up now. No, *you* hang up.'

You looked to Dex for support, but he was laughing and flexing his knuckles for the next set. 'Was it cute?' Dex asked.

'What?'

'The dog. Was it cute?'

You shrugged. 'It was a dog with a party hat.' Dex didn't seem to have heard. He was fiddling with the gamepad, trying to work out the glitch that had cost him the last game. 'I saw something interesting, though,' you said. It was pathetic, really, the way you kept trying to get our attention like a child tugging at his mother's skirts. Neither of us showed any interest, so you continued alone: 'We're suing the government for trying to stop climate change,' you said. 'Well, some oil companies are, and Fay is representing them. I saw all the files on her computer.'

Dex put his controller down and looked up sharply. 'What's your point?' he asked. 'Did this stop you from changing her wallpaper to the cute little doggy photo?'

'No, but... '

'Then I don't want to hear no more about it, alright? We could be suing Mother Bleeding Teresa for all I care. Our job is to keep the computers running. Don't start getting all philosophical on me, okay? Didn't think you were into that shit.'

'Maybe Marie's into that shit,' I said, and although for a moment you seemed on the point of responding, in the end you did the only thing possible: you looked at the floor, half-heartedly trying to laugh along with us. Dex seemed satisfied, and went back to examining the wiring on his gamepad.

I waited patiently. Dex was an obsessive man, and I knew it would be several minutes before he was ready to play again. I have to admit to feeling a little sorry for you as I watched you poke around listlessly on your desk, moving a few things around and sipping the tea. I thought back to when I first started. You seemed so much younger then. I think you'd only started a month or two before me. It was your first job after university, and mine too. You looked lost all the time, as if you were waiting for the term to end and the parties to begin. When we were introduced, you blushed a little and dropped your eyes to the floor as you shook my hand. Your hand felt hot, as if you had a fever. I knew immediately that you liked me. You were too shy to say it, but I could see it from the way you sneaked glances at me during the day when you thought I was immersed in my computer, then turned away as soon as I looked up. Dex saw it, too. He'd barely noticed me until then, but soon he began looking over as well. Sometimes, as I watched the two of you subtly posturing in front of me, it would remind me of a TV nature programme about a pair of male iguanas putting on their best displays to win the female. So, although obviously I had no real interest in either of you, I let it continue and, in little ways, encouraged it.

Then came Cristina's leaving party and your confession. And from that moment, the atmosphere in the little room changed. The comfortable pattern of shy flirtation was broken immediately by the word 'Marie'. You started to treat me like a mere work colleague, while Dex reverted to his default mode of disdain. Nobody looked at me any more. You had a new confidence about you. You didn't need me any more. Without you and Dex as my audience, the days started to drag, and the ways of filling them seemed pointless. So now whenever I looked at you, I felt something missing. I wanted the early days back, the days before that word 'Marie' broke everything.

I'm sorry for telling Dex, and I'm even sorrier for all the times I threatened to tell Marie. I suppose I was jealous, in a stupid way. I loved to see the fear in your face every time I said I'd tell Marie everything. You begged me not to, said you'd do anything. It made me feel like I had some power again. The things I forced you to do were not too bad, I could have been nastier. I just showed you the photos I'd posted online, the ones that I had thought were a bit sexy. There's nothing worse than posting photos of yourself online and getting no response. Not one. Even the spammers maintained an embarrassed silence. You told me I looked fantastic, and so I told you to post that online. Set up as many different screen names as you could, then post admiring comments, share the link with your friends, tag it, Digg it, Fave it, Mixx it, StumbleUpon it and whatever else you could think of.

Of course, the comments wouldn't be believable if it was obvious the profiles were set up just for that purpose. So you needed to comment on other photos too, and make friends, and list interests. Each of the profiles had to become a person in its own right, so that when I posted a new photo I'd wait eagerly for the comments from each one. Yeah, pathetic, I know. But like I said, it had been a tough year, and I just wanted to feel better about myself. And sure enough, the attention began to come, most of it good, some of it a little twisted, but at least it was attention. People just need a little prompting, they'll follow whatever other commenters have said for the most part. So with you setting the tone, and marketing me as much as you could, I was all set. I posted more photos, revealed more about myself, and more people came to visit.

Even after I had a following, I still forced you to put up your own comments. Don't know why really. I know I put a lot of extra pressure on you, when you were already struggling just to keep Marie thinking you were that blogger. Now you had to keep up a whole load more identities, and worry about Dex finding out as well. The photos were not porn, but they probably violated company policy in a few different ways. And if he did ask, you'd have to explain why you were doing it, and that was the very last thing you wanted. I knew that constantly asking you about Marie was pretty cruel too. As I looked at you poking around on your desk I did feel guilty, but I reminded myself it was your fault to begin with. You were the liar, not me.

'Why don't we play the shoot 'em up like normal?' you asked in a slightly wheedling voice.

'Fuck off,' Dex said, still fiddling with his gamepad. 'You can't just abandon the Wimbledon final to go and shoot zombies. It's finely poised.'

'Yeah, between defeat and annihilation,' I said. 'Come on, let's get on with it.'

The phone rang. For a moment you seemed tempted to pick it up, but a sharp look from Dex made you drop your hand. The umpire said 'Quiet please' and I began bouncing the ball on the perfect green turf, ready to serve for a 4-2 lead. You slipped out quietly, and I served into the net.

Chapter 13

The clock ticked loudly in the silent front room, and I just started babbling, saying anything and everything to drown it out. There was just something awful about the silence. I was finally meeting your grandparents, and I wanted it to be wonderful. I wanted your granddad to like me, and most of all I wanted to end up feeling that I knew you better, more deeply. I desperately wanted that. So every time silence filled the room, I felt as if things were going wrong, and did anything I could to puncture it. I grasped at whatever came into my head and threw it out there, not caring what it sounded like. Anything was better than silence and a ticking clock.

You'd warned me about it on the way down the M1. 'Granddad moves at a different pace,' you said. 'Sometimes you ask him a question, and he can take ten minutes to think of the right answer, and all you can do in the meantime is sit there and listen to the bloody clock ticking your life away.' I'd thought you were exaggerating, but it really was true. The old man seemed to have no sense of time whatsoever. He'd sit there smiling benignly and clearly off in his head somewhere forming the idea that would one day lead to a thought and then a logical argument and finally spoken words. It was true that what he did say in the end often made a lot of sense, but anyways it made me real uncomfortable, so I filled the silences with random brain droppings and your grandfather probably thought I was an idiot.

I'll give the old guy credit, though, he had too much class to show what he really thought of me. While I rattled on about everything and nothing, he just sat there smiling at me and then said how glad he was that Jeff had found such a lovely girl. Then he proceeded to say what he'd been thinking about all along, which was usually a delayed response to something you or I had said half an hour earlier.

After a while, he hobbled off to the kitchen to refill the pot. You smiled and put your hand on my knee. 'He really likes you.'

'You're kidding,' I whispered back. 'I've done nothing but babble ever since I got here.'

'I'm telling you, he likes you. It was only a few minutes before he told you to call him Arthur. With most people he insists on Mr Standhope until they've known him for years.'

'He's just being nice, Jeff. He must think I'm an idiot, all the garbage I've been talking. I just can't take sitting here with nothing but the ticking of the clock.'

You squeezed my knee, and leaned over to kiss me on the cheek. After that there was just that unbearable ticking again, interrupted only by the drumming of your heel on the threadbare Persian rug. I gestured with my head towards the armchair where Daisy was sitting in an old blue dress and pearls. Her body had slumped in the soft fabric and her head was lolling back on a cushion, making it look like she was staring at something on the ceiling. 'Should we talk to her?' I whispered. 'It feels weird, sitting here and just ignoring her.'

'She can't understand anything,' you said. 'It's pointless. Granddad likes to treat her as if she's still there, and it seems to help him deal with it so I go along with it. But when he's not here, I don't talk to her. There's just no point.'

You didn't even lower your voice. I didn't understand how you could talk about Daisy like that with her sitting there. I mean, you never know, do you? I got up and walked over to her. Up close, she looked more alive somehow. I could see her chest rise and fall, could even hear the slight rasping of the air passing through her throat. Leaning closer, I smelt the staleness of tea and, just behind it, minty toothpaste. I knelt down and held her hand. It was cold and soft, like Play-Doh. The skin on her face fell in loose folds, but on top I could see white flecks of foundation and some light rouge. From her neck came the scent of lavender perfume. Her eyebrows had been drawn on her face with great care. Not just a crude pencil line, but a series of individual strokes tapering down to the ends. I thought of Arthur bending over her, slowly drawing each line from memory. On her chin the foundation lay a little thicker, and beneath it I could just make out the pockmarks it was designed to cover.

I looked over her shoulder and saw propped up on the shelf a picture of Daisy as Arthur still saw her, a slim brunette doing a handstand on the beach, her long hair tumbling down to the sand, her mouth open in laughter, her long legs reaching up to the sun. I understood then that his life's labour each day in this chilly suburban semi consisted of washing Daisy, forcing her limp body into a blue dress and slipping pearls around her neck, spraying her with lavender perfume, plucking the hairs from her chin, dabbing foundation onto her cracked skin, applying rouge to her faded cheeks, trying doggedly to restore something that each day slipped further away.

'Are you okay in there?' I whispered.

In the moment afterwards I got the weirdest feeling that something in her face had changed. Then I heard the shuffling of feet behind me, and looked around to see Arthur passing through with the tea. 'Don't mind me,' he said cheerfully. 'I'll just rest this down on the table while you chat with Daisy.' When I looked back at her face, it looked the same as always, her eyes staring vacantly at the ceiling, her slack jaw sagging towards her chest, a suggestion of saliva at the corner of her mouth. The change had just been Arthur blocking the light. You were right, of course. I put her hand carefully back where

I'd found it on the arm of the chair, and started to get up.

'Please, please, don't let me disturb you,' Arthur said. 'I know what women are like, always got plenty to talk about when the menfolk are not around, eh, Jeff?' You gave him a thin smile that seemed as if it cost you a lot to produce, and Arthur strained to increase his own cheerfulness to compensate. 'You can stay over there and talk about women's things, and we'll talk football and politics and all that.'

He was trying so hard that I wanted to cry. 'Sure thing,' I said, and perched on the arm of the chair, holding Daisy's soft, cold hand in my lap.

The poor guy looked happier than I've ever seen anyone look. I mean, he just sat there looking at Daisy and then at me, then back at Daisy, with this huge smile on his face and the hint of a tear in his eye. 'I'll just get some more biscuits,' he said.

'It's all right,' you said, 'I'll get them. The HobNobs, yeah?'

'Yes, yes, that's kind of you, son. Yes, the HobNobs. They're in the... '

'... cupboard above the kettle, where they've always been,' you said, and rolled your eyes at me as you walked past.

I turned to Daisy and squeezed her hand. 'Your dress looks lovely,' I said.

'Yes, it's your favourite, isn't it, love?' Arthur said, and started telling me all about the history of the dress and the times she'd worn it, and for a few minutes it really felt like Daisy was part of the conversation, even though she didn't utter a word. Then you came back in with the biscuits spread out on a plate, and Arthur began the long palaver over who wanted more tea.

As I sat there on the arm of the chair, holding Daisy's hand and sipping tea with my free hand, I began to give myself up to the silences. I knew I'd already made Arthur happy just by sitting with his wife and pretending she was more than just a vacant mind in a failing body. If nobody spoke, it didn't mean the visit was a disaster. I knew now that you were telling the truth. He liked me. I sat and held Daisy's hand and allowed the conversation to meander around in the gathering gloom. Because the clock was so far off the actual time, I soon gave up trying to add five and a quarter hours or whatever it was, and relied instead on the height of the sun in the sky, like it was the Middle Ages or something. With nothing else happening, I noticed more precisely than usual how the light changed. I saw Arthur's hunched figure on the sofa at first bathed in light as the setting sun slanted in through the front window, and then gradually becoming more indistinct as the whole room faded to grey. Just at the moment when it was becoming uncomfortably dark, Arthur got up automatically, in the middle of a sentence, and pottered across to switch on the overhead light, finishing his thought as he returned to the sofa and eased himself creaking into it. I couldn't even say how long the silences lasted. Time seemed altered in that room. At home I can lose three hours on the internet without blinking, but in Arthur's front room each minute seemed to have a character of its own. The ticking of the clock seemed to slow as the light faded. As I gradually forgot about the passing of time, the regular ticking began to mesmerise me. It gave a rhythm and shape to my thoughts.

I remembered our months together, the gradual way in which Milton Keynes became my home. At first the place drove me crazy. It felt like being controlled by a well-meaning parent. As you're walking around, you can feel what they want you to do, and the wide streets and well-lit pedestrian walkways are all very logical and sensible. But it's just not what you want, and as much sense as it makes, something in you rebels against being planned for. You want to go down dead ends, take pointless detours, cross anywhere but at the carefully labelled crossings. There's something threatening about so much reason.

But after a while, I got used to it. I began to go out for

drinks with Jason and Jerry and the rest of them after work. With familiarity, the city softened. Grafton Gate was not an anonymous, windswept piece of concrete any more, but the place where Martin had fallen over as he was trying to hail a late-night taxi. The Costas and Wetherspoons held memories of people and conversations, good times and bad. I understood now why you'd moved back there when you were old enough to leave Arthur's draughty old semi behind. Milton Keynes was not a rootless, historyless place as I had first thought. It had a history for you, memories of places you'd been with your parents, the school you'd gone to, the old skateboard park where you and Jon had first discovered the joys of sniffing glue. Like you, I was now accumulating my own history there.

It was a surprise to me when you stood up and said we should be going. Only when I looked at the clock did I realise hours had passed. In the car on the way back, you complained that we'd stayed longer than usual, and would hit traffic on the M1, which we did. But I didn't care. I felt like I'd passed a test. I knew that the next Sunday, when you went to visit Arthur and Daisy again, you'd take me with you, and that it would be the same every Sunday after that. It would become our first ritual as a couple. I would learn more about you, hear stories of your childhood, perhaps come to understand you better. As Arthur said, you can do anything if you take it slowly enough. Perhaps even Daisy would show a flicker of recognition one day. I was so excited I didn't shut up the whole way back, even though you were just grimly gripping the wheel and muttering about the traffic. I didn't need a response. I was just happy. I felt closer to you already. Seeing you with your granddad showed me a different side of you. Despite your frustration with him, you clearly loved him. You helped him, worried about him. It was nice to see. It was a strange kind of relationship, but I was beginning to understand it. I thought of you as a freshly orphaned teenager, moving to this cold house and piecing together a new life with two old people who didn't know or understand you but clearly loved you. I imagined you slowly forging a bond based on nothing but this strange love founded on mutual incomprehension. Still, it was strong enough to keep you coming back Sunday after Sunday, year after year, drinking tea and talking about the traffic on the M1. All of this was nothing to do with 'the famous Jeff Brennan', the blogger I'd initially fallen for. This was a deeper, more intimate part of you, and I was glad I'd found it.

Over the next few weekends, it turned out more or less like I'd expected. I went with you every time, and every time it became easier. In a way I seemed to get on better with him than you did. I suppose the two of you had too much history, whereas I was just new to the whole thing and thought he was a really sweet old man. I guess being brought up by him as a teenager would be a different thing, and that's why there was always this vein of frustration through your conversations, like everything was being said under the shadow of a thousand old arguments. But with me, it was easier.

He was always so self-effacing. From the way he talked about his boring work life, I assumed at first he'd been an insurance clerk or something. Only on the fourth or fifth Sunday did I discover that he'd been a journalist. A real journalist, too, for the nationals. He'd started out covering fires and break-ins for the *Camden Chronicle*, and had worked his way up to be courts correspondent for *The Times*. It was hard to picture this gentle, tea-drinking old man shouting questions at a convicted murderer on the steps of the Old Bailey, but I guess when people get to a certain age it's hard to picture them doing anything. Besides, he said, he was never part of that hard-drinking, macho Fleet Street crowd. He did his work, got his story, and went home to his wife. He was only interested in telling the truth.

'Of course,' he said, sipping his tea, 'the truth is relative.

News is made up of exceptions to the rule. That's what makes it news. So I spent a lifetime writing about exceptions and oddities. Anyone reading my stories would think Britain was a nation of rapists and paedophiles. I got every fact right, but I was telling a very distorted truth. We all were. I don't know if we could have done anything differently.'

It was hard to answer him when he got like this. Fortunately he didn't seem to expect an answer. He'd already thought it all out anyway in the long days sipping tea in a silent front room, and we all knew that you and I couldn't say anything he hadn't already thought of, analysed thoroughly, and either accepted or despatched. So he just mused on his life, and then said it didn't matter really anyway, and started talking about his roses or the weeds growing through the cracks in the path.

Towards the end of the afternoon, I usually left the two of you in the living room and went off to clean up around the house. Arthur said it wasn't necessary, and mostly it wasn't, but still I liked to help out. I put the stepladder up in the kitchen and cleaned the cupboards he couldn't reach. I vacuumed the stairs, something I was relieved to hear him admit he couldn't manage any more, because even I almost lost my balance a couple of times as I fumbled on those narrow steps with the cumbersome old machine. I got down on my hands and knees and scrubbed the tattered kitchen lino to a lighter shade of grey. Sometimes I ventured upstairs, but there was not much I could do up there. Every room, apart from the one he'd cleared, was full of memories. Nothing much with any practical use or monetary value, but I couldn't possibly throw anything out either. I knew there was a story behind every old ticket, broken lampshade and tacky souvenir plate. In Arthur's head they had a different existence. They took him far from this cold suburban semi, far from this Britain he didn't understand any more, back to a time and a place that belonged to him. So I didn't touch them, I just tried to dust around the edges.

It made you mad that your grandfather always refused your offers of help, but gratefully accepted mine. You said it was sexist, and you were probably right, but I didn't care. Arthur was from a different time, and I had no interest in questioning his motives. I just wanted to help out. Sometimes I took Daisy into the back room and gave her a pedicure. Afterwards, in the car, you asked me how I could stand to handle those swollen old feet with their corns and bunions. You didn't understand. As the dead skin came off in my hands, as I moisturised and lotioned the cracked soles, as I clipped at the talon-like nails and removed yellow crud from between the toes, I felt something I hadn't felt since I worked at the homeless shelter. There's an intimacy you feel when everything else is stripped away and you're confronted with the dirty, foul-smelling reality of another human being. It's like the closeness of a mother and child, steeped in all the years of shit and vomit. It's impossible to maintain distance or pretence after that kind of closeness. It feels more real than anything else. I was helping Arthur and Daisy with the real stuff of life – keeping their bodies groomed and their house clean. That was more of a contribution than I made in all my days at my charity job.

On the sixth Sunday, Arthur asked me to teach him the computer. He asked it quite nonchalantly, like he was offering another cup of tea. I hesitated, and looked at you. I knew about all the times you'd tried to teach him, and how his reluctance and apathy frustrated you. I'd heard you rail on about how much he could get out of the internet if only he'd give it a try. I knew how hurt you were that he never seemed to take it seriously. And now he was looking straight past you, and calmly asking me to teach him.

Your face showed no particular reaction, but when you spoke your voice was dry and cracked. 'I didn't think you were interested.' You clearly wanted to say more, but didn't trust your voice with the words.

Arthur didn't reply for a long time. He stared out of the

window with his elbows on the arms of the chair and his fingertips meeting in front of his chest, as if in prayer. The silence was so long that it seemed like he was ignoring you, and I began to be afraid of how you would react. But finally he spoke. 'I never saw the real effects of it before,' he said. 'It was as if you were just typing into a computer and never got anything out again. But I remember that afternoon you made friends with Marie on the computer, and she didn't stay on the computer – she emerged into the real world, and now I see this lovely young lady sitting on my sofa, drinking tea, talking to me, cleaning my cupboards, being good to Daisy. It made me want to understand it more.'

'I could teach you,' you said, your voice still weak.

'I think perhaps a different teacher would be good for me,' Arthur replied. 'There was nothing wrong with how you taught me, of course. It was entirely my own stubbornness. But I think a new approach would help.'

After that, the computer sessions became another regular feature of the Sunday afternoons, like the ticking of the clock and the pouring of tea. Arthur was a slow learner, but I slowed myself down as much as I could. We just did half an hour each time, and concentrated on one thing until he could master it. We spent three weeks just on mouse control. After that it was how to open programs, then how to operate a menu, then how to get on the internet, and so on. I had to keep reminding myself that time didn't matter, and to stop you from looking over our shoulders and explaining something five steps ahead of where Arthur was. And, slowly and painfully, he did learn. After a few months he was able to get on the internet by himself, and a little later he could send and receive emails, and after that he could find news that interested him, and then I introduced him to Facebook and explained slowly, over several Sundays, exactly how it worked and how you and I had used it to exchange those first messages and then arrange our real-world meeting. Only when I was sure he understood did I offer to help him set up his own account, and to my surprise he was keen to do it. He let me photograph him for a profile picture, and only later, shyly, like a little boy, did he ask, 'I suppose it has to be a computer picture, does it? I mean, it couldn't be an old paper one?' He was delighted and I think slightly in awe of me when, one Sunday, I took one of his old black-and-white photos away with me, scanned it in and uploaded it as his new profile picture. The following Sunday, his eyes filled with tears as he looked at himself on the screen, young and handsome in his National Service uniform, his beret at a jaunty angle, a cigarette dangling from his fingers. 'I wish I could show Daisy,' he said, 'but I don't think she'd understand.'

Every Sunday afternoon as I cleaned up, I would notice small absences, accumulated clutter gradually replaced and reclaimed by empty space. It was sometimes hard to be certain of exactly what was missing. When I cleaned the kitchen cupboards, for example, I would notice gaps in the rows of old cans, and only later would I remember the three ancient little bottles of vanilla essence, their labels stained almost to the dark brown of the glass. In the dining room, a whole drawer-full of placemats, corkscrews, salad tongs and serving spoons disappeared one week, only a single folded tablecloth remaining. The piles of yellowing books, magazines and newspaper clippings shrank Sunday by Sunday. In some of the rooms upstairs, whole cupboards were gone, grime-edged rectangles in the carpet the only reminder of their existence.

When you asked him about it, Arthur said he'd got some local lads to help him clear out. 'The Owen boys, remember them? They're quite big these days, but not big enough to be afraid of a few hours of hard work.'

'I would have helped,' you said.

'I can still manage a thing or two by myself,' Arthur said. 'I just did it gradually, a little at a time. You can do anything if you take it slowly enough.'

Each disappearance seemed like an act of surrender, a recognition that neither he nor Daisy would ever again bake a cake, entertain dinner guests or read the article that had once seemed so important. Even memories seemed to be losing their significance. Pictures disappeared from the mantelpiece in the living room and the little shelf above the radiator in the hall, and it took genuine effort for you or me to recall whose image had once been smiling out at us. When asked, Arthur just smiled and said it wasn't important. He had spent his life accumulating memories, only to forget what they were for. He and Daisy had plenty between them: he just had to squeeze her hand a certain way to take him back to a romantic walk along Blackpool Promenade, and by the time he emerged again into the present, the sun had almost set and he had to rush to make dinner before it got too late.

One Sunday, the mantelpiece in the living room was completely bare. Beneath it was a large cardboard box covered in old-fashioned writing: *Gamages - An Unlimited Variety of Attractive Merchandise at Money-Saving Prices.*

'It's for you,' Arthur said, beaming. 'Now I've packed it carefully – I've been saving up copies of *The Times* all week to use as padding – but even so, be careful not to knock it against anything. The mechanism is rather old, and... well, I'm sure you'll be careful. Don't take any notice of me. Perhaps you could put it on the floor in the back of the car, though, rather than in the boot, that way the front seat can wedge it in. Well, whatever you think's best. I put a bottle of oil in the bottom of the box so that you know which brand to use. I mean, that's the one which works best for me, but I'm sure you'll decide for yourself. If you could try to remember to clean it every few months or so, although I know you're busy but just try if you can.' He said a few more things, then stopped, flustered, and looked at his hands. 'Well, it's yours now.'

'I couldn't possibly,' you said. 'I mean, it's your clock, not mine.'

'Not any more,' Arthur said. 'I've packed it up now, and it's going out, either to you this afternoon or to the dustmen tomorrow morning.'

It was probably a bluff, but it was an effective one. Even the most callous grandson could not have let an ancient family heirloom go to the dump. You did a decent impersonation of someone overwhelmed with gratitude, and a few hours later we lugged the surprisingly heavy box out to the front drive and inched it carefully into the jeep while Arthur fussed and fretted in the background.

Chapter 14

Marcus Higgins @marcushig	**1h**
@JeffB yeh had a good time too m8, feel rough now tho lol	

Marcus Higgins @marcushig	**54m**
@JeffB U remembr that document u talked about in pub? I need it.	

Marcus Higgins @marcushig	**53m**
@FrenchFrank yeh did u see video? Fckd up!	

Marcus Higgins @marcushig	**52m**
@JeffB Don't care how u get it. We NEED it, nobdy'll do anythg without proof	

Marcus Higgins @marcushig	**48m**
@JeffB Yeh risky but weve got no choice, nobody's coming to protests any more. Need sthg big	

Marcus Higgins @marcushig	**47m**
@HouseFanLester Lol yeh, nice pic man, lk yr styel	

Marcus Higgins @marcushig	**46m**
@JeffB cant believe u wont do it. Wot abt all that stuff we said in pub? People lk FD are the problem	

Marcus Higgins @marcushig	**44m**
@JeffB Dont care if shes nice. Thats exactly the problem, nice people like FD doing thr jobs n letting world get fucked	

Marcus Higgins @marcushig	**42m**
@JeffB u have to	

Marcus Higgins @marcushig	**42m**
@JeffB Or what? Or I tell yr secret	

Marcus Higgins @marcushig	**41m**
@JeffB U hv no choice. Get it in 1 week or I tell her whole thg	

Marcus Higgins @marcushig	**15m**
Next protest: Smith & Jefferson law firm, Milton Keynes, MONDAY at midday. Protest S&J's support for corporate polluters!	

Chapter 15

I suppose I should be flattered, in a way. I mean, you have to be quite famous before people start wanting to be you. I've had several impostors over the last few years. You were the sixth I think, or even the seventh. There was the guy who set up a 'Jeff Brennan' profile on LinkedIn, making business contacts and getting them to pay him for product placement on my blog. Then there was the slightly seedier site which claimed to be my 'private, personal blog' but in fact linked to some pretty nasty pornography. And there were a few people who just set up sites or Facebook profiles or Twitter accounts in my name out of little more than boredom and loneliness as far as I could tell. They were easy to find, and easy for my lawyers to shut down.

You, however, were different. You were the first person to imitate me not on the web but in person. Your web presences had always used my name, your name, but never claimed to be linked to the blog. I had already checked them and decided they were legitimate. But how could I know that somewhere in Milton Keynes you were passing yourself off as me, just to get a girl? I'm so used to being able to access everything through Google that it still seems odd to me that for so long I didn't know. I know now, of course, but it occurs to me that maybe you don't know how I found out. From your point of view I must have appeared out of nowhere, just when you thought you had everything under control. So allow me to explain.

For seven years my life was simple. I lived in the same flat, following current affairs and writing a daily blog post. At first it was just for enjoyment, and to give me something to do every day at a time in my life when I really didn't feel like doing anything. But the blog seemed to become popular for some reason, and as I gained popularity I started to receive press releases, and then later to get the real news: exclusive scoops and leaks fed to me by anonymous insiders. One day I realised that, without meaning to, I had created the most popular political blog in Britain. And, having created it, I was stuck with it. I became slowly crushed by the weight of daily expectation, and began to devote more and more of my life to the task of creating something that tens of thousands of readers around the world would appreciate. The writing itself was not the hardest part, and even the research was not difficult. The hard part was getting myself to the computer when everything inside me resisted. Waiting for me, along with the hundreds of appreciative comments, would be a healthy dose of abuse and ridicule, and that's not a pleasant thing to face every morning. What I was posting on the web was not really my political views but myself. I put myself up there every day for the world to judge.

To compensate for this unintended exhibitionism, I protected myself in real life with a fervour bordering on the obsessive. I had a wonderful flat in an old converted warehouse, and rarely left it. Every day I followed exactly the same routine, starting with a cup of coffee on the balcony overlooking the Regent's Canal, just letting the peace and stillness settle on me. Then I would go inside and sit down at my antique writing desk, the kind with endless secret compartments and a beautiful sloping surface perfectly inclined for the writing of flowing letters in elegant script. Underneath it sat my old computer, a big ugly box, the same one I had when I first started writing the blog seven years ago. On top were the keyboard, mouse and screen, slightly incongruous I'll admit, but so familiar to me that I didn't notice any more. Beyond them was the canal, a constant presence in my life. You can't actually see it when you're sitting at the desk, but somehow you're aware of its presence below your line of sight. You can almost hear the shouts of long-dead canal workers unloading barges of grain from rural Buckinghamshire. There's a strange sense of space and peace that can only come from water, whether it's the Atlantic Ocean or an urban canal. If the council filled in the canal and built a park instead, the quality of the light would be different.

I would always begin by perusing the news sites, bringing myself swiftly up-to-date with everything I needed to know. Then I visited other blogs, not with the intention of jumping on the hot story of the day as most people do, but in order to avoid it and write about something fresh. After that I went to my own blog and scanned through all the new comments. This took a while, of course: I averaged hundreds of comments a day, and made a point of reading every one. To respond to them all would have been impossible, but I wanted to be aware of what people were saying. Only then did I start to plan the day's post.

In the seven years since Paola left me, I had not taken a single holiday. I had got up, written my blog post and then enjoyed the safety of my own company for the rest of the day. My passport had expired at some point and I hadn't bothered to renew it. Leaving England held no appeal and, as the years went by, even leaving my flat became something of a struggle. After all, I had everything I needed. If I ran out of food or household supplies, I ordered online and had them delivered. Books and music I downloaded. With a limitless supply not only of the basic necessities of life but also of all kinds of entertainment, what need was there to venture out into the dirty, crowded city? Human company was all I was missing, and after what Paola did to me I was convinced that human company was vastly overrated. I stuck to my own company and was happy. The balcony marked one extent of my territory, the front door the other.

I never felt as if I was missing anything; to the contrary, I felt lucky. My routine was ideal, my life in perfect harmony. Nothing could disturb it. Nobody could judge it and find it lacking. I still remember that look on Paola's face as she looked around the flat one final time, with her bags in hand and the taxi waiting outside. She took it all in with a sweeping glance of disdain and told me none of it was real. Where she was going, the man she was going to (the man she had been fucking every Wednesday and Friday afternoon for the last two years of our marriage), it was different, she said. He was real. There wasn't so much stuff, but all of it was earned. He had worked for it, saved for it, in some cases even built it with his own hands. Not like me, where it was just the result of privilege. She spat the word at me. Privilege. I didn't know what reply to make. She smiled viciously, as if my silence confirmed something about me, walked out and quietly shut the door.

Seven years on, the door is still closed and I still don't know what reply to make. I still don't know what I could have done to be more real in Paola's eyes. Give away everything my parents and grandparents worked for? Pretend I never had it, pretend I never had the public school education or the good degree either? Find work as a brickie and slowly save up over decades to have a fraction of what I have right now? Would that be more real, pretending to be someone else? I suspect I'd be mocked as a posh-boy wannabe, slumming it for fun. I can't win, it seems. But neither can I forget that look on Paola's face. So I hide away year after year, following the same routine every morning, writing the same blog on the same clockwork schedule.

Then someone walks in. Not into my life, of course, because that's too well protected. But she walks into my blog, as anyone can, and starts to leave comments every day. For a year or so I don't notice her really. Her comments are much like anyone else's, anodyne praise with a subtext of self-interest, hoping for a piece of my fame to rub off on her or, more importantly, for a piece of my daily traffic to be diverted her way. But then something changes. Her comments come to seem more intimate. It's as if she knows me, in a way that is impossible for a mere blog reader. There's nothing overt, nothing I could point to as indisputably flirtatious. But there seems to be something there each time, some private joke she is sharing with me. The subtext of self-interest has gone, replaced by something deeper and more genuine.

So I try to find out more about this woman. I begin visiting her blog, even though it's more or less identical to a thousand others. Sometimes I imagine I see something, but it could just as easily not have been there. So I lurk, and read, and re-read, staring into the screen for hours, searching for something between the lines that just isn't there. I look at her profile photo more times than I like to admit, squinting at the small image to make out details: the earring nestling in her long black hair, the slight smudge of bright red lipstick on the side of her mouth. I even download it once, put it into Photoshop and try to see more, although all I manage to do is transform her smooth, beautiful face into a grid of big, square pixels. I visit her Facebook page, but learn nothing. She has recently moved to Milton Keynes, and has posted a series of photos with ironic titles like 'Culture in Milton Keynes' (a bowling alley), 'Architecture in Milton Keynes' (a boxy concrete megastore), and so on. But she doesn't say why she has moved there, or what she is doing. She could be a rocket scientist, a stay-at-home mother of two, a waitress or a ski instructor for all I know. Her Twitter feed is no more enlightening. Everything is immediate, so nothing is permanent. I persist, thinking that if I keep adding up all of the hourly thoughts, experiences and comments, her picture will gradually become sharper and less pixellated. But the accumulation of minutiae obscures rather than clarifies. The more I read, the more she comes to sound like everybody else. I don't know this woman at all. And yet, every morning, I still anticipate her comments on my blog more than anything else. There is something in them. She seems to know me, better than anyone.

Of course, you know why. You know that there really was something in those comments; it wasn't a random infatuation, born of loneliness. It wasn't all in my head. There was a real intimacy there, a real love. The woman I knew only as a name and a photo was real to you in ways I can only imagine. And she loved you. And that love came across in her comments, as much as she tried to hide it. The wires were crossed, the love letter delivered into the wrong hands, but it was still love. It wasn't all in my head. Perhaps if I had known all this, I would have been able to forget her, to keep the door closed, to go on with my routine. But I didn't know. I thought there was something wrong with me, and that the only way out of the obsession was to meet her in person. I would either live happily ever after or, more likely, be disappointed. Either way the disturbing obsession with an internet screen name would soon be over.

One morning, the opportunity came. As soon as I saw her comment, I knew what I would do. Of course, I didn't act right away. I went about my normal routine as if nothing had happened. I spent the morning researching a post about the shameful treatment of the Diego Garcia islanders, compiled facts and quotes with all my usual care, condensed my argument on the trusty A4 pad next to my computer, wrote it up and released it to the world just after lunchtime. Then I made a light lunch, went back to the computer and left comments on the blogs of people I thought would be particularly interested in my Diego Garcia post. Although I'm already popular, it doesn't hurt to keep drawing new readers. Even Coca Cola still advertises.

At three thirty I shut the computer down, sat down in my

favourite leather armchair and watched *Countdown*. It's more or less the only programme I watch these days, but it's well worth the licence fee. My score that day, though, was below average. I ended up trailing the two real contestants by quite a distance, whereas usually I beat either one or both. Even then, though, I refused to admit what was really happening. I stuck to my routine, switching the television off and the stereo on, settling in my favourite armchair and cracking the spine of a good book. But the music failed to soothe me, and I barely got through the first chapter of the book, so often did I have to stop and reread a page I'd just finished.

I surfed the web aimlessly late into the night, something I never normally do. Eventually, of course, I found my way back to my blog, back to the comment from Marie. What was different about that day's comment was that, instead of referring back to her blog or to another website, she referred for the first time to a real-world event. A protest outside Smith & Jefferson law firm in Milton Keynes. I scanned the details quickly, but didn't take them in. All I cared about was that Marie would be there. She would be standing in front of me in full 3D, in a graphic resolution more perfect than anything that's been invented yet. There would be no tightly-cropped edges leaving me to guess at her surroundings. I would see her full body, the way she moved, her mannerisms. I would hear her real voice, not the imagined one that I always conjured up out of the lines of text on my computer screen. Perhaps, if I got close enough, I could smell her. Perhaps, even, touch her.

Just the thought of her smooth skin caressing my fingertips was enough to remove any remaining shred of doubt. I clicked on the link in her comment and read about the event. It sounded standard enough: a march from A to B, a few speeches and home again in time for *Countdown*. The whole thing was backed by solid, reputable non-profits and was fully approved by the police, so there would be little risk of arrest. The only remaining question was who to go as: myself, or another?

Anonymity was my automatic choice, one that I had used once or twice to attend major events without compromising my blog's perceived impartiality. It was a simple enough matter since nobody knew my appearance. All I had to do was avoid identifying myself as Jeff Brennan, and that could be achieved by using my real name. It wasn't even a lie.

But then I realised that by donning my usual cloak of anonymity, I would defeat the object of attending. I would be a face in a crowd, with no chance of meeting Marie. I might see her from afar and, perhaps, if I wormed my way through the bodies, I might even get close enough to smell her, to hear her voice, but I knew that this would not be enough. I had gone too far to be satisfied with voyeurism. I needed to meet her, and I knew that without Jeff Brennan's name I had no chance. I played out a thousand scenarios for provoking an encounter, and all of them ended in defeat.

There was no other possibility. I had to go as Jeff Brennan. I had to do what I had never done before: use my fame as currency. My exchange rate was high. Success was certain. She would want to meet me and, what's more important, so would others. It would be my first outing, the appearance of a famous recluse. There would be crowds, cameras, microphones. And through it all, I would select her, Marie, to speak to. I would tell the world that she was the one who had lured me out of my lair and, by her principled example, convinced me to fight the good fight on the front lines. She would be overcome with gratitude, and mistake it for love. I ran through the strategy in the delicious early-hours stillness, imagining disruptions, looking for flaws. I found none. It was perfect.

I went to the blog's dashboard and started a new post. Something in me baulked at the enormity of what I was doing and urged caution. Hesitating for a moment, I almost shut down again and postponed the post for the morning. Coffee on the balcony, the faint mist hanging over the canal, the wide open sky, the memory of canal boats and the shouts of boatmen.

The thought of it was enticing, but I soon recognised it for a snare. The decision to act was what had given me clarity; return to indecision and I would return to that state of unease, of emptiness. I pressed on. The post itself was quick to write. In five minutes at the most, it was done. I hit 'Publish', shut down, went to bed and immediately fell into the deepest, most refreshing sleep I'd experienced for months.

Chapter 16

| **Marcus Higgins** @marcushig | **44m** |

BIG NEWS! The blogger Jeff Brennan will be at Monday's protest! See announcemnent on his official website

| **Marcus Higgins** @marcushig | **43m** |

@IrishDan glad you can make it this time. Bring loads of friends

| **Marcus Higgins** @marcushig | **39m** |

For more details of protest, see #Mkprotest, + retweet n tell all yr friends, lets make it a top trending topic!!!

| **Marcus Higgins** @marcushig | **38m** |

@IrishDan Great, c u there!

| **Marcus Higgins** @marcushig | **37m** |

@Jane4evr Yeh itll be huge, and we DO have a permit! Bring as many as the bus can hold :-)

| **Marcus Higgins** @marcushig | **27m** |

@JeffB Any progress on yr little project??? Stakes r getting higher...

| **Marcus Higgins** @marcushig | **22m** |

@JulieGemmill Cool, looks like everyone can come this time ;-)

Chapter 17

I still remember that initial excitement when I saw you'd published a new post. It was after midnight by then, and you were asleep. It was so rare for you to schedule a post to come out at that sort of time, and it felt like a treat. It was like you were beside me on the couch, talking to me in the early hours stillness.

As I read your words, though, the excitement turned to confusion, then to a burning anger. I smacked my laptop shut and marched into the bedroom to wake you up. But when I got there, something stopped me. I looked at your sleeping form and was scared of it. You were like a stranger sleeping in my bed. I ran back out to the living room, lay down on the couch and read the post again. Maybe I'd misunderstood. I read again and again and again, until my eyes throbbed and the letters became a blurred jumble. I just couldn't believe that you'd made such a big decision without telling me. Did you think that by having it come out in the middle of the night, you could slip it past me?

I mean, I was used to being left out of things by now. I'd given up on those early dreams of you discussing your ideas with me before posting. But this wasn't just any old blog post. This was a change in your whole way of life. What was more, it was the very thing I had been urging you to do for a long time. I remembered all the times I'd talked to you about it, and you'd waved me away. 'I like to keep the blog separate from my life and my life separate from the blog,' you'd say. You repeated it so often that it came to sound like a prayer. You began to say it faster, to run the words together and slur the syllables, to mutter it like an invocation to ward off evil spirits. I kept asking and you kept pushing me away.

And now, suddenly, without even mentioning it to me, you'd changed your mind. You'd announced to the world that you would be attending the protest at Smith & Jefferson on Friday. You'd even had the gall to thank me for inspiring you to go to it, but only identified me as a 'loyal reader and commenter'. Did you think this would make me happy? A token acknowledgement, and everything would be alright? You didn't even consult me, Jeff. And it was so dishonest, as if you'd never heard of the protest before, as if you didn't know Marcus or anyone else, as if it was only my chance comment on your blog that had persuaded you to go. Really, how could you? After all those times I'd tried to get you to open up to me, and all the times you'd said you'd never change. Now suddenly you'd gone and done it and I had to learn about it second-hand from your blog? What was the point of being in a relationship if I knew no more about you than when I was just one of your readers?

I went to the kitchen and boiled the kettle, using the shaft of light from the open fridge to locate a cup, pour in milk and three heaped spoons of sugar. Standing in the dark kitchen, with toast crumbs and grains of rice digging into my soft bare soles, I was overcome with fatigue. For a moment I was in bed with you again, the warm duvet wrapped around, its soft creases and folds snuggling perfectly into the creases and folds of my body. My arm was draped over your shoulder, and I sank into the soft pillow, drowsily kissing the wispy hairs at the nape of your neck and feeling warm and safe.

I shivered. The kitchen was cold and dark. I raised a foot to pick out the crunchy bits of dried food and toss them into the sink. I couldn't go back to your bed. I knew that I wouldn't be able to sleep, and that I wouldn't be able to hug you or kiss your neck either. So I stayed in the cold kitchen, and took a sip of scalding tea. It tasted of nothing.

I walked back to the living room, with both hands wrapped around the steaming cup. On the way, I reached down to touch the radiator: stone cold. You always turned off the heating, saying you hated 'fuggy' rooms because they reminded you of moving to your grandparents' house. Nothing to do with saving money. 'Put on a jumper if you're cold,' you said, and it always made me feel accused of something, as if wanting to be comfortable at home was unforgivably extravagant. I turned the radiator up to maximum and settled into the biggest, warmest armchair, blowing across the surface of the tea and staring out over the dimly-lit room.

Even after months of cohabiting, there was still little of me in this room. The few things I had brought with me from my flat were stowed in cupboards or hidden away on the lowest shelves. When I bought something to brighten the place up – a vase of flowers, or a print for the wall – you acted pleased but I could see you weren't. Later you'd say you already had one like it, and pull out some cracked old vase or tattered student poster, and my bright new things were stowed quietly away in cupboards. Sometimes I wanted to complain, but then I remembered that it was your flat, not mine. I remembered that I was always too quick to impose myself, and tried to hold back. It was your right to have the flat reflect your own tastes.

But as I looked around the room, I realised that there was little of you in it, either. The furniture was the same Ikea stuff that I'd seen in my friends' places. On the large whitewashed walls only a few pictures hung, and they seemed randomly assembled. A psychedelic poster of Jimi Hendrix was straddled by a couple of twee watercolour landscapes that your parents had bought years ago from a tourist-trap teashop in the Cotswolds. On another wall was a small print of abstract red and black dots; other walls were blank apart from old nail holes and blue-tack marks. On top of the bookcases stood some superficially interesting ornaments. I'd imagined at first that I could learn something of your life from them, and was disappointed to discover that the ornaments, like the pictures on the wall, had no real stories attached to them. The carved wooden elephant had been given to you by a friend who you'd now lost touch with, the African sculpture of a long, impossibly thin man with a stick was picked up cheap from some jumble sale, and a similar tale of random chance or forgetfulness applied to all the other sculptures and trinkets around the flat. Even these minimal stories had to be extracted from you phrase by phrase. I was always the one to press, while you answered in bemusement, as if unable to understand how anyone could attach importance to such things.

The only item with a real history and relevance was the clock that now ticked in the stillness, giving shape to my thoughts. Your devotion to that thing surprised me. You seemed childlike, almost, as if you wanted to rebel but drew back at the brink, afraid of the consequences. I guess you did it out of love for your grandfather, but still it surprised me: you weren't that kind of sentimental person. After we brought it home, I'd expected to see a listing on eBay: Antique Clock, No Reserve, MUST SEE!!! But you'd unwrapped it, checked it carefully, brushed off the dust and installed it on the top of our stereo unit, where it looked completely out of place, dominating the living room as it had dominated Arthur's.

The ticking at first drove me totally crazy, intruding on everything from TV to music to sex. There was always this heavy mechanical rhythm in my ears, and I even asked you if there was some way of muting it. You laughed at me. 'I'll see if it's got a snooze button,' you said. Very funny. I only said that because what I really wanted to ask you – to get rid of the thing – was impossible. It was a family heirloom, and I had no right to get you to junk it. What if we'd broken up right after that, and you'd hated me for making you throw out a link with your ancestors? Love can be temporary, but family is permanent. You hated the ticking too, but you loved your grandfather too much to do anything about it. I knew that if I couldn't take the clock, I'd have to move out. The thing became a kind of challenge for me. Tick, tock, tick, tock, all day and all night for the rest of my life with you. The thought terrified me, but I took a deep breath, squared my shoulders and faced it. Tick, tock, tick, tock, over breakfast, in our conversations, as we cuddled in bed, when I woke up in the morning and hovered above sleep at night, tick, tock, tick, tock, always exactly the same steady, plodding rhythm that had counted out the seconds and the centuries since some ancient clockmaker set it in motion.

Then, one day, I was sitting on the sofa staring out of the window at the pale blue sky, and thoughts began to come to me. It felt like that, not that I was thinking, but that thoughts were coming to me. If I was thinking about anything at all, in fact, it was about the ticking that was interrupting my life as usual, but in the middle of it a whole load of thoughts came to me, memories of my family in America, images of you and me together. I felt clear and clean inside, like I'd reached an understanding, not in my head but unconsciously. The clock seemed to help me in doing that, in becoming clearer. It provided a steady tempo for my mind, stopping it from running ahead of itself or getting stuck in circles. It ordered my life into neat, regular chunks. I stopped immersing myself so much in TV, music, internet, video, chat, blogs and all the rest of it, and began to spend more of my time sitting on the sofa, listening to the clock. You began to ask me irritably what I was doing, wasting so much time just doing nothing. I didn't know what to reply, because I didn't really understand it myself. All I knew was that I was beginning to understand those long silences in your grandfather's front room. I knew what he was doing while he sat there with his elbows on the arms of the chair, his fingers meeting in front of his face as if in prayer. I knew that something was happening, even though nothing was happening.

For you, it was different. The clock was always a burden. You couldn't decide whether your grandfather had given it to you out of wicked malice or simply a complete misunderstanding of who you were. The ticking grated on you, making you irritable with me and perpetually distracted from whatever you were trying to concentrate on. The chimes bothered you particularly. The mechanism was old and worn, and designed in any case for an age with few competing sounds, so they really weren't that loud. Just a tinny little bell every hour, counting out the passing of time. I suppose it was that part of it that you resented, the passing of time. You always looked up in disbelief from your computer, unable to accept that another hour had passed. You resented the clock for reminding you of the accumulation of wasted hours as you clicked around on the internet, constantly trying and failing to stay focused on what you'd gone on there for. You'd have preferred to remain ignorant, only looking up from the screen when darkness had fallen and you were too tired and hungry to care any more about the wasted time. Having it shoved down your throat every hour was unbearable. You said the ticking made you feel the same way, reminding you of each passing second. 'It's not right,' you said. 'I just want to relax, and I have this noise in my ears all the time, I can't escape for a moment.'

When I suggested you could stay in bed one Sunday, though, and let the old mechanism slowly fail, you looked like I'd proposed smothering our first-born child with a cushion. Clearly the thought hadn't occurred to you. You looked back at me as your brain slowly tried to process the idea. The silence was long and strange. Finally I just said to forget it, and you looked relieved. I knew you couldn't justify to me why it was impossible, but it was. You had to get up every Sunday morning and wind the clock, and you had to get up a little earlier once a month and clean it. You didn't know why, any more than most people know why they go to church. The weight of centuries just didn't let you out. You hated the clock, but in a way I think you needed it too. It gave you a connection to something you'd never had before, something solid and lasting. You had no way to understand it or express it, but it meant something to you. As you sat there looking blankly at me, you were considering not the guilt you'd feel over letting down your grandfather, but the loss you'd feel from the removal of your new Sunday-morning ritual. I knew you well enough to see things you couldn't see yourself. At least, I thought I did. That night, though, as I sat sleepless in the semi-gloom, I doubted whether I'd ever really known you at all.

I took another sip of tea and stared solemnly through the steam at the generic furniture, the meaningless ornaments. I knew there must be something more to you than this. I'd seen it constantly in your writing, and glimpsed it occasionally in your speech. You understood the world at a deeper level, somehow: that was why your blog was so popular. I sipped my tea again, even though there was nothing left but the sugary dregs. Perhaps to look for you in your furniture or ornaments was simply superficial. Perhaps you existed beyond these things. You were always criticising consumerism, but it occurred to me suddenly that perhaps I had never really heard or understood you fully. I'd assumed you were like all the others, criticising the excess of those 'five for the price of four' Primark aficionados, but not hesitating to clutter your own house with more expensive, exclusive, fairtrade tat. Perhaps you were different, though. Perhaps you really had learned to move beyond identification with things altogether.

But where, then, could I find you? Your blog gave hints, but it was a public persona. You said nothing of your personal life, and in your personal life, you said little of your blog. I pressed and pressed, but you never told me anything. I tried to remember my resolution that day on the promontory in Milton

Keynes looking out over the sheep on the hillside. I tried to be as patient as I could, but it was no use. Even as weeks and months went by, I saw no change at all. If anything, you got even more closed and defensive. I guess it was because I was asking so much. You just shut me down whenever I mentioned the blog, said you didn't want to talk about it. It was like it didn't exist for you, like you left it in that office downtown and when you got home you were someone else, only interested in what we could have for dinner or watch on TV. As for the question of going public, that was completely off-limits. Sometimes I lay awake at night and just watched you sleeping and tried to figure out what I could do to prise you open and uncover the man I knew was in there, the Jeff Brennan I knew so well from his blog. I thought about packing my bags and going back down the M1 to London and my friends at the Chestnut Tree Café. I even thought about going all the way home, back to Beechwood, California. I could stay with my parents, start over. But then I remembered how I'd left, so full of hope and ideas, determined to show them all that I could do something big. I thought of the calls home, the envy I could hear in my friends' voices and the pride in my parents'. I couldn't go back there with nothing but a string of failed jobs and failed relationships. So I stayed in the flat, and waited.

I raised the cup to my lips again, and realised now that it was empty. In my head I went to the kitchen and boiled more water, but somehow my body refused to follow, instead nestling into the soft, warm armchair and promising to get up soon, very soon, any time now, and go to the kitchen and do everything that was required of it, only now it had to sit just a little longer in the soft, warm armchair.

You were kissing me. I felt your lips on my forehead first, then my nose, my lips, my cheeks and my ears. Normally your lips were a little too wet for my liking, and I had to restrain the impulse to wipe off the excess saliva, a gesture which I knew would be seen as unromantic. Now, though, your lips were dry and cracked from the night. I had the sensation of parched earth, something dry, hard and lifeless, desperately seeking my warmth and moisture. I turned my head away and moaned softly.

You laughed a dry, whispery laugh. 'It's okay, sweetheart. It's only me.'

'I'm getting up,' I mumbled. 'In a minute.'

You laughed again and left me in the armchair.

The next time my eyes opened, a harsher light greeted them. The sun had burned through the early cloud, just as the weatherman predicted, and it was a bright winter morning. You were in the kitchen, frying up a veggie scramble. You looked across at me and smiled. 'Something I said?'

'What's that?' I replied, feeling that it took a great effort to force the words out across the room.

'I mean, you slept in an armchair, curled up around an empty cup of tea. I was worried when I woke up and saw the bed empty. Thought you'd left me.'

Despite the words, your tone was teasing. It clearly hadn't occurred to you that any of these things might be true. You were making a joke out of something you didn't understand. I knew this, and recognised it as your way of making things safe. I smiled slightly at the recognition of the familiar, and you smiled back, relieved to have had confirmation that nothing was wrong.

'We can talk over breakfast,' I called out. 'I'm too tired now. Bring me a cup of tea, will you? I was going to make another one, but I fell asleep.'

'Sure,' you said. 'And I'll have breakfast ready in a minute.'

By the time you'd finished in the kitchen, I was ready for you. I hadn't had the solitude I wanted, but still I had worked out what I would say. I went straight to the point.

'It's more something you didn't say,' I said as I cut into a tomato.

You stared at me in silence, watching the gooey centre of the tomato spill out across the plate as if you'd never seen such a thing before. 'What do you mean?' you asked, smiling nervously.

'You asked if it was something you said, the reason I slept on the armchair. It wasn't. It was something you didn't say.'

Dread clouded your face. You looked down at your food and started hacking at a burnt piece of potato with your blunt knife. 'What do you mean?'

'There's something big you haven't told me, Jeff. You know there is.' You swallowed hard, and pushed some vegetables around on your plate. 'But if you don't want to tell me even now, then let me tell you.' You put a hand up to stop me, as if hearing it would make it true, but I ignored you. 'The protest, Jeff.'

Your face was a mask. I had no idea what you were thinking. You were looking at me now, not avoiding my gaze, but your eyes were blank. You put a new piece of veggie scramble in your mouth, and your knife scraped loudly on the plate as you prepared the next one. Something bulged on the side of your head as your jaws worked up and down, up and down. You looked, now, as if you were genuinely not avoiding me any more: you seemed more like an animal, chewing on its food, not comprehending anything but the feeling of nourishment entering its body and the buildup of saliva at the prospect of a new bite.

Suddenly I lost the heart for accusing you. It seemed pointless, like accusing a dog of chewing on a bone. It was who you were, the way you operated. Secretive, furtive, keeping your thoughts hidden from everyone, perhaps even from yourself. I felt as if I'd been in the same situation too many times. It was like when I read your blog and saw posts that seemed to have no connection with the person you really were. I remembered the naïve expectations I used to have, early on, when I thought you would start to share your secret thoughts with me. I thought that's what real couples did, shared things with each other. Instead you went to work every day, producing the most popular political blog in the country, and when you came home you just wanted to hear about my day of petty office drama.

I forced myself to go on. I couldn't let you off the hook. This was different. I thought of how I'd felt that night, reading the post: the anger, the sense of betrayal. I slammed my fork down on the plate, and jabbed my knife in the air towards you. 'Well, Jeff? What's going on?'

The worst of it was that you didn't even know what to say. You just sat there with your mouth flapping open. Under the table your hands were fumbling with your iPhone.

'Jesus, Jeff, please tell me you're not tweeting this conversation,' I said.

'No, sorry, just habit.'

'Well can you put it away for two seconds and talk to me? To me, remember me? Your loyal reader and commenter?'

You sat there for what seemed like hours, saying nothing, maybe hoping I'd give up. But I didn't give up. I sat there and waited, didn't say a word. You said nothing for ages, and then eventually you opened your mouth and said something that made me want to take that knife and jam it down your throat.

Chapter 18

I still remember that night. Bright lights, music, beer, whisky chasers, Red Bull and vodka, cigarette smoke curling up into the dark damp air. You and me together through it all. Downing shots, shouting over music, running across four-lane streets. Dodging cars and laughing at death. Your face like a dead man bolting his last meal. Drinking faster, dancing harder, running further than ever before or since. Smoking each fag down to the filter, sucking it until the tar seared into your fingertips. Letting the stub tumble to the gutter and lighting another. Popping pills that turned your face sallow and your eyes feverish. Sweating like a dog all through the cold winter night. Puking in an alley and coming out bouncing on your toes like a boxer, ready to start all over again.

Yeah, I know why. You explained it to me over a Happy Meal at the 24-hour McDonald's drive-thru on Portway. We didn't drive thru ourselves, could barely walk in our state, could we? Just crossing the huge concrete forecourt almost got us hit by some horn-honking driver. We staggered all around that low brick building, fumbling in the dark and laughing at ourselves, before we finally found the pedestrian entrance tucked away down the side. Whole place was empty except for four servers stood at their terminals, backs straight, staring forward, like a row of tin soldiers. You said something about throwing coconuts at them, and the mood you were in it was probably lucky that there was nothing to hand. They must've seen people like us before. Everything plastic and bolted to the floor, all the surfaces smooth and clear. Nothing heavy or sharp in the whole place. Ketchup in sachets, food in boxes, drinks in sippy-cups. Like a crèche in a nuthouse.

Maybe it was this safe, soothing atmosphere that made you more reflective as you ate your cheeseburger Happy Meal and slurped on your Coke. Maybe that's why you started talking for the first time. Up until then I couldn't get a serious word out of you. Could see something had happened, knew it from your voice when you called me up last minute and said you wanted to get completely laggered. But when I asked what was up you just waved the question away like you were swatting a fly or something. Would've poked my eye out with your lit cigarette if I hadn't been on my toes. 'It's Saturday night,' you said. 'It's Saturday night, Jon!' Later on I tried a few times in different ways, but you always just said, 'It's Saturday night.'

Couldn't complain, could I? Got what I wanted. Saturday night with you, getting wasted and forgetting the week. Reaching for anything we could get our hands on and pouring it down our throats, knowing it'd cure anything, at least for a while. The blankness. Space to escape and breathe again, if only for a night. And this time we were even leaving our flats, so we'd have some photos to post for a change. But still, you scared me that night. That desperation in your eyes. It was something I hadn't seen before. Stopped me from escaping the way you were escaping. Kept me wondering what was behind it, what had happened, what thing in the real world was weighing on you so hard that you had to keep drinking and drinking and drinking to make it go away.

In McDonald's, though, where we sat with our Happy Meals and plastic straws and the panpipe tones of *Killing Me Softly* in the air, it was like you were just really tired. The wild desperation had faded into the beige walls, the restless energy had been sapped by the soft music that smothered us like a blanket. Your head was bent, your eyes hooded, your movements slow and dreamlike.

'It's all over,' you said through a mouthful of mangled chips.

Surprise sur-fucking-prise. I mean, it was the only explanation. But still, I couldn't imagine how you'd let it happen. Thought you had it all under control. Even that crazy bitch Annie at work seemed to be keeping quiet as long as you kept bigging her up online. Didn't want to make you clam up again, though, so I just waited for you to finish your mouthful, then suck loudly on your straw as you tried to vacuum up drops of Coke from the sides of the ice cubes. Finally you spoke again. Told me about Marcus threatening to tell Marie if you didn't steal some document for him from work, about the real Jeff Brennan and his post, about Marie and her accusations.

I wanted to be a friend. Do what I always did, tell you it would all work out. But I couldn't lie to you, could I? You were completely fucked. You knew it, I knew it. I mean, Marcus and Marie you could maybe have dealt with, but not the real Jeff Brennan. There was just no way the two of you could co-exist. His appearance on the stage meant your exit. When he turned up at the protest, Marie would see all the lies you'd told her. If all she did was spit in your face and walk off arm in arm into the sunset with the real Jeff Brennan, it'd be a result. If I was her, I'd probably kill you. No, I'd chop your balls off. Then I'd kill you.

Of course, I didn't tell you any of this. Didn't lie to you neither. Just sat listening. Trying to keep my face neutral. Spewing a few sympathetic noises from my mouth. But there was really no hiding from it, and you knew it as well as I did. The only thing to do was get completely wasted and forget about it for as long as possible. I understood it now. The frenetic drinking, the desperate sucking on the cigarettes. Like a drowning man grabbing for a passing log. You were doomed, and all I could do was help you enjoy your last supper.

'Want another Happy Meal?' I asked. 'On me.'

You sat back in your chair, stomach stretched like a balloon, hands resting on either side as you considered the offer. 'Nah, I'm alright, thanks,' you said finally. 'I could go for some nuggets though. Want to share a big box?'

I smiled. 'Yeah, why not.' When we were kids, we used to get the box of six nuggets that only came with one packet of sauce, and always argued over which one to get. Now we could afford more, and I went to get the twenty-pack, with barbecue sauce for you and sweet'n'sour for me. There was a bit of a wait, and I stood face to face with the cashier, pretending to read the menu so that I didn't have to make eye contact. The fluorescent lights behind the pictures of crispy lettuce and succulent burgers began to hurt my eyes. I felt suddenly sober. Saw myself for a moment through the jaded eyes of the cashier. A swaying, sick-looking drunk ordering chicken nuggets in an empty McDonald's on the edge of Milton Keynes in the dead of night. Then the nuggets came and it was over. The familiar oily smell made me salivate like a dog, and I crammed a hot nugget into my mouth before taking the box back to the table where you were sitting with your head in your hands.

The nuggets had the same effect on you as they'd had on me. You raised your head, your eyes regained focus and your hands grabbed greedily at the box. 'The worst of it,' you said through mouthfuls of chicken, 'was that I had no idea what she was angry about. I mean, why did that prick have to post at one in the morning?'

'Should have told her you did it for her sake, mate. That always works. They love to think they're the centre of the universe.'

You laughed bitterly and took another sip at your empty Coke. 'Tried that. But of course that prick had to go and mention Marie, didn't he? Not as a lover or anything, but as a 'loyal reader'. She kept saying I was trying to pretend I didn't know her, like I was ashamed or something. I mean, of all the hundreds of comments he gets, why did he have to pick hers to reply to?'

I ate another nugget. Nothing else to say, was there? When I thought of the protest coming up on Monday, I cringed for you.

'Then I made it worse by blaming it on Marcus. I thought that was what had happened, that he'd decided I wasn't going to get the document and told her everything. After that she went absolutely ballistic, waving her knife at me and saying I was always trying to blame someone else, that it was nothing to do with him, that I'd written it myself in black and white on my own blog. That was when I realised it was him, the real Jeff Brennan, and I knew I was fucked.'

I tried to tell you it'd be okay, but the words wouldn't come out. I munched on another nugget and hoped you'd say something so that I didn't have to, but it seemed like you were finished. 'At least you've got your Saturday nights back,' I said finally.

You smiled weakly. 'Yep. I've missed them.'

Bullshit. Still, I smiled back anyway. 'Let's go home and kick some jihadist ass. I left it where it was last time we played together, haven't done any missions on my own. We can pick up from before. Like none of it ever happened. I recorded *Match of the Day* as well. Spurs v Chelsea, should be a good one.'

I don't remember leaving McDonald's. Next thing I remember is walking up Midsummer Boulevard towards some night club. You'd got a second wind, you said. Remembered that gang of girls dressed as mini-skirted nuns who said they'd be ending their hen night at Oblivion. I tried to tell you they wouldn't be there any more. Tried to say the place was way out of town, it cost fifteen quid on the door and as much as that again for a couple of drinks. Said that for all the sexy outfits and giggling innuendo, girls on a hen night are only interested in the idea of men, not our reality. But you didn't listen to any of it, so there we were lurching down a wide empty street at one in the morning, heading for a club on the edge of town and the dream of drunk girls in nuns' outfits.

'We're lost,' I said.

'We're not lost.'

'You said that before.'

'It's just up here a bit.'

I peeled back the sleeve of my coat with shivering fingers, held my watch up to the street lamp and peered at the dim face while a cold rain trickled down my arm. 'One thirty,' I said. 'This place'll be closed by the time we find it.'

'It won't. It's just up here.'

'Up where?' I asked, looking around at the wide, barren boulevard. Offices long-closed, restaurants and pubs shuttered. Everything and everyone was asleep. On the higher floors of the office buildings a few lights had been left on, like some lame attempt at a Manhattan-style skyline. Wasn't working. There's nowhere in Milton Keynes where you can get far enough away from the buildings to see a real skyline. They just crowd the avenues, looming over you wherever you go until, when you get a mile or two away from them, they disappear behind hedgerows and darkened suburban homes and you realise they weren't so tall after all. Just an optical illusion.

We kept walking fast along Midsummer Boulevard. Hands stuffed into pockets and white headphones stuffed in our ears. Rain getting steadily harder. Wide, empty roads covered with sheets of water rippling in the wind. Pavements swept clean of their usual Saturday night mess. The chip wrappers, stray gherkins and chicken bones now clogging the drains instead, forming bubbling pools along the sides of the road. Too-bright streetlights making it look like daylight in a black-and-white world. Just this broad strip of shimmering white against a backdrop of black desolation. It was apocalyptic. Like something from a film. It was also proper cold, and I was getting more sober with every step.

'You're completely fucked,' I said in modest revenge. You pressed the white buds deeper into your ears and said nothing.

It was true, though, and you knew it. Each of your problems on its own was enough to stop your new life dead. Marcus was behaving like the smacktard I'd always said he was. One day I'd say I told you so, but not tonight. I mean, threatening you like that is just wrong. If I had to blackmail you to save the world, I'd let the world burn. He'd say I lack 'vision', I suppose. But thinking big is what's caused all the problems in the first place, and thinking even bigger won't solve them. Just makes you crazy, twists you up until you don't know what's right any more. I prefer to be narrow-minded, as he'd put it, and do right by my friends. I was proud of you for telling him you wouldn't do it. I mean, I know it had more to do with fear than principle. You couldn't risk trying to steal a document from work. Your boss was a dick, but he wasn't stupid. He'd catch you and hang you out to dry. You'd lose everything. Of course, if you didn't do what Marcus wanted, he'd tell Marie and you'd lose her. But at least you'd still have a job.

Marcus could ruin that too. He was bringing all your wacko eco-warrior friends along to the place where you pretended to be a sensible IT consultant. Bringing Marie along too. Deliberately taking the worlds you'd kept separate and smashing them together like a destructive child. Couldn't say what would happen when he did that. He might not even have to tell Marie anything, or tell your boss anything. He might be able to maintain his purity, the hypocritical prick, just standing in the background and watching everything fall apart. You remember that afternoon when we were about twelve or thirteen? When we stood on that bridge over the M1 and fantasised about throwing things down on the cars below? Well, Marcus wouldn't have chickened out like we did. He'd have let the brick fall, and watched the carnage with a smile on his face. That's the kind of person he is.

Even if you managed to steer through the pile-up, though, there was still the situation with Marie. She hated you already for making a decision like that without her. More importantly, it showed up the difference between you and your blog, and every time that happened you lost a bit of credibility. Surely by now a few doubts were appearing in her mind? Hadn't it at least occurred to her that she could have been wrong all along? That you were not, and never had been, the real Jeff Brennan? Weren't the differences too obvious? Wasn't she wondering? Or had she gone too far to let herself wonder?

Then there was Annie. As unpredictable as ever. I felt a bit sorry for her to be honest. Funny thing is, if you hadn't got shacked up with Marie, you'd have jumped at the chance of going out with Annie. She was cute in a Taylor Swift sort of way, and when I met her once at some piss-up in Milton Keynes she'd seemed like she was up for a laugh. When you first met her you even told me about her one Saturday night, but thought she was out of your league. Funny how things work out. Still, maybe the only reason she was interested in you was because she could tell you had a girlfriend already. Women are weird like that. The only thing predictable about Annie was that she would keep posting photos online, and that if you weren't enthusiastic enough about her in enough different voices, she'd ruin everything. She might even get there before Marcus.

But the situation with Annie, with Marie, even with Marcus, could maybe have been managed. The real Jeff Brennan appearing on the scene, though, that was different. You could talk your way out of most things, but not that. When Marie saw him at the protest while you skulked in your office, even she couldn't avoid seeing the truth. There was just no room for two Jeff Brennans. Didn't even matter any more what Marcus said or didn't say. Jeff Brennan's appearance would kill you.

A cold gust cut through my coat. I stopped under a street lamp. 'Too much,' I said. 'Let's just call a cab.'

Didn't even break your stride. 'It's just a bit further up,' you called out over your shoulder. 'I'm sure of it.'

I looked ahead down the wide, empty street. Nothing but

big, dark concrete blocks on both sides, stretching off to the horizon. No bright lights, no queues. No velvet rope or stocky bouncers. No groups of people standing around waiting for friends. No shouting, no broken glass. No kebab shops or chicken shacks, no stink of grease. Nothing but the road, the echo of footsteps, the jangle of music in my ear, the cold, the rain and the big dark boxes of long-closed shops. Nothing familiar. It was like we were walking the same stretch of road again and again in an endless loop. I pulled out my mobile.

'But we're so close now,' you shouted. I turned away from you, hunching my body over the phone to shield it from the wind and the loud drumming of rain. This bored night-shift taxi controller mumbled in my ear while you pulled at my arm. Only a bit further up, you said. Made no sense to give up after coming so far. Mini-skirted nuns were waiting for us. A load of other shit, too, but I booked the cab and let it all float away on the wind.

Ten minutes later a car appeared on the empty street and started to slow. You put your hand out in the road like a policeman directing traffic. The car crawled along the kerb. Through the dim windscreen, behind the blinding headlights and the frenetic wipers, a small, round face peered suspiciously. I stood up a little straighter and pulled my hands out of my pockets. The car stopped for a moment, still a few yards short of the street corner. The small, round face moved closer to the windscreen. Chubby hand reached forward to wipe mist from the glass. Small, dark, round eyes flicked from you to me, from me to you. We know this game so well, don't we? Stand up straight, hands where they can be seen, eyes forward. Smile just enough to seem friendly but not so broadly that it's like you're trying to hide something. No sudden moves. The car's engine ground into gear and the wheels rolled slowly forward to the corner where we stood. The window jerked open a centimetre. Then a centimetre more. 'Your name, please?'

'Jon.'

'Destination?'

'14 Willow Drive.'

The head turned to face forward. A click of the central locking system and in a few seconds we were in the back seat. Another click and we were locked in. Hot and clammy suddenly, choking on nicotine and pine. A smooth male voice introducing a soothing jazz classic that was quickly drowned out by the roar of the engine. At a red light, the fizz of a can, loud slurping, the metallic stench of Red Bull. Behind it all, a strange, burnt aroma I couldn't place. More jerking forward, crunching through the gears.

'Do you know Oblivion?' you shouted suddenly.

The driver braked instinctively. 'What?' he shouted back.

'Oblivion. The night club.'

'No, no,' he shouted. 'Car was booked for Willow Drive. That's a twenty pound journey. Oblivion is just round the corner.'

'Told you we were close,' you hissed at me. 'Can we just go past it?' you shouted.

'Cost extra.'

'No problem.'

'Okay,' the driver said. 'But you don't get out. I keep the doors locked.'

'No problem.'

I sighed, and tried to stifle a belch. 'I hope you know you're paying for this shit,' I said as the car turned sharp left onto another wide, empty avenue.

'No problem,' you said again.

Silence again as the car zipped through empty streets. The driver rubbing holes in the misted-up windows, looking for the club. You and me doing the same, saying nothing. Ten minutes passed.

'Almost there,' said the driver, sensing our doubt. 'It's just up here somewhere.'

I sighed. 'Look, can we just go home?'

The driver touched the brakes and half-turned. 'Look, which you want?' he demanded angrily. 'You say Willow Drive, then you say Oblivion, now you say no Oblivion. Which is it?'

'Oblivion,' you said firmly.

I slumped back in the seat, shaking my head. When you got an idea in your head, there was no talking to you. 'Whatever. You're paying for this whole trip, okay?'

'No problem.'

The car built up speed again, spraying water up into the deserted night. 'Don't worry, we'll think of something,' I said. The car sped through another red light.

'There's nothing to think of,' you said calmly.

I looked out of the window. Thinking of all the times you'd helped me out of some problem or another over the years. How I'd never done anything for you except take the piss. I wasn't sure whose fault that was, mine or yours. 'Are we nearly there?' I shouted at the driver.

'Just a bit further,' the driver shouted back as we passed the street corner he'd picked us up from.

It was inevitable, I suppose. That big a lie. It's just not sustainable. You'd done well to survive for so long. A few months with the woman of your dreams. Better than nothing, wasn't it? Then again, if there was nothing, there'd be nothing to regret. 'Better to have loved and lost' was bullshit, written by someone who'd never lost very much. The reality of losing is it makes you bitter, and loving just leaves you wanting more love. You'd probably have been better off living those months as an IT consultant, drinking and dreaming.

'Let's just go home,' I said.

'Not yet,' you replied. Rubbed another hole in the misty window. 'Almost there now. Almost there.'

Chapter 19

Marcus Higgins @marcushig 6m
@JeffB I still need that thing we talked about, can u get it?

Marcus Higgins @marcushig 5m
@JeffB No choice m8, I know its hard but we need it, remember?

Marcus Higgins @marcushig 3m
@JeffB Yeh we're friends but the cause comes first. Hv to make sacrifices

Marcus Higgins @marcushig 2m
@JeffB Try harder. Otherwise next time I see her I tell everything

Chapter 20

I knew something was wrong immediately. You tried to pretend everything was normal, but you forget sometimes how well I know you. I saw you sitting on that same sofa when you were four years old, your chubby hand spread out across the cushion in a vain attempt to hide the pen marks. I saw you sitting there at eight, pretending to have done well at school even though your mother had already shown me the report littered with Cs. I saw you sitting there again at fourteen, pretending not to care that your parents had died, and again at sixteen, swearing you weren't drunk and then vomiting into the wastepaper basket. I saw you now, at twenty-three, sipping tea and making conversation, still believing as certainly as when you were four that you could conceal your secret from me.

Even before you arrived, I knew something was wrong. As Daisy and I sat in the living room waiting for you, I looked at my watch and said, 'Not like Jeff to be this late.' A few more minutes passed in a silence that still sounded foreign without the ticking of the clock. 'Yes, I know, there were those few times, but he always called to tell us. He knows how much you worry about him driving down the motorway every Sunday, when the news is full of pile-ups, tail-backs, jack-knifed lorries and head-on collisions. He's always called before. Something's different this time.' More minutes passed, and I began to wish the clock was once again on our mantelpiece, breaking the world up into regular, manageable chunks. Without it there was nothing to bring order to my thoughts. I walked over to Daisy's chair, perched on the edge of it and held her hand. It trembled slightly, and I stroked it softly until she calmed down.

Soon, of course, your red brake lights appeared in our driveway, and the darker visions of blood on tarmac were swiftly dispelled. But when you walked through the door, the lies started.

'Where's Marie?' I asked.

'She couldn't make it this week,' you said as you took off your coat and hung it on the end of the banister. 'She's meeting friends.'

'That's strange, she didn't mention anything about it last week. As she was leaving she said she would see us next Sunday. I remember she did.'

You walked into the living room, and I trailed along behind you. 'Well, she must have forgotten, Granddad. Or perhaps you did.'

That was a low blow. I do have the occasional lapse, but I'm sure I have a better memory than many people half my age. It was a familiar strategy, though. You did the same when you were four, blaming your cousin Jamie for scribbling on the sofa. Attack is the best form of defence. You came out swinging, and I knew immediately that you were hiding something.

You looked awful, too. Pale, unshaven, red-eyed, your crumpled clothes clearly flung on in a hurry. Your voice was lower than usual, and the words seemed to scrape against your throat as they came out. You breathed something sour and stale over me, a smell reminiscent of passing The Plough too early on a Sunday morning. 'Would you like some breakfast, Jeff?'

You looked at me sharply through those reddened, sunken eyes. 'It's the afternoon, Granddad. Why are you offering me breakfast?'

'I thought you might have skipped it this morning.'

'Oh yeah, I forgot, you know everything about me, don't you? What I had for breakfast, what's on my mind, what colour underwear I'm wearing.'

The sarcasm reminded me of your teenage years. Always angry, but never really knowing why. Spitting sarcasm and injustice. Reminding us at every opportunity how old we were, how out of touch. If you could have spoken about your parents even in passing, I'm sure you would have listed all the ways in which they were better at bringing you up than we were. Even though you couldn't do that, and still haven't to this day, the implication was there in everything we did. Your parents would have let you stay up late, or go to the party, or smoke or drink. Your parents would have understood you. Their presence haunted us all, as you appealed constantly to their memory without ever speaking their names. You tolerated Daisy and me, but our authority was always temporary. Your real allegiance was to them.

'At least let me make you one of my cures,' I said with as much warmth as I could muster. I felt awkward again, like in the early days when you came to live here and the three of us sat around the dining room table night after night. You and Daisy just slumped silently in your chairs, and it was left to me to live for three people. I told stories to the walls, full of false cheer and hollow optimism. You looked at me as if I were stupid, but what else could I do? All the wise friends and relations said how horrible it was for you, how I must try to lift you out of it. It never seemed to occur to them that I had lost a daughter, too. Two parents trumps a daughter, it seems, and so I injected my voice with good humour and tried to keep you going, even though I heard my voice ring out fake across the silent dining room and knew you hated me for it almost as much as I hated myself.

'I don't need a cure,' you said. 'There's nothing wrong with me. Just the usual gallon of tea would be fine.' As I walked to the kitchen, you called out after me, 'And no extra sugar, I know you were going to add it.'

You came out soon after to apologise, but it wasn't necessary. I knew it wasn't me you were angry at. 'You were right, anyway,' I said. 'I was going to give you extra sugar.'

You laughed and put your hand on my shoulder. 'You see, I know a few things about you, too. All these years and you still think a cup of strong, sweet tea will cure the world's problems.'

'Gives you energy, that's all,' I said. 'You look as if you need building up.'

'I'm fine,' you insisted. 'Had a few drinks with Jon last night, that's all.'

'Oh, how is Jon?' I asked, and we were back on safe ground again as I made the tea and you told me Jon's news, such as it was. Back in the living room again with Daisy, we played the familiar game of asking about old friends, and it didn't matter that most of yours were stuck in boring jobs and most of mine were dead. We didn't really care about the present, but were asking about the past, and finding common footing again in our shared memories.

Inevitably, though, we ran out of friends to ask about, and silence returned. An occasional car rumbled past, and somewhere in the distance screaming children played. From an adjacent garden came the buzz of a lawnmower, and the scent of freshly cut grass seemed to fill the living room. I thought of my roses, which had looked lifeless recently, and of the weeds growing through the cracks in the path. The afternoon was tolerably warm, and I had been planning to ask Marie to help me with a few things in the garden. The girl likes to be useful, I can see that, and I'm running out of tasks around the house with which to occupy her. I wanted to ask whether she'd be back next weekend, but felt it would be out of place.

'It feels strange without the clock,' you said.

'Really?' I said. 'I've got used to it myself. Funny how you could have something around for so long, and then not miss it a jot when it's gone.' Silence fell again, so I added, 'Have you found a place for it in your flat yet?'

For a few moments I could hear once again the screams of children playing, and then you finished sipping your tea and replied, 'Yes, Granddad. Pride of place. We don't have a mantelpiece – the place is too new for that – but we've put it on top of our stereo unit. It looks great. Here, I've got a photo here somewhere to show you.'

You reached for your mobile phone and began staring at it intently while your thumbs alternately stroked and prodded at it. You handed me the phone, and I saw a brightly-lit square in which the clock appeared to be floating in space. Only when I squinted a little did I make out the square white table – presumably the stereo unit – which until then had been invisible against the white walls. On the shelf below was a small white oblong, and two tiny boxes. 'Stereo systems are small these days,' I said.

You laughed, and I wasn't sure what I'd said. 'Yes, Granddad,' you said. 'That's why we had space for your clock on top.'

'It's yours now, not mine,' I said absent-mindedly, staring at this strange scene. The clock looked absurd in its new setting. The tiny oblong probably contained a thousand times the technology of the clunky, awkward monstrosity above it. It could probably even tell the time as well. I regretted having saddled you with this burden. Its dark oak casing and traditional curves, which had always struck me as rather elegant and imposing on my mantelpiece and my father's before, looked ugly and awkward in your place of clean, straight white lines. Even the mechanism, for which I'd maintained such reverence over the decades of careful cleaning, now seemed unnecessarily cumbersome. I couldn't imagine what the inside of your stereo looked like, but I knew it would make my clock look as modern as a flint axe. I handed the phone back, feeling a little dizzy.

'I've been taking good care of it,' you said. 'Winding it

every Sunday morning, and cleaning it once a month, just like you always did.'

'That's good of you,' I said. 'Did you manage all right? It's quite intricate, so don't take it all apart until you're sure you understand it.'

'Too late,' you said. 'First time I cleaned it, I found myself dismantling the whole thing. I mean, I hadn't intended to, I was just going to clean the bits I could see, and squirt a bit more oil. But it was weird, I just started taking it apart.'

I felt an unexpected surge of relief at the thought of the clock in a million pieces on your living room floor. You'd taken it apart, and now you'd never find anyone to fix it for you, or to make a new part to replace the one that had probably disappeared under the sofa. 'It's not worth it,' they'd say. 'Cheaper to buy a new one.' It's how the world is these days. I felt sorry for you, though, because I now understood what was wrong all along. You'd probably been up all night trying to fix it, and had arrived late because you didn't want to have to face your grandfather and admit that you'd broken his old clock. If only you knew how little it mattered to me. 'It's all right,' I said. 'It really doesn't matter. I shouldn't have given it to you in the first place.'

'No, you don't understand. It was the weirdest thing. All the time I was taking it apart, I knew exactly what I was doing. I don't know the names for all the parts, but I knew what order to take them out in. I knew how to arrange them on the table the way you used to, I knew where the old oil would be crusted on, where I'd have to clean a little harder and then spread more new oil on top. I mean, I didn't know in advance, if you'd asked me what I was going to do next, I wouldn't have had a clue. But when I got to each new stage, my fingers just did the right thing. I cleaned all the parts, then slotted them back together as if I'd been doing it all my life.'

As you were talking, I remembered all those times on the first Sunday of the month when you came downstairs and watched me winding or cleaning the clock. From the first Sunday you came to live with us, you always sat on the chair next to me and watched silently as I took the clock down from the mantelpiece, spread out the oilcloth and began the familiar process. It was more or less the only time we spent together that was comfortable. I never tried to make you speak, and you never complained that I was ruining your life. For that brief time on a Sunday morning, an unspoken truce was called. I sat and cleaned, and you sat and watched. Then, when I'd put the clock back on the mantelpiece and turned around to speak to you, you'd have disappeared. A little later I'd go up to your room and find you in front of your computer, surly and resentful again, refusing lunch or tea or whatever I was offering, and I'd wonder if I had imagined your presence. But on the first Sunday of the following month you'd appear again. 'I never realised you were memorising it all,' I said.

'Neither did I. Funny, isn't it?'

'Yes, I suppose so. Well, are you sure you put the escapement back right? It can be tricky, you know, you have to jiggle it a little to get it to seat properly.'

I went on with a few more questions, and I suppose I must have asked too much, because you said with a sneaky smile, 'Thought you didn't miss it, Granddad.'

'Not in the least,' I said, and left it at that. But as I drank my tea and then got up to help Daisy sit a little more comfortably in her chair, I began to feel uneasy again. If you hadn't broken the clock, then something else must have happened. 'How does Marie like the clock?' I asked.

'Fine.'

'I mean, it's not very contemporary, is it? I wasn't sure if it was her style.'

'She likes it,' you said. 'Says it's nice to have a rhythm to her life, feels like a heartbeat.'

'That's nice,' I said. 'So everything's fine with the two of you?'

'Everything's fine,' you said. 'Listen, why don't we have a go on the computer? Don't want you to miss out on your lesson, just because Marie's not here.'

I wanted to say no, but how could I? How could I tell you that when Marie explained things I understood them, whereas when you did, it felt like a lecture I had no interest in attending? How could I tell you that you always made me feel rushed and flustered, whereas she seemed infinitely patient? 'That would be nice,' I said.

In the dining room, with you breathing over my shoulder, I immediately felt rushed again. The keys merged and jumbled before my eyes, and I couldn't remember what to do. The room felt cold. I began to remember the chill of my piano teacher's draughty annex, the smell of his cough sweets, and to wait for the sharp rap of ruler across chapped knuckles. 'I haven't practised,' I admitted.

'It's okay,' you said softly. 'To start, you click on 'Start', remember?'

I fumbled for the mouse, and began to feel better about myself as I found my way onto the internet and checked my email. There were five new messages, and I remembered the excitement of new post clattering through the letterbox in the morning.

'They're just spam,' you said. 'Delete them.'

I searched my brain, dismissing cans of sliced meat and rummaging for the updated meaning, which I knew was in there somewhere. Marie had explained the whole thing when I first got my email account, and I thought I'd understood it then.

Sensing my hesitation, you prompted: 'Junk mail. Like those annoying pizza menus and holiday brochures you're always getting through the front door.'

'Ah yes. But how do you know?'

You sighed. 'Trust me.'

'But how will I know, when you're not here?'

You sighed again, and leaned forward. 'This one says

you've got a problem with your HSBC bank account. Do you have an HSBC bank account?'

'No, but surely I should at least read it.'

'Why?'

'Well, perhaps there's been a mix-up, and... '

'There's no mix-up. Reply to that email and they'll get into your bank account and take your life savings, okay? Next, 'Re: hi', from someone called Daria. Do you know someone called Daria?'

'No,' I said again, feeling like a schoolboy, only being asked questions with one possible answer, and feeling the urge to say yes just to annoy you. Instead I highlighted all the messages and silently clicked 'Delete'.

That seemed to make you suitably guilty, and you injected a note of patience into your voice as you asked, 'Where do you want to go next?'

I thought of my garden, the sun striking my face as I stepped through the back door. Leaning on the cold stone of the bird bath to catch my breath, the moss tickling my palms. I heard the chair behind me creaking, as if your impatience had seeped into the old teak joints. 'Facebook,' I said hurriedly.

The answer seemed to please you, because you relaxed in your chair again and waited patiently while I searched for the bookmark. 'You know, everyone's been telling me what you've been up to on Facebook.' My hand froze on the mouse, and I turned to face you and explain, but saw with relief that you were just joking. I turned hastily back to the screen and let you continue. 'Jon says you've written on his wall a few times now. Marcus says you've exchanged a few messages. Even Dex and Annie at work both asked me who Arthur Standhope was.'

'I've embarrassed you.'

'Not at all. They all thought it was great, someone your age getting involved with Facebook. Just funny, that's all. What did you do, go through my friend list and make friends with everyone on there?'

I shrugged, and continued to click through to the site. 'What else could I do? None of my friends are likely to be on Facebook, are they?'

You pointed to the screen, and began to lecture me on its contents, and tell me where to click, and I felt hot pressure on the back of my neck. My hand began to falter on the mouse, and the movements of the little black arrow on the screen became more erratic as you leaned closer to me and pointed and corrected. 'No, not there,' you said, but it was too late. I had clicked on the wrong thing. A little red heart, broken in two – the colour must have attracted my wandering mouse as it crossed my news feed, looking for whatever it was you wanted me to click on. I read the text next to it:

'Marie has changed her relationship status from 'In a relationship' to 'It's complicated'.'

I asked you what it meant. You just sat there, looking once again like the guilty four year old covering pen marks on the sofa with a chubby hand. 'It means it's complicated,' you said finally.

This I couldn't understand. I understood being together, and I understood breaking things off. But this vague middle ground of complications was something around which, although I'd heard mention of it on television, I had never been able to wrap my mind. 'So are you still together, or have you broken things off?'

'We haven't broken up completely, but we had an argument, and I haven't seen her since.'

'Will she come here next weekend?'

'I don't know, Granddad.'

You looked tired, and I had to restrain the impulse to offer you more tea. You said nothing more, and I tried to remain silent too as you stared at the screen and stroked your cheek, your hand scraping on the unshaven spikes. It was as if you were trying to understand the little red heart as well, staring at it until it made some sort of sense. So curt and impersonal, this sudden change of status. Was that how things were done these days? Marie had burst out of the image on the computer screen and had, for several months, been a real human being, sitting on my sofa, drinking my tea, teaching me about email and spam and menus and bookmarks. Then one day her status changed and she was gone again, back to where she came from, a little image on a screen. It made no sense to me, but then very little seems to these days. 'What caused it?' I asked.

You sighed, blowing stale, sour air over the backs of my hands. 'She thought I was someone else,' you said in a weak, scratchy voice.

'I remember,' I said. 'From the first time, you said that. I told you it didn't matter.'

Your face brightened a little. 'I remember.'

'So you never told her?'

'No.'

'Ah. Who did she think you were?'

You smiled and leaned forward, your hands taking control of the keyboard and gently easing mine away. 'I suppose you might understand now,' you said. Your hands skated across the keyboard, so fast that I couldn't make out the individual keystrokes. I looked at the screen, and your name had appeared at the top. Below it was a tagline: 'Britain's #1 political blog.'

'A blog is just a type of website,' you said, anticipating my question. 'He writes about political news, and publishes it here.'

'Another Jeff Brennan.'

'Yes. You'd probably like his site, actually. He's a journalist, like you. You'd be proud of him if he was your grandson.'

'I'm proud of you,' I said, my voice faltering slightly. I dislike that kind of thing, but you'd left me little choice. There was an awkward silence, and I filled it by saying, 'A bit boastful, isn't it, calling himself the number one political whatever? He's probably not very nice in real life.'

You clicked a few buttons, and the machine began to shut

down. 'Grandma must be getting lonely in there,' you said.

'Yes, must be. Good lad, always thinking of us. Marie's lucky to have you, even if you're not this 'number one' person. She'll realise it soon, and come back.'

'Thanks Granddad. But it's not really about that.' Then you told me the whole sorry tale, about the 'real' Jeff Brennan appearing in public for the first time, Marie's anger at his post because she thought it was yours, an anger that would multiply manifold when she discovered you were not, and never had been, the famous Jeff Brennan. You told me about Marcus blackmailing you, and Annie threatening you. 'So you see there's really no hope. If one thing doesn't get me, another will.'

For a moment or two I said nothing. I was shaken, to be honest, by this sudden blizzard of lies and threats. Every Sunday you sat on my sofa sipping tea and asking politely after my roses, and yet this was the world you inhabited, this world where friends were not really friends, where reality changed from one week to the next. 'You must tell her first,' I said. It was all I could think of. 'Explain everything. Tell her you love her anyway.'

'She'll kill me.'

'She'll be angry, but it's better than her finding out from someone else. In public, where she'll be humiliated as well.'

You stood up abruptly, as if trying to escape physically from the thought. 'It's all right, Granddad,' you said, taking my arm. 'I'll just lie low for a while, and it'll all blow over. Here, let me help you up.'

'I'm fine.' I let you help, though, to make you feel better. 'It's just a little cold in this back room. My knees seize up a bit.' With a loud crack, I was upright. 'Don't you want to at least try?'

You looked pleadingly at me. I remembered when you were about fifteen, and you'd planned a camping trip with a group of friends, but at the last minute you got cold feet. I told you to call and tell them, but you refused. Stubborn as your mother at the same age, you said you'd just stay in your room and play computer games, and when you didn't turn up they'd go without you. I tried everything I could think of to force you to call them, but nothing worked. You stayed in your room, hiding, pleading with your eyes in the same way that you pleaded with me now. I picked up the phone and told your friends you were ill. Perhaps that was a mistake. Perhaps I made many mistakes, both with you and your mother. Perhaps if I'd been tougher with you both, as my father was with me, then things would have been different. But how could I inflict that on you, when you already resented me for not being your parents? How could I enforce on you that Spartan discipline I'd detested, those long, lonely hours of bowling at a single stump, waiting in vain for the day when everything would be child's play? I couldn't, and so now you were facing a crisis in complete inertia, waiting pointlessly for someone to make the magic phone call to bail you out, as I'd always done but couldn't any more. I'd failed you.

As we left the room, you looked around for the first time. 'How much stuff have you thrown out, Granddad? You'll have nothing left at this rate.'

My brain took a while to adjust from the past to the present, and I had to look around the room to remind myself what you were talking about. The sight of so much empty space pleased me, and the prospect of having nothing left at all was even more enticing. An empty house, just me and Daisy in it together, back to where we'd come from, free of all the things which had dazzled us with their seeming importance for so many years. 'I have everything I need,' I said. 'Everything essential. None of that stuff had any real value any more.'

'I don't understand why you're keeping this old thing, then,' you said, pointing disdainfully at the Olivetti typewriter on the table. I was a little offended, I must say. Despite everything, I still saw it as a gleaming slice of the modern world, the elegant piece of machinery I'd eagerly unwrapped from its packaging in November 1957. I still remember when I loaded the first ribbon, fed in the first sheet of crisp white paper and filled it with the words: 'Daisy I love you, I love you Daisy, DAISY I love you, Love you I do Daisy,' and so on for a whole page. When I pulled it out and gave it to her with a flourish, she laughed and said, 'I love you too, Arthur. But perhaps you should try out some different letters. Half of them could be missing for all you know.' And I replied, 'Those are all the letters I need, my love.' We had such fun in those days. Still do, of course, but it was different then. And in my youthful, faux-gallant way, I'd hit on the truth. For all the millions of words I typed out on that machine over the next half a century, none would matter as much as the first.

'It's okay, Granddad. Keep it if you want. I just don't get why, when you're throwing out so much else.'

'I'm using it. Don't you see the piles of paper beside it? One fresh, one used. Every day the fresh pile gets shorter and the used pile gets larger.'

You looked at the piles with shock. Clearly it hadn't occurred to you that I might have something to say at my age. 'I didn't realise,' you said. 'But why don't you just use the computer? I can show you... '

'It's all right,' I snapped. 'The typewriter is just fine.' You reached forward to ruffle the sheets. 'No reading,' I said. 'It's personal. Come on, you're right, Grandma must be getting lonely.'

'But what is it?' you insisted, your hand still hovering over the pages as if refusing to accept that it couldn't have just one quick peek. I'd never seen you so curious. Even as a child you lacked a child's curiosity. When I hopefully showed you my old cricket gear, you said it looked old and dusty. My collection of postcards from far-flung imperial outposts failed to ignite your interest; you'd seen the Taj Mahal already, and in colour. Nothing I said or did was new to you, and if you did see anything unfamiliar in my house you just dismissed it as old-fashioned. But this manuscript had instilled in your eyes that inquisitive sparkle I'd long given up on seeing.

'It's a kind of memoir,' I said.

The sparkle disappeared from your eyes, and the usual cynicism returned. 'I thought only famous people wrote memoirs.' A thousand responses crowded my mouth, jostling to get out first. In the end they blocked each other, and I said nothing. 'I didn't mean to be cruel,' you continued. 'I know you were a journalist and everything, but I think people might not remember you any more.'

'Who said anything about other people?' I said. 'I'm writing it for me, and perhaps one day for you.'

Your face brightened. 'Self-publishing,' you said. 'Yes, that's more realistic. There are some websites where you can do it really cheaply.'

'I don't need websites,' I snapped. 'I've got my two piles of paper, one fresh, one used. One day the used pile will get higher, and I'll know I'm halfway through. Then one day I'll use the final sheet of fresh paper, and I'll know I'm finished. I'll secure the pile with two large red rubber bands, one lengthwise and one crosswise, and dispose of the old typewriter.'

You shrugged. 'Whatever makes you happy, Granddad.' You didn't understand that I was doing it all for you.

Chapter 21

Marcus Higgins   @marcushig   1h
#MKprotest Reminder BIG PROTEST today. Stand up for climate sanity. SEE JEFF BRENNAN IN PERSON!! Details here

Marcus Higgins   @marcushig   54m
#MKprotest Listen to my interview on BBC Three Counties radio

Marcus Higgins   @marcushig   27m
@CalifM Sorry to here about yr marital probs. Glad u can come anywya. C u there

Marcus Higgins   @marcushig   26m
#MKprotest is one of top trending topics on Twitter, keep it moving up! This is gonna be HUGE!!!

Marcus Higgins   @marcushig   24m
#MKprotest Loads of coverage in papers, see Guardian, Independent, Indymedia, SchNEWS, BBC n more

Marcus Higgins   @marcushig   22m
@CalifM I know, cant believe he didnt consult u. Always was a bit selfish IMHO

Marcus Higgins   @marcushig   21m
#MKprotest See also our Facebook group, Meetup group, Flashmob event, spread the word any way u can, even IRL if u want!

Marcus Higgins   @marcushig   11m
#MKprotest REMINDER: ASSEMBLE MIDSUMMER ARCADE 9AM, JUST FOLLOW THE CROWDS AND THE NOISE!!

Marcus Higgins   @marcushig   8m
#MKprotest TO ALL PEOPLE WHOVE SAID YOULL BE THERE THX!! CANT REPLY TO ALL, TOO MUCH GOING

ON! SEE YOU ALL THERE, MIDSUMMER ARCADE 9AM

Marcus Higgins @marcushig　　　　　　　　**7m**
Tweet todays protest at #MKprotest! We need pics, vids, words, eevrything!

Marcus Higgins @marcushig　　　　　　　　**7m**
#MKprotest Tens of thousands expeected, big charities signed up, BIG celebrities coming, TV coverage a certainty. BE THERE!!

Marcus Higgins @marcushig　　　　　　　　**4m**
@JeffB Last chance m8, think about it

Chapter 22

Obviously it's all a bit strange in the office this morning, you know? I mean, in our little room it's all as per usual: you surfing the web, Annie reading a magazine, me throwing paper balls into an imaginary bin. But in the main office, where I spent half the bloody morning on account of all the security meetings, it's a bit like Christmas, or a snow day. Everything feels a bit different, you know? People making all these loud jokes about the protesters, all trying to show they're not afraid of a bunch of dope-smoking wasters with nothing better to do on a Monday morning than block up traffic and shout at people for doing their jobs. Saying they could of worked from home, but they wanted to come in anyway. Wanted to show they wouldn't surrender, couldn't be defeated. The phrases people use, they've all got this familiar sound to them, but don't ask me if it's from 7/7, the IRA, the unions, the Blitz, the Empire or what. They're all defiant like, determined to 'just get on with it'. Hey, that should be Britain's motto, shouldn't it? We should just have this sign outside the Channel Tunnel that says, 'Welcome to Britain: Just get on with it'. We're proud of it, aren't we? Like life is some shitty endurance test that you just have to grit your teeth and get through.

Mind you, in spite of all the talk, I saw that everyone got to work earlier than usual, and no-one parked in the company carpark. And even from the safety of the third floor, people are sneaking these little glances out into the streets, waiting for the angry mob to turn up. Security guards are patrolling the floors to reassure people, but the sight of all them fluorescent jackets they've got on over their usual uniforms only makes it a million times worse. Obviously no work gets done. As per bloody usual, you might say, but usually they do a better job of hiding it.

Fay Dunwood's a bit of a celebrity that day. Normally she was only known for the stink of them chicken tikkas she heated up in the office microwave at lunchtime. She got in at nine, left at five, and spent most of the time in between either gabbing on the phone with her husband or forwarding joke emails to the other people in her team. In the 'Getting to Know You...' section of the office newsletter, she said her hobbies was hillwalking and bell-ringing, and her proudest achievement was 'my two lovely children Harry and Emily'. Like she had a bloody point to prove, her desk was covered with photos of her and her family standing on hillsides in orange raingear. She joined in the office banter, came along to the socials for a swift one before catching her train. Did nothing, in other words, to draw attention to herself.

But obviously that day she's the person everyone wants to talk to. 'How does it feel to be an evil corporate conspirater?' they ask. That and 'Hey Fay, so *you're* the one to blame for global warming!' There wasn't nothing meant by it. Everyone knew Fay wouldn't hurt a fly. She was just doing her job. She was the one who'd helped draft the government's climate-change laws, so it stands to reason she was the one they picked to challenge them. Besides, if she hadn't done it, someone else would of, wouldn't they? If not in our company then in another one. There was no way to stop it, so what was she supposed to do, fuck up her career for nothing? The whole idea of protesting against someone like Fay was bloody ridiculous. Some people don't need a reason, though, do they?

Full credit to her, though, Fay laughs along with all the jokes. But when no-one's speaking to her, I catch her looking nervously out of the window at the empty streets. I wonder to myself what she's really thinking about, the thousands of people who'll soon be filling them streets, shouting angry slogans about her, Fay Dunwood, hillwalker, bell-ringer and proud parent of Harry and Emily. Obviously they won't use her name, will they? I mean, she's safe behind the office glass like the rest of us. Outside the company, nobody knows it was her client, her account from start to finish. It's only us inside what know. When people shout 'Smith & Jefferson, shame, shame,' it'll really mean 'Fay Dunwood, shame, shame.' Is she feeling any shame? Don't know. If she is, she's not showing it, but then she wouldn't, would she? She might whisper it to her husband, when Harry and Emily are all tucked up in bed. But while she's stood there looking out of the window, I can only guess what she's thinking.

For us, though, the day's not that different from any other day. Like Annie said, I make a point of avoiding work wherever possible. She got the reason wrong, though. Truth is I do it to improve team morale. I've worked in IT teams where everyone was running around all day fighting fires, and most of them turned out to be false alarms. When a real, serious problem come along, we couldn't tell the difference from all the shit we'd been drowning in all day, and so it never got dealt with.

Now I'm in charge, I do things differently. I'm not lazy, I'm strategic. I'm like a football manager, resting his best players in the pointless midseason games to keep them fresh for the Cup Final. When the servers went down, we swung into action. Obviously that was only possible because we were fresh from all the months of video games and cups of tea. With all the clutter cleared away, I can see the important things. Say what you like about me, but I'm good at my job. I even had a contingency plan for that day, in case the protesters managed to damage any equipment or cut the power or phone lines. I'd thought of everything. None of it was written down, obviously, but in my head I had it all worked out. It's amazing what you can do while you're throwing a paper ball into a bin for hours on end. You and Annie never got it, you thought I was just wasting time. Fine. I know nobody understands me, and it don't bother me. I know what works.

Anyway, that morning as I'm sat there throwing paper balls into the bin, I keep an eye on you over the top of my screen. You're all hunched over the computer, your shoulders up around your ears, all tense like. I can see the screen in front of you changing constantly as you hop from site to site like a bird. Sometimes you stop for a while, but I can tell from the angle of your head, or from the fact that you never scroll down, that you're not really reading nothing much.

Obviously at the time I never knew why. Thought you was just worried about the protest, like the rest of us. Now I know what must have been going through your head that morning, it all makes sense. I have to hand it to you, mate, I never would of thought you could pull off a lie like that. I mean, taking on a whole new identity. It's one thing on the web, but in real life it's a lot more complicated. To be honest you never struck me as even having one personality, let alone two. Don't know how you managed it.

Suddenly I notice something. It's nothing to see really, just a quick motion of your head, an even bigger tensing of your shoulders and a quick click of the mouse. Annie don't even look up from her magazine. That's why she'll never get nowhere much beyond where she is right now. To be fair, most people would be the same as her. Or even if they thought they seen something in that moment, they'd tell themselves their mind was playing tricks. But I've been in this game a long time and I've seen that same movement a million times over the years. Some people are better at hiding it than others, but everyone does it. Soon as their eyes read something racist, sexist, insulting or pornographic, they can't help looking over their shoulder to see if anyone caught them. Their shoulders always tense up, and they quickly click away.

Thing is, they never actually close the page. Don't matter if it's a rant about the boss, an un-PC joke or a jpeg of a woman's tits, obviously they want to look again. So they hide it under this Word document or Excel spreadsheet and pretend to work, all the time thinking about what's sitting under them boring work files. They always go back to it in the end, and obviously that's when you've got them by the balls. If they deleted it immediately, they could claim they never done nothing wrong. But they always go back and look again.

So I pause my game, leaving the paper ball hanging in mid air on a specially tricky shot, with a strong cross-wind. I'm close to a high score by now, but it don't matter. I switch instantly from play to work. I move quick, silent, like a hunter in the forest. A couple of keystrokes bring up the right program. To cover my tracks while I key in your information, I ask Annie what's new in the world of celebrity gossip. As per usual, the silly cow has to flick back through the magazine to remind herself what she's just read. Then she fires out some stupid list of trivia, and by the time she's stopped for breath I'm looking at a page showing all your recently received emails and instant messages, your sent items, and a log of all your keystrokes. I've also opened up the audio file I've created of my paper-ball game, just for times like these, and the soothing little rattle of ball in basket begins to loop endlessly.

'Interesting,' I says to her. 'Thanks for the education.' Annie then starts in on the predictable bloody tirade about what an arsehole I am and why I ask questions if I don't want to hear the answers, and obviously I wind her up with some more sarcastic responses until she marches out to get a cup of tea, slamming the door behind her. By that time I've found out that your emails are clean, but you've received an instant message from an external source with some suspicious content: 'I've worked out how to save you.'

My first thought is you've found religion, and I says to

myself what a bloody letdown. But it don't fit, somehow. I mean, even if the saving part makes sense (I get saved about once a week by email, although the churches are always short of cash), the wording's wrong. Religious people don't 'work out' how to save you, do they? They just know, or believe, or are told by the Supreme Bloody Cloud-Dweller. The whole point of religion is not needing to work nothing out, just having it all handed to you on a two-thousand-year-old plate. So it must mean you're really being saved from something. But from what, the protesters? Not likely. In all my security meetings, the police never said there was no real danger. Just a whole lot of marching and shouting and then everything back to normal in time for the evening rush hour. No, you had to be in some other kind of trouble, and that was a whole lot more interesting. Best case you was doing drugs and I could turn you in to the Managing Partner and get a bonus. Worst case, it was the usual sort of trouble with a woman (or man), and it would make for some good office gossip.

All I need is your response, and obviously I've just got to be patient. I pause the audio file of my paper-ball game and go back to the real thing. Annie came back, glaring at me. I give her a sweet smile and tell her how nice she looks that morning. She fires back some abusive response, but still blushes to her blond roots, poor thing. I chuckle to myself and make another successful shot.

Fair play to you, you took your time, and when you made your move it was nicely done. Most people wouldn't of seen that little instant-message window that come up at the bottom-left of your screen for a second or two before disappearing again behind your internet browser. Obviously you wasn't stupid enough to reply, but you had to look. People always have to look. The more time passes, the more they begin to doubt themselves, wonder if they misread the message, second-guess who it come from. The more important the message, the more times they read it. That second look is always the giveaway.

A few minutes later, you get up and say in this gruff voice, like you've got something in your throat, 'Anybody want anything from the kitchen?'

Annie says nothing, but I says, 'Eggs Benedict on lightly toasted muffins with extra hollandaise sauce.' You roll your eyes and walk out.

'Why can't you ever just give a straight bloody answer to a straight bloody question?' Annie says into her magazine.

'What makes you think it was a straight question?'

She shakes her head sadly. 'That's just what I mean. You're bloody exasperating sometimes, Dex.'

For a few minutes nothing happens, but then I think of something, 'Hey Annie, do you know what Jeff's secret is?'

Obviously it's just a shot in the dark really. I mean, I never thought Annie would of been involved in whatever it was you were up to. But you should of seen her response. This deep, blotchy red colour spreads across her skin, from her forehead right down her face and across her neck and what I can see of her shoulders. She keeps her head fixed on the magazine but can't stop her eyes from flicking up to look at me, to see what I know. Obviously she denies it all, but by then it's hopeless. She's hiding something, that much is bloody obvious, and soon as I find out what you're involved in, she'll pay for it and all.

Meantime, you're still making these pathetic efforts to escape. From the amount of time you're gone, I guess you've gone to your usual spot on the stairs, found out you can't get no signal on your mobile, then tried a few different places around the building and maybe even gone outside. Then you've admitted defeat and run back to your desk, all out of breath. If you'd asked, I could of told you why. Signal jamming technology is simple to come by on the web these days. It's just a box with a switch on it that can block mobile phone signals for a good few hundred metres in all directions. It's also illegal, but when I was going over security procedures with the police and asked what would happen if, just supposing, someone was to use a signal blocker to disrupt the protests, the superintendent said that, just supposing of course, anything to stop the bastards talking to each other was fine with him. While you was gone I activated another one of my security measures, putting a temporary block on external calls from office phones in case you was desperate enough to slide into an empty cubicle and call from there. As for payphones, the nearest one's so far away that, even if you knew where it was, you could never make it there and back in time to avoid suspicion. In fact, you probably never even thought of looking for one. So you had no choice but to come slinking back here, all defeated.

'Where are my eggs?' I demand. Got to admit, I'm enjoying myself now.

You don't even look at me, let alone reply. You're scared now, I can see it. Your struggles to escape are going to get more sudden and desperate, and as you thrash around, you'll only tighten the noose. For a few minutes, you sit there trying not to go back to the message in the bottom-left corner of your screen, but I know you will. You've got no choice, have you? The window appears with a quick click of the mouse, your fingers sweep across the keyboard, and then it disappears again. A few seconds later the monitoring software spits out your message on my screen: 'Tell me wot 2 do.'

The reply, though, is not as damning as what I'd hoped. 'Just do what we discussed. Trust me.'

You think for a minute or two, then fire back another response: 'Email me. Personal, not work.'

I smile to myself. Your attempts are so feeble. You must of known I could monitor anything coming in or out of the company, no matter what software was used. An email's like a postcard: to get from one person to someone else, it's got to pass through a lot of hands. Since I'm in charge of the sorting office, I can read what I like. Obviously you know this, but you're on the run now, just running wildly and making only a token effort to throw me off the scent. All I've got to do is trot after you, keeping you in sight all the time, picking the best moment to complete the kill.

'It's simple,' the email says. 'Nobody's seen this 'real' Jeff Brennan. He's never posted a photo of himself online. So if I denounce him as an impostor, how will he prove who he is? Marie will back me up, she still believes in you. Together we can turn the crowd against him, no problem. But first, you have to do what we agreed. Otherwise I take his side. Sorry, mate, but that file is too important to let go of. The movement comes before friendship, it's a sacrifice I have to make. Marcus.'

At the time, I've got to admit, I didn't have the foggiest what he was talking about. But I didn't have to. I knew something was happening, and that was all I really needed to know. A good hunter doesn't ask why he hunts, he just completes the kill. For the next few minutes, I bide my time. You don't reply to the email, or send any more instant messages. Annie keeps on flicking angrily through the pages of her magazine. I start to throw paper balls again, letting the rhythmic rattle of ball on basket settle my nerves and keep my mind clear.

Then it happens. In a quick motion, you drop your pen and bend down to pick it up. When you sit up straight, though, there's this little flash drive sticking out of the USB port. I start to salivate. Few minutes later you copy a file from the server onto the drive, then bend down again to scratch your ankle, leaving an empty USB slot when you sit up again. I have to say, it's almost impressive. Still, identifying the file you've copied is easy. When I see it's from Fay Dunwood's folder, I know it's game over.

I fire off a quick email to the Managing Partner, marked urgent, and a few minutes later in walk these two security guards. They look more scared of you than you are of them, but you let them take the flash drive out of your pocket and stand at your desk, all pale and ashy, packing your things into the plastic bag provided while the guards watch your movements. Obviously I keep on playing my game, throwing the paper balls into the basket. I'm proud to say that in spite of all the distractions, I never missed a single shot. I did look over the top of my screen a few times to see if you'd look back, and what kind of look would be in your eye if you did. But you never looked back.

When the guards have finished with you, a couple of female guards turn up to deal with Annie. Sensitive way of doing it, the company's good at things like that. Unlike you, Annie breaks into sobs at the first sight of them fluorescent jackets in the doorway. Turns and pleads with me, she does. Quite sad really. At first she can't say nothing more than 'Dex, Dex, Dex,' between all the crying. Then eventually she manages to say, 'They're just photos, Dex.' Obviously it makes no sense to me, but it don't matter, I just ignore her. A good manager don't look back or second-guess himself. He just decides, and moves forward. I mean, what kind of authority would I of had after that if I'd of caved in and let her stay? Sign of weakness, it would of been, and after that she and everyone else would know they could take the piss. Can't have that, can I? So I just make her voice like background noise, throwing my paper balls and watching the score mount up. Soon she's gone, and I've got the office to myself. I close my eyes and enjoy the quiet.

Chapter 23

I followed my routine that morning, but sipping coffee on the balcony did not bring the usual sense of peace. I stared at the canal but saw nothing of its beauty. I went inside and made more coffee, even though I knew it would only make me jittery, and I went out onto the balcony again to drink it, searching for something that wasn't there. Everything was altered slightly, as if in a bad dream. I went back in and paced about in my flat for a while, changing my shirt a couple of times, packing and unpacking my bag for the trip to Milton Keynes, the trip I'd been both looking forward to and dreading all weekend.

I looked at my watch and saw that it was already ten minutes past the time I had planned to leave. I checked my email. Nothing of note. I read the news, clicking absently from site to site. After a while I stumbled upon a piece (in *The Guardian*, no less) about my appearance at the protest later that day. It shocked me to see such interest, not just in my opinions but in me. In fact I remember how my whole body curved inwards over my collapsing stomach. I don't know why, but that's how it happened. It was a completely physical reaction, not a mental one. My knees rolled up towards my chest, my shoulders rounded, my head fell down, and my stomach felt like a punctured tyre. For a few moments I was unable to breathe, unable to think, unable to sense anything other than the deafening roar of blood. Then, after a few moments in which I thought I was dying, I felt breath return to my lungs and my pulse return to a rate at which, though it was quick, I could at least distinguish between the individual beats. I clicked on a few more links and saw that my appearance today was already in danger of going viral. I began to lose control of my breathing again, and shut down as quickly as I could.

My first thought was to put an end to this nonsense. This attention, this obsession with celebrity, this feeling of distraction was precisely what I had striven so hard over the last seven years to avoid. I had overturned seven years of wisdom on a momentary whim, to satisfy an absurd fascination with a woman I had never met. I would sit down at the old wooden desk, fire up the trusty old computer again, write a new post backing out of the protest, and return to my life. I would not have to go out, to face the world, the cameras, the questions, the stupid, puerile interest in the body of a 'celebrity'. I would return to the world where body was irrelevant and only the mind was on display, the world where nobody expected anything of me beyond what I was capable of: the steady daily production of well-written, well-informed blog posts. Anonymity beckoned, and if I closed my eyes I could feel its welcoming warmth wrap around me like a blanket.

I even sat down at the old desk, but that was as far as I got. As I reached to switch on the machine, I thought of Marie, of how excited she must be and of how much I would disappoint her by backing out. I thought of how it would look to the rest of the world, too. How it would smack of cowardice and indecision, two failings to which my online self, Jeff Brennan the blogger, had never succumbed. I thought of being stuck again in that painful self-consciousness, obsessed with an imaginary woman. But more than all that, I thought of Marie's body extending beyond the tight confines of thumbnail photos, extending into the real world and acquiring shape and form. I thought of how her voice would sound, how her neck would smell, how her skin would feel against mine.

After that, there was no chance I would switch on the computer. Feeling suddenly calm, or perhaps just numb, I stood up from the desk, put on my jacket, took up my bag from the sofa and walked slowly to the door. As I opened it, I felt the air being sucked into the flat as if into a vacuum, the fresh air mingling with the stale, new with old, old with new. I stood at the sill between these two worlds, closing my eyes and feeling the worlds mingling and crossing around me, passing in both directions. After a while the sensation stopped and I knew the air was now thoroughly mixed, the old distinctions erased. Return was impossible. I opened my eyes and stepped into the corridor, closing the door behind me.

I remember little about my journey. I felt like a child being taken out by my mother into a world I didn't understand, seeing it from behind the clear plastic cover of my buggy but not knowing what the signs meant or how the different parts of the city were linked to each other. My impressions of that trip are blurred, dreamlike. There was some kind of argument with the bus driver over his refusal to let me pay in cash, and then various other delays and distractions before, finally, I was settled on the train to Milton Keynes. For a while I began to relax, but then the carriage filled up with the chatter of people on mobile phones, the screams of children, the smell of fried chicken, the steady steaming-up of the windows, the constant movement of people up and down the narrow aisle, their bulging hips brushing my shoulder, loud ringtones, the slopping of cheap coffee in plastic cups, the rustling of paper bags and napkins, the chomping of teeth on processed meat, the scattering of flakes of Cornish pasty over the sticky floor. I shut down again, and remember nothing of the rest of the journey, or Milton Keynes station. My next memory is of stepping out of a taxi on the edge of a large crowd.

I say it was large, but of course these things are relative. To estimate the numbers is a political act in which I won't even engage. Suffice it to say that the police estimate was 500 while the protesters' estimate was 10,000, and the truth, as always, lies somewhere in the middle. I was surprised, though, and not a little encouraged. I couldn't imagine a regional protest of this sort attracting such numbers in the usual course of events, and took it as a sign that my presence could really achieve something. Perhaps, I thought, blogging was merely a phase in my life whose only purpose was to get me to a place where I could have a greater impact. Certainly I had been dissatisfied, sometimes, with blogging as a way to effect change. As much as my blog shaped other blogs, it had only a sporadic effect on the outside world. Sometimes I broke scandals and sometimes corrupt ministers were even brought down as a result, but they were simply replaced by other ministers who, in due course, became embroiled in scandals of their own. The scandals themselves seemed to sustain the system rather than threaten it, distracting us all with a well-oiled cycle of outrage while the essence of things remained unchanged. Most of the time, I just wrote blog posts to draw attention to one issue or another, which spawned other impassioned posts by the school of minor bloggers swimming in my wake. Much was written, but I had come to doubt if it ever led anybody to do much.

As I looked out over the crowd, though, I felt a renewed surge of power. These people were here partly because of me. Some, surely, would have attended anyway, outraged by whatever issue it was. But many of them were there to see me, drawn to my celebrity. In a world where so much is unreal, the real event holds unprecedented power. To catch a glimpse even of a minor TV presenter or soap star gives a thrill. For a moment the unreal becomes real, the flickering image or anonymous screen name is made into flesh and bones. Our ancestors knelt at the communion rail for wine and wafer, but we cannot allow ourselves such unabashed awe, of course. So we clothe ourselves in ironic detachment as we crowd forward with camera phones, our hearts secretly pounding at the miracle.

I was expecting such a crowd to form immediately but, of course, nobody knew me. At that time I was just a man stepping out of a taxi. If anyone even noticed me, they'd have seen nothing more than a tall, thin, slightly awkward-looking man stooping to the window to pay the bill, embarrassing the taxi driver with the unexpected size of the tip and having to assure him that there was no mistake. At the mention of my name they would go wild. I would no longer be a man but that other thing, a celebrity. They wouldn't see my awkwardness any more than they saw the cracks in the Mona Lisa's paint. The image would blind them to reality and they would see what they wanted to see.

To put off this moment for as long as possible, I did not identify myself immediately. I simply pushed through to the front of the crowd. I would announce myself to Marie and Marie alone. She could then decide whether to share her discovery with the world or keep it to herself. She could hold my fate in her hands, weigh it, feel its contours, decide on its worth. Even if only for a few seconds, she would be the only one to see the miracle.

The avenue was wide enough to allow me to slip through at the sides, squeezing up against the railings and sidling forward with whistle-blowing, chanting protesters to my left and bored police officers to my right. At several points along the way, we had to stop to allow cars from side streets to cross, and we all waited obediently behind the invisible line until the police gave us permission to move again. Later on, I noticed the railings changing course slightly, channelling us into a concrete plaza, the kind that at this time of day would normally be covered with office workers perching on the contoured edges of its fountains and flowerbeds, munching on designer sandwiches as they tried to stop their rubbish blowing away in the breeze. Today, though, it was the property of the protesters: a stage had been set up at one end, the fountains were dry, and most of the cafés and restaurants around the edges had pulled down their metal shutters. Only Starbucks was open, doing a brisk trade in takeaway coffees served through a narrow hatch in its boarded-up windows with a heavy police presence.

I scanned the crowd for a sign of Marie, consulting the small image in my head and trying to match it with any of the hundreds of faces I saw in the crowd. It wasn't easy. Although I had studied her picture more times than I care to mention, it was low resolution, cropped close and shot from a strange angle. For all I knew, it could have been shot years ago. The real Marie could have a nose ring, or blond hair, or a fake tan or a new chin. She could be tall or short. She could walk with crutches, or use a wheelchair. She could have put on weight or lost it since the photo was taken. She might never even have looked like her photo. She could be a middle-aged man, hiding behind a photo of a beautiful woman. She might be called Stan. She might be dead. Still I pressed on, pushing relentlessly through the crowd, feeling that, no matter what, I would recognise her. Even if she looked different, I would recognise something about her. I felt that I knew her so well from her presence on my blog that it would be impossible not to recognise her now.

The stage was close now. I had worked my way over to the opposite side of the square, avoiding the bottleneck around Starbucks, and just had a few rows of people to get past. I could see the organisers and professional speech-givers up on stage, preparing to start. Between me and them was just a thin line of humanity. The journey that had begun in the glowing pixels of Marie's avatar on the computer screen in my flat had now almost reached completion on a strange Milton Keynes lunchtime. I knew that my life was about to change, and strangely the thought fascinated rather than frightened me. I was ready for it.

It occurred to me at that moment that I would certainly give up my blog. With Marie, I would no longer need it. I would have an identity far superior to that which I had constructed.

I would still make public appearances, using my fame for the social good, but my blogging days were over. I might even get rid of my computers, disconnect my phone line, cancel my mobile contract. With Marie, I would not need them any more. I would devote every minute of every day to being in her presence. We would go for brunch at all the best spots in London, would take long walks and leisurely holidays. We'd sit on the balcony all day, or curl up in bed reading a good book together. The flat would be full of flowers, and we'd plant herbs in the empty pots on the balcony. We'd see all the best plays, go to all the best concerts, enjoy romantic dinners in all the best restaurants.

At the last moment, as I was about to push through the last row and climb up on the stage, a strong arm reached right across my chest and gripped me. I felt its fingers pressing into my left upper arm, establishing a lock that barred my progress as effectively as any iron turnstile. I looked to my right to see who was blocking my way, and I saw the face I had dreamt of for so long. Its eyes were wide and dark, its lashes long, its skin smooth and slightly flushed, wide cheekbones framed by perfectly straight black hair. Just as on the web, the image was cropped close. Although in theory her whole body was now there for me to savour, my eyes could not get beyond her eyes, her lips, her soft skin, her straight black hair. For long seconds, I remained like that, locked in her grip, staring into her face and drinking in every detail as I used to on those lonely nights at home.

The strange thing was that although at first she opened her mouth to speak, no sound came out. She stared at me with – I'm sure of it – a kind of recognition. It was more confused, of course, than my recognition of her. She had never seen either me or my image, and yet there was something in me that she knew so well, better than she's ever known you or anyone else. After all, it was me she initially fell in love with, not you, and I'm sure that in that moment she sensed it. She'll deny it now, of course, and perhaps she'll even believe her denials. But I saw the look on her face in that moment when we were frozen in each other's arms and the surging crowd and the whistles and the horns and the chants melted away and all that existed in the world was her face and mine. I heard her voice falter and die. I remember the strange silence of those long moments when she just looked at me, struggling to understand what she was feeling. If she doesn't remember, or has chosen to forget, then it's no concern of mine. I remember, so it will always be true for me.

'Where do you think you're going?' she said finally, although her voice shook slightly and I'm sure was weaker than she'd intended.

'You're American,' was all I could think of to say. 'I never knew you were American.'

I often think about that moment. Perhaps if I'd said something different, things would have changed. I could have proved to her that she knew me, recalled something that only the real Jeff Brennan would know. But I just said that she was American.

Emboldened by my own uncertainty, she adopted a more aggressive tone. 'Listen, buddy, stage is for speakers only. Who do you think you are?'

'I'm Jeff Brennan,' I said quietly.

She looked at me closely. 'What did you say?'

This was my moment, the moment I had dreamt of, but I was unable to imbue my voice with the confidence it deserved. As I spoke the words, I didn't sound as if even I believed them. 'I'm Jeff Brennan,' I said again. 'I'm Jeff Brennan.'

She smiled, but it was not the smile I had expected. There was no joy in it, no sudden spark of love. It was the cruel, lopsided smile of someone who takes pleasure in swatting a fly. 'You're Jeff Brennan?' she said. 'You're Jeff Brennan?'

'Yes,' I replied. 'I'm Jeff Brennan.' I should have said: and you're Marie, and I know you better than I know myself, and your comments are the only reason I blog any more. But I didn't. In all my imagined versions of this scene, the simple announcement of my identity was always enough to produce the desired reaction. Nothing beyond that was ever necessary. Without anything prepared, I was stuck. 'I'm Jeff Brennan,' I said again.

Her smile now became horrifically twisted, so twisted and cruel that I barely recognised her. 'You're the second one today,' she said. 'A whiff of celebrity brings out all the insects.'

I was stunned. 'But I'm Jeff Brennan,' I said.

'Yeah, and I'm Marilyn Monroe. Beat it, we've got an event to organise.'

She relaxed her grip on my arm, evidently expecting me to melt back into the crowd, but instead I pressed forward again. 'I'm Jeff Brennan,' I said, with such determination that she stopped smiling and looked at me seriously.

'Look, you really need to get with the times,' she said impatiently. 'If you're going to pass yourself off as a celebrity, get a damn iPhone so that you know when the celebrity's cancelled his appearance.'

She shoved her phone in my face, and I saw an image of what looked like my blog. It had all the elements of my blog, the simple header I'd spent so long designing, the off-white background, the well-spaced text, the sidebar with links to my favoured blogs. But something was wrong. 'That's not my blog,' I said.

'Damn right,' Marie replied. 'It's Jeff Brennan's.'

'I mean, I didn't write that last post.'

'No shit.'

I felt my heart rate increasing and my breath becoming short. 'It's my blog,' I said. 'It's mine. Just that last post, I didn't write that.'

'How convenient,' Marie said. She actually seemed to be enjoying herself. Nothing made sense to me. My blog didn't look how it should look, and my Marie wasn't behaving as she should behave. My Marie would never take pleasure in something like this, would never smile with such twisted cruelty. My Marie was not like this.

'I don't understand,' I said. 'It's my blog.'

'Oh yeah? Well, I might believe you, but, you see, this Marie that Jeff mentions in his last post? 'My girlfriend Marie'? That's me. I'm Marie. I've lived with Jeff Brennan for the last few months, as it happens. I know what Jeff Brennan looks like, what he smells like, what he eats for breakfast, what he mumbles in his sleep. And I'm pretty sure that you're not the man I woke up with this morning, so get out of here and stop wasting time. Capisce?'

At this, Marie whipped away the phone and slipped it back into her pocket, folding her arms and looking at me triumphantly. Everything I said in my defence after that seemed to cement my guilt in her eyes. Not that I said very much, I was in such shock that mostly my mouth just flapped impotently. I couldn't understand how the fantasy life I'd concocted with Marie appeared to have become a reality, but with somebody else in the lead role, and how this creature of my imagination now appeared to have taken over even my own blog. Marie just watched me floundering, her arms folded, that cruel smile distorting her face, and spoke the words that ended my life. 'Like I said, beat it. We've got a show to run.' She turned her back on me, and my limp body fell further and further back into the crowd until all I could see of her was the straight black hair on the top of her head, then a memory of where she used to be, then nothing.

Chapter 24

To be honest, I did it as much for me as for you. I woke up that day feeling like shit. Went through my usual Sunday morning routine: pint of milk and some toast to test the stomach, then a massive fry-up and a mug of strong sweet tea, then a brisk walk to the newsagent's to slap the sweat from my face, and back home for a shower and a clean shirt and ready to start all over again. Yeah, I know. Not anyone's idea of glamour, is it? But I was used to it. It was as much a part of my life as the Saturday night haze. Definitely wouldn't have swapped it for a dull Sunday trying to fill time. May have felt like death, but at least I felt something.

But that day it was different. The physical pain didn't stop the chatter in my head. I thought of all the hundreds of Sundays that had gone past in exactly this way. I could have done so much, if only I'd started. I thought of ten more years going by like this and it seemed impossible. The familiar sickness felt suddenly like a poison spreading through my body, killing me Sunday by Sunday.

It was while I was in the newsagent's that I made the decision to do what I did. I never bought anything anyway. Only went there to have somewhere to walk to, or maybe because that was always my dad's Sunday morning routine too. Brisk walk, back with the *Mirror* rolled up under his arm, cheerful whistle and a packet or two of Wine Gums if I'd been a good boy. For me, as an adult, it made no sense. All the stuff I wanted to read was free online, and in my state, sweets were the last things I wanted. Cigarettes I bought online by the carton. No reason for me to be there, was there? I drifted through the aisles, flicked through a magazine or two under the eye of the owner. Not wanting to buy anything but not wanting to go back home either. Maybe it was the same for my dad. He always seemed to be gone a long time, and never spent much time reading the paper when he got home. But to me, in that moment, my life blood was flowing away in that newsagent's. I could see it pooling on the floor in front of me like spilt milk. What a fucking waste. I decided what I'd do. I put the copy of *Nuts* back on the shelf and marched out with a new purpose.

'Nothing today, sir?' said the newsagent, as he said every Sunday.

The usual accusation in his voice, but this time I didn't feel guilty. 'No, thanks,' I replied, and marched on out of there, not stopping until I got back to my flat.

More tea and a few biscuits, then I sat down at the computer with the cup and plate on one side of the keyboard and a pack of cigarettes on the other. Long day and a long night ahead of me, I knew that. The job I'd taken on was not a simple one. Matter of fact I didn't even know if it was possible. That was the attraction. That's why I said I did it for me as much as for you. For the first time in years, I was doing something difficult. It was like being at school or college again. A mountain of work, a tight deadline, an uncertain outcome. Nothing like anything I'd experienced in adult life. Working for Hertfordshire's leading chain of curtain and blind specialists doesn't provide much of a thrill. I mean, people either need curtains or they don't. I use the same lines, and sometimes they buy and sometimes they don't. Even if I make a sale, I can never tell if it was because of me or in spite of me. For a deal to be made, both sides have to feel like they're cheating the other one, don't they? The trick of salesmanship is to be the one who's right. It's not much of a way to live.

That day, though, as I sat at the computer with tea steaming on one side and a cigarette smoking on the other, I could feel the blood moving in my veins for the first time in years. Impatience, not for time to pass but for my great task to start. I'd be up all night, I knew that, and would probably have to call in sick on Monday morning too. Might not be enough time even then. But I'd do it anyway. I'd try for once. Would be good to say it was all for you. But mostly it was for me, for the feeling it gave me.

The afternoon went on. So lost in my work I didn't see the sun go down. Just darkness at some point, so dark I couldn't see the keyboard even in the reflected glow from the screen, and had to get up and switch on a light. The stiffness of my body telling me hours had passed. Light on now, a new pack of cigarettes on the go and a fresh pot of tea, then back to my work and I was gone again for hours more. All I remember of that night is a few little snatches like that, the minute or two when I came up for air. More pain at each break-time. Like I was hollow, beaten, bruised. Lay down on my bed once, let myself sink into the softness of the mattress, the warmth of the pillow, just for a minute, just for a minute, but with a sudden jolt I realised I was lying to myself again, like I'd lied my whole life. If I'd let myself sleep even for a minute, it would have been Monday again. Stinking headache, ashy breath, too late to save you and probably too late even to pull a sickie. Everything ruined as usual, nothing left but more Saturday nights and Sunday mornings, week after week, decade after decade. I jerked my body upright and forced it back to the computer.

Strange that I never had the usual temptations. No clicking from site to site, no blankness, no lost time. I had a purpose, and more or less I stuck to it. It was natural, of course, to have a few different windows open at once, to relax from time to time by playing some online baseball or voting on the top 50 hottest chicks of 2010. But I didn't let that shit take over.

Just let myself go for a few minutes, then back to my work. I was relentless. Unstoppable. Really late now, that strange early-hours silence when all the soft background noises you never noticed before gradually die off and you realise what real quiet is like. The world sleeping. Not me though. For the first time I'd be different from the rest of the world. Wouldn't take the easy path. I'd achieve something.

Even stayed off the booze. It called to me a few times. Just a beer to help me relax, or a whisky to help me think, or some shots of vodka to stop me thinking and make me run off pure inspiration. But instead I brewed up more tea. Fucking murdered the fags though. A whole cereal bowl full of ash and crumpled butts in no time, and soon had to start using the empty tea mugs as well. Knew it'd all stick to the remnants of tea and be a bitch to clean out in the morning, but I didn't care. The morning didn't exist for me. My only life was the night. Empty packs piling up on the table with empty mugs and used-up butts and oceans of ash. Nervous and light-headed but alive. When the tea stopped working I switched to ProPlus, each tablet like an adrenalin shot to the heart.

Morning light: new energy but also a dose of panic. Time was running out. Events were in motion. I saw the real Jeff Brennan in a swanky flat somewhere, having his breakfast, drinking his coffee, fucking his wife, all the time rehearsing in his head the speech that would destroy you. Soon he'd be on the train, on his way to the protest. So would thousands of people, coming from all over the country to see you get punked live on stage. I saw you on your way to work, a condemned man, commuting because there was nothing else you could do. Queuing on the A5 with everyone else. Feeling sick, dead, worse than in McDonald's. No hope in your head, no idea that I could save you. If I failed, you'd never even know I'd tried. You'd just lose the one good thing in your life, and drink with me on a Saturday night to take away the feeling.

The panic crippled me for a while, but was probably

good in the end. When I managed to get my head out of my hands, I attacked my work again like a madman. I'd faced the possibility of failure, and it was horrible. I'd do anything to avoid it. I did anything. I did the best thing I've done in my life. At about ten thirty on Monday morning, after a day and a night of intense work, I got the breakthrough. It's like that, sometimes. Trying a hundred different possibilities, none of them working, and then suddenly you get that moment, a chink in the door, and you know you've done it. Best feeling in the world. The thrill of a lottery win, except it's not just blind luck that got you there. It's skill, intuition and, yeah, maybe a little bit of luck as well.

For a long time, it seemed impossible. I'd got off to a good start. The idiot had left the default script in his footer telling me what blogging software he was using, and the meta generator tag told me which version he was on. After that I'd thought it would be simple enough to look up all the known vulnerabilities until I found one that worked. Even thought I might get it done in an hour or two, no need for a sleepless night and another Monday off sick. Started planning a trip in my head, a reward, using the recouped sick day for a long weekend in Amsterdam. But of course it didn't work out like that. There's this complex kind of a dance going on all the time between the software companies and a loose network of talented amateurs in bedrooms and garages from Moldova to Ecuador. A new release, new vulnerabilities which are exploited and publicised and then quickly remedied, before new holes are discovered and the process begins all over again. People who don't understand these things talk about evil hackers or evil corporations, but that's just to sell newspapers. Really they depend on each other. Take away the guy in Moldova and the vulnerability still exists, you just don't find out about it.

Point is, in the original spirit of the web, these guys share their information with the world. They maintain complex sites for no pay, and put up with the constant risk of arrest for 'damaging' something they're actually helping to fix. Information can be used in a lot of ways, though, so if you have bad intentions, like I did that night, you can trawl through these lists of discoveries and test out the vulnerabilities to see if any of them still work. Usually you find the holes have been patched up and so you just move on to the next one and the next one and the next one until you hit the jackpot. Or if, like me, you're on a higher level (what I would once have called 1337), you can improvise on other people's ideas to find a new vulnerability of your own.

That's exactly what happened that Monday morning. I'd been aiming lower. Just some way to bypass the security checks long enough to upload or alter a post. Maybe target one of his plug-ins, or use the file upload functionality to sneak in a malicious script. But none of it worked. The amateurs may have the talent and the enthusiasm, but the companies have the resources, and they work fast to patch up any problems. Whatever I tried, the company was a step ahead. That's why I had that panic attack on Monday morning. Thought for a while they'd beaten me. Beautiful thing about software code, though, the possibilities are limitless. If you're trying to break through an iron gate, there are only so many things you can try before you have to give up. With a website, you can keep going forever. If you hammer away long enough, with enough determination and enough skills, you'll find a way in.

When it happened, it was beautiful. Instead of just being able to upload a post, I was able to get Jeff Brennan's login details. I'd thought about that possibility earlier, but quickly rejected it as unrealistic. An SQL injection attack had failed, and after that I'd got discouraged and decided to aim lower. But in a fit of desperation at the passing time, I tried on Monday morning to access the server log files. A longshot, but sometimes you can get into them, and sometimes you can extract login credentials. I tried several known routes and none of them worked, but in a flash of inspiration I saw a way through. My chink in the door. Granted, there might be another level of encryption, or the credentials might not be stored in the files I was accessing. While I was searching through, though, I felt my heart beating and the blood flowing fast and thick through my veins, and I knew I was close. When I saw the text I was looking for, it felt unreal. My hands were shaking as I went to the admin folder and tried it.

With those two short strings of text, the world of Jeff Brennan's blog opened up to me. I could write new posts, rewrite past ones, alter his identity in whatever way I wanted. The whole past, present and future of one of the biggest blogs in Britain belonged to me. Soon I'd give it to you as a gift. But at that time, at ten thirty on Monday morning, it belonged to me. The power surged within me. The presence of my readers, all around the world. People staring into the screens of laptops or desktops or smart phones, waiting for me to tell them what to think. The temptation, the strong, strong temptation to write my own post. Share my night's achievement with the world. Get the fame. The respect. Even take over the blog altogether. Let you twist in the wind and become Jeff Brennan myself. Convince Marie it had been my blog all along, you were just my cover. I thought it all out. The power was mine, now. I'd earned it. You'd done nothing. Why should you get the fame, get the girl, get to ditch me again, to leave me to my lonely Saturday-night fantasies?

Yeah, Jeff, I thought it all out. I want you to know that, so that you appreciate what I did for you. I gave it all up. The fame, the girl, everything. Gave it all up for you. I'd done something good for once, and I wasn't going to let myself fuck it up at the last minute. So I wrote the post I'd planned from the start, from that moment in the newsagent's when I was flicking through the pages of *Nuts* and letting the idea form in my aching head. Short, but saying everything it needed to. Your appearance at the protest was cancelled, you'd realised that you should not have taken such a big step without consulting the love of your life, Marie. Laid it on a bit thick at that point, but I'm sure she loved it when I said how there would be other protests, but there would never be another Marie. Regular fucking poet, I was. Even added in that you'd heard of impostors planning to attend the protest and leech off your fame, and this had made you rethink the whole idea of appearing in public. You'd stay anonymous for now, only appearing in public when you had thought it through and, most importantly, discussed it with Marie.

I checked it carefully, hit 'Publish' and it was done. A weird feeling after that, going back to the blog and seeing my own words there in black and white. People all over the world reading them right now on their phones or laptops or at their desk at work. I thought about taking them back, but it was too late. As soon as I'd published, the words had been sent to RSS feeds and search engines, cached and replicated and stored forever. I could delete the post from the blog, but not from the web. People had seen it by now, no matter what. After a minute or two, the comments began appearing. I read them obsessively, couldn't stop myself. No need for sleep now, no more temptation to sink into the mattress. I just wanted to stay up, writing more, reading the comments, just being Jeff Brennan, even if it was only for a while. I'd still give you the blog. Had to, didn't I? But for a few hours, while events in the real world played themselves out, I'd be the most famous blogger in Britain. I'd earned it, after all. I'd done something for once, something good. I changed the password to pwn3d, changed the registered email address to one I'd just set up, lit another cigarette and enjoyed my new identity.

Chapter 25

All the way back to London, I still didn't realise what had happened. I just sat in the corner of the carriage, watching the fields flash by, and let my mind play a continuous loop of that terrible scene at the protest. I had met my Marie. It was just as in my dreams, except that in real life everything was warped. Marie was cruel and aggressive, my blog didn't look quite like my blog any more, and someone else was living my life. All the way from Milton Keynes Central to Watford Junction, the same scene looped in my mind, the crowds, the arm across my chest, the cruel smile, the iPhone with the weirdly distorted version of my blog, the crowds, Marie receding, and then back to the beginning again. What stuck in my mind was that look on Marie's face, so reminiscent of Paola's, seeing me and being filled with disgust. Leaving my flat had been a mistake. I had spent seven years trying to get over that look, and as soon as I left the flat, I encountered it again. All that remained now was to go home, to lick my wounds and slowly reconstruct the feeling of safety it had taken me so many years to build.

The closer I got to home, the stronger the pull it exerted on me. As the scene beyond the scratched train window changed from open fields to suburban semis, then terraces and cuttings and finally the blackness of tunnels, my impatience grew. I willed the train onwards, and it responded by grinding to a halt. A deeply depressed driver announced over crackling speakers that we were being held at a red signal; a few minutes later he returned, slightly more animated, to say that there was a person under a train at Euston, and we wouldn't be moving for a while. Tuts and sighs escaped briefly from pursed lips. Newspapers were shaken and rearranged, seats creaked and the soles of shoes scraped on the floor. All of this activity seemed to come not from individual people but from the train itself, as if it were a strange animal emitting various noises before finding a comfortable place to settle down. Finally the noises stopped and all that remained was the low throb of the diesel engine and the soft pitter-patter of thumbs on keypads. I had no keypad, so was at a loss. I somehow passed the time – I have no idea how long it was – by staring out of the window at a nineteenth-century brick wall. I felt a strange affinity for the anonymous person under the train. I knew how he had come to that place. On another day, perhaps, it would be me, or the train driver, or the red-faced man opposite. One day the urge would be too strong, the promise of release too tempting. One day the finger that had hovered for so long over the Escape key would spasm, and the program would end. The data would be erased, the disk formatted ready for the next user. The mess of a life would end in the greater, but mercifully short, mess of being sliced apart by two hundred tonnes of steel. Not today, though. Today it was someone else's turn to be a service disruption.

After some time, the train abruptly jolted forward again, and began to crawl towards its destination. As it pulled slowly in to Euston, I stood at the door jabbing at the 'Open' button, my anxiety rising until finally the doors opened and I was out onto the platform and pushing my way through the crowds, past the pushchairs and the suitcases and the slow-moving tourists, through the ticket gate and out into the street to take a taxi home. The driver spent the journey complaining about Oyster cards, speed cameras and the demise of all things British, but I didn't care. All that mattered was that with every complaint, with every set of traffic lights, with every recycled opinion, I was steadily moving closer to home. I could see the moment when I stepped over the threshold and closed the door behind me. I could feel the rush of air as the edges of the door sealed in place, and wallow in the silence and peace that would follow. As the driver talked about asylum seekers living in palaces, I closed my eyes and ran my hand over the surface of the antique wooden desk, feeling the grain, the roughness, the familiar scratches in the expected places where two hundred years ago the warehouse overseer had let his penknife slip.

Soon the taxi swung off the clogged main road and into the quiet cobbled mews that led to the canal, the old converted warehouse, the silent flat waiting for me with everything just as I'd left it. The taxi stopped, the doorman rushed out and opened the door, I emptied my wallet and thrust a handful of notes at the driver, and then I walked into the temperature-controlled lobby and felt the door close behind me, the quiet cool stillness of the lobby and the slow trickle of water from the artificial waterfall embracing me and excluding the world outside.

I opened the door to my flat and breathed in deeply, searching for the aroma of my morning coffee. Of course, it was gone, long since swept away down the air ducts and replaced with the scent of freshly-cut grass pumped out from wall-socket air-fresheners. But as I looked around, everything was as I had left it. The Brugnetti espresso machine was on the counter, the silver filter and holder lying next to it where I had cleaned and dried them that morning. Close to the window was my beautiful scratched writing desk and the reassuring bulk of my old desktop computer. I walked across the polished floorboards, breathing in the silence, the stillness, bathing in the warm afternoon sun that poured in through the huge windows. I sat down at the desk, turned on the computer and watched the familiar start-up sequence as my fingers traced ancient lines in the wood. I was truly home.

Only as I opened the internet browser did I start to doubt.

I looked through the window at the grey buildings of north London, and began to realise that something had changed, even here, even at home. For a while I clicked around, reading the news and retaining the sense of normality. But after a few minutes I clicked on my blog. The look was still the same as ever, the same as it had been from the moment I set it up years before, but the top post was still not mine. It didn't even sound like my voice: the sentences were clunky, the grammar was dubious and clichés abounded. 'At the end of the day I've decided its best not to appear.' It was the voice of a football manager, not Britain's number one political blogger. I felt an immense anger, seeing this alien presence on my blog. It was the same post I'd seen on Marie's iPhone, of course, but reading it on my own trusty computer, in the familiar surroundings of my flat, was a thousand times worse. It was as if I'd been burgled, and was looking around at foreign footprints on my hardwood floor, a gap where my espresso machine used to be, a crack in the coffee table's glass top.

I tried to log into my blog, already knowing the outcome. Access denied. I went back to my blog's main page, and read the comments. It was the usual stale blog fare, telling me I had done the right thing, wishing me well, and so on. Not a single one of my loyal readers had noticed the difference between this sloppy, hackneyed post and all the others. For all these years I had been pouring my soul into the blog, shutting out the world and focusing only on creating the sharpest posts, believing it all made a difference. But nobody cared. I could have dashed off a few sloppy sentences, run the spellcheck and hit 'Publish', and the comments would still have been the same. The accumulated weight of all that wasted time hit me with a colossal force, and I quickly shut down.

I paced the floorboards, hoping that from the regular smack of leather on wood I would derive some sense of order. Usually it worked, but this time there was no chance. Nothing worked. Everything I had built to protect myself was now worthless.

I paced anyway. I couldn't think what else to do. I paced and paced from window to wall, window to wall. I would call the police. I would call my lawyers. I would call my service provider. I would call you. I would kill you. No, too extreme. I would start a campaign, rally support. I would start up a rival blog, let people decide which was real. Too long, I needed to do something right now. I had to call you, to speak to you and find out why you had done this, how you had done this. I would call you. I would kill you. I would kill you, and I would kill Marie. I would do nothing.

I stopped pacing. The flat was gloomy and still. The afternoon sun had disappeared, replaced by the dim reflected glow of distant streetlights. In the sudden silence, I let the idea sit. I would do nothing. The anger and anxiety, which a moment ago had seemed unbearable, now were gone. The force that had driven my pacing feet from window to wall, window to wall, was suddenly absent. I stood still, and listened to the silence. I would do nothing. Such a simple thing, and yet I felt as if I had made a discovery to rank alongside the great achievements of science.

I remembered how, earlier that day, in a place and time that already seemed remote, I had been prepared to give up the blog for Marie. If for her, then why not for me? I had already been starting to feel obsolescence growing on me like moss on a fallen tree. The new thing is micro-blogging, the world summed up in 140 characters or less. People don't want to read real arguments. They don't have time for well-constructed thoughts, or for sentences polished to a sheen. They want the intellectual equivalent of a Happy Meal. Blogs like mine, nutritious but sometimes a little stodgy, are losing favour. I still get visits and comments, but only because people want to trade off my popularity. I attract traffic, and so other bloggers gather greedily on my site, hoping to siphon off some of my visitors with a well-timed or well-phrased or just deliberately provocative comment.

Balance, too, is going out of style. My new readers get impatient with me: they want a ready-made opinion, something they can just shove in the microwave, reheat and serve out whenever necessary. They want me to think for them and tell them what to say. They don't care about hearing both sides. They want only one side, their own chosen side, and the more extreme the better. Extremists are certain, and that's always been their appeal. I'm right and you're wrong, and if you don't agree you're a fascist, or a communist, or an elitist, or all three.

I would do nothing. I would do nothing, and all of my problems would end. I would do nothing, and you would be the one with the problems. You would be the one facing an empty page every morning, searching for brilliance with which to fill it. You would be the one fending off trolls, deleting hate mail, discouraging weirdos and patiently arguing with people who seemed to delight in being obtuse. You would be the one accumulating rituals to protect you from all this, while I could discard mine like a heavy winter coat in the first days of spring. I wouldn't have to lock myself away any more.

I went and sat by the window, and looked down over the dark space where I knew the canal was. I didn't have to worry about any of that any more. I didn't have to stay current, to stay popular, to adapt to changing times. I could be myself. I could straighten my back and walk on, leaving you to carry the burden. For the first time in my new life as the ex-blogger Jeff Brennan, I smiled. In fact, I had to try hard to suppress outright laughter as I pictured you sitting in front of a blank screen, the cursor blinking at you mercilessly, the crushing weight of thousands of expectant readers choking the life out of every original thought the moment it occurred. You didn't have my experience. You hadn't lived, as I have, with that suffocating pressure every day for the last seven years. You hadn't developed an elaborate web of defence mechanisms to still the demons whispering doubts in your ear. The blogging world is harsh and unforgiving. Anonymity empowers cowards to ejaculate their bitterness over the screen, abusing you in terms they'd never dream of using in person. You didn't have any rituals to instil faith in your ability, the unshakeable faith you'd need to rise above these barbs with your self-belief intact. You were naked, defenceless. They'd crucify you.

You could probably write a decent blog post. Most people can. Your first attempt was pretty poor, but nobody seemed to notice. Grammar and elegance don't matter much on a blog. But to write the kind of blog post that approaches an idea in a completely new way, while also guarding against as many lines of criticism as possible, is an art that few possess. You would make all the usual mistakes: you would be too ideological, too literal, too wedded to one camp or another, and the other camp would set upon you like a horde of barbarians, slicing your argument to pieces amid the deafening roar of angry war cries. And your camp, seeing the carnage, would swerve away, not wanting to get involved. The bravest would involve themselves in the bloody, increasingly pointless war of attrition. But most would leave you to die slowly. There are plenty more blogs out there, and the primary allegiance of any blogger is to himself. He will support you vehemently as long as he thinks he can gain popularity by it, but as soon as you become a liability, he'll instantly switch allegiance. The blogging world is too young to have developed rules of war. No prisoners are taken. The wounded are shot, their bloody carcasses left on the web for all to see, and the horde moves on.

I remembered Marie's reality, so harsh and unforgiving, so different from how I had imagined her. I remembered her speech earlier that day, so vulgar and self-aggrandising, so full of pride over her newfound fame. I had stood in the audience amid the clapping and whooping and whistling and seen not the woman of my dreams but a fame whore. She had probably sought you out. Sought me out, really, but found you. She didn't care about either of us. It was the stage she wanted, the cameras, the attention, the momentary feeling of being raised above life into something more meaningful. In other words, she was a fool. Standing in that crowd watching her prance and preen before the cameras, I no longer felt bitter, but realised I'd had a lucky escape. In the absence of belief, Marie had, for a time, become my reason for blogging. But that time had now passed. I had seen the reality and recognised it for what it was. You were the one who had what you wanted, and you had to live with it now. If by some inevitable law of our shared fates Marie did come to me now, I would reject her, and this would perhaps give me some small satisfaction.

The biggest satisfaction, though, would come from watching you step into my shoes as Jeff Brennan the blogger. You would die, slowly, and I would watch. Perhaps I would even set up a new blog of my own and participate in your dismemberment. No. I was finished with that world. I would watch from the sidelines, like those wealthy tourists who sat on a hill at Borodino eating hard-boiled eggs and passing the binoculars around as ten thousand men hacked each other to death in the field below. But most of all, I would live, as I had not been able to live before. I put my shoes on, opened the door and went out.

Chapter 26

Marcus Higgins   @marcushig   **1h**
Thanks to all people who came to #MKprotest. It was HUGE!!! See media coverage

Marcus Higgins   @marcushig   **24m**
See positive coverage on Jeff Brennan's site. Says he will definitely come to our next event! Looks like we have our first celebrity endorsement!!!

Marcus Higgins   @marcushig   **17m**
#MKprotest so many pics n vids that ive set up a dedicated site here: bit.ly/mkprotest. Keep em coming!!

Chapter 27

You did put me in rather an awkward position. Sunday morning came, and you'd given me no indication of whether you would be coming alone, or with Marie, or not at all. I presumed that, if things were so bad that you couldn't come at all, you would at least have telephoned. So I tidied up as usual, and helped Daisy into her best blue dress. I hesitated for a while over the teacups, and finally put out four. If she didn't arrive, I could discreetly remove one before serving. If she did come, and I'd only put out three, there would be a certain awkwardness. She would be reminded of the break-up, or 'complications' as they call it these days, and would be embarrassed to think that I knew all about it. So I put out four teacups, and opened a second packet of Bourbon biscuits.

Still, as I sat in the front room with Daisy, waiting for your car to arrive, I felt quite perplexed. I wanted Marie to come, but didn't know what I would say to her if she did. Should I intimate to her that I knew what had happened, or feign ignorance? Should I offer sympathy, or happiness, or indifference? Should I enquire about her supposed meeting with friends the previous Sunday? Not to do so would appear rude, but doing so would put her on the spot and force her into a lie. On the other hand, saying nothing about it might embarrass her too, making it appear that I knew it was a lie all along. All of these thoughts and dozens more jangled around in my mind as I sat there in the silence waiting for you to arrive. The clock would have calmed me, but the clock was gone. Without an anchor, my thoughts drifted hopelessly. I sat there and looked out of the window, willing your jeep to appear in the driveway. I kept thinking you were late, but when I got up to check the clock in the hall, I saw that you weren't. It was just my anxiety. My hands were shaking more than usual, and I had to keep reassuring Daisy. I knew she could feel that something was wrong. Such a state you had me in, when a simple phone call would have solved everything. I'm not used to such 'complications', and the possible outcomes multiplied in my mind, completely overwhelming me.

Even when your jeep appeared in the road outside, nervous moments still awaited me. You backed into the driveway slowly, far more slowly than usual. 'They're here,' I said to Daisy, but thanks to the dark tinted windows of your jeep I couldn't yet tell whether the use of the plural was justified. I began to read things into your slow progress down the driveway. Were you tired? Injured, perhaps? Upset? Were you trying to postpone for as long as possible the moment when you had to face me and say it was all over? Or perhaps Marie was with you, telling you to be careful. She always did worry over those stone pillars at either side of the driveway and the damage they might do to the side of the jeep. Looking back now, I think probably you backed in at the same speed as you had done every Sunday morning for years. You see what an unusual state of worry I was in?

Finally you emerged from one side of the dark jeep and Marie from the other. I rushed to the front door, all the while trying to remember what I had planned to do and say if Marie did turn up. I was pleased to see her, but also in a panic. For a moment, the hallway seemed to tilt to one side, as if on a ship in stormy seas, and I had to grab the radiator shelf until the feeling passed. By that time you were already ringing the bell impatiently and peering through the letter-box. 'Coming,' I tried to call out, but I made no sound.

The day continued in similar vein even after I let you in. All of the topics of conversation I'd prepared flew out of my head, and I just looked awkwardly from you to Marie, from Marie back to you. I wasn't even a very good host, I'm afraid: you had to prompt me to go and make the tea, and then when I came back I'd forgotten the plate of biscuits. You began to squint at me, turning your head slightly to one side, as if inspecting a faulty toaster and wondering whether to send it back. That look only sent me into more of a panic as I thought of the dreaded 'assisted living' conversation, and the more I tried to behave normally, the more eccentric I must have appeared.

Fortunately, Marie talked a lot to fill the gaps. She seemed once again like the nervous girl I'd met the very first time she came, babbling on charmingly but inconsequentially about whatever came into her head. I was grateful to her. The pressure began to lift, as nothing seemed to be required of me but the occasional response. The more she talked, the less important my worries seemed. Even if I'd wanted to bring up her previous weekend's absence, I would have struggled to work it into the conversation. Marie was taking the decisions out of my hands, and I sat gratefully on the sofa and drank my tea, feeling better.

You, however, were far from comfortable. You perched right on the outer edge of the sofa, your shoulders hunched, the muscles in your back tense under your thin shirt, your heel drumming on the carpet even more frenetically than usual. You gulped your tea rather boorishly, I have to say, and greedily finished off the biscuits before Marie had even had a bite. You said almost nothing. You kept looking at the space on the mantelpiece where the clock used to be, then reaching irritably into your pocket for your mobile phone and checking the time on that. Marie must have sensed your mood too, but she chattered on anyway, and the time passed quite agreeably.

As soon as I got up to make more tea, you sprang up and said you'd help. I told you it wasn't necessary, but quickly saw that you had no intention of helping. You wanted to talk, away from Marie. 'Well, I'm sure you ladies can keep each other company,' I said. 'We won't be long.'

'Sure thing,' Marie said with an easy smile, and we departed like two conspirators into the kitchen.

To make things even more obvious, you closed the kitchen door behind us. 'I like to be able to hear,' I complained, 'in case Daisy needs help.'

'Marie's with her,' you said. 'She'll be fine.'

'The kitchen will get all steamed up now.'

'It's fine,' you said impatiently. 'Granddad, I need to talk to you. I've lost my job.'

So abrupt, so clinical. You told me as if it was a trifle, the loss of a job. I remember my father losing his job in the thirties, and it was like a death in the family. The spectre of hunger and destitution hung over our family for the years until things picked up. It's something I never forgot, and I spent my whole life ensuring that under no circumstances would I ever lose my job. I was successful, and so was my daughter, and I was delighted when my grandson found a job that, although it seemed not to make him happy, was at least quite stable. And now you stood in the kitchen, casually telling me you'd lost it. You made it sound as if it were a minor irritation, like a flat tyre.

'That's terrible,' I said. 'What did Marie say? She seems so cheerful, how can she be so cheerful?'

You rolled your eyes. 'She doesn't know, Granddad. Remember? It was only last week I explained it to you. She thinks I'm someone else. She never knew about my real job in the first place. She thinks I work full-time on that website I showed you.'

This was all too much for me. I couldn't understand how one could make money from a website where nothing was sold. I had, after all, visited it with you the previous weekend, and after you'd gone I read a few of the articles and quite enjoyed them. But I'd paid nothing. 'Will I be charged?' I blurted out. 'I read a few of his articles, I thought they were free.'

You looked exasperated. 'Look, that's not the point, Granddad. No, you won't be charged. Can we just focus on my problems for a minute? We don't have much time, Marie will get suspicious if we're out here too long.'

'She probably already is,' I said. 'I never normally shut the door, you know that. Haven't shut it in fifty years, the kitchen gets so hot with it closed.'

'Fine. I'm sorry for shutting it. Now can we move on, please?'

'I'll just put the kettle on,' I said, and while I did you told me all about the previous Monday when you thought everything would end. I didn't understand all of it, but I grasped enough. Marie had not found you out after all. You had tried to do what Marcus asked of you, and had been fired for it. The security guards had taken you out by a back door to avoid the protest, and you'd spent the day in Starbucks, imagining the terrible scenes at the protest: the real Jeff Brennan appearing, Marie realising your deception and hating you, Marcus sticking the knife in because you'd failed in what he asked you to do. You thought you'd lost your job, Marie, everything. Then, on your fifth or sixth double espresso, you received a text from Marie: 'Love you, love you, love you. Come home soon, got a treat for you :-)'

Your first response was that Marie wanted to lure you back home to kill you. The treat would be a kitchen knife through the heart, or poison in your drink. You didn't reply, but still you were unable to stay away from your iPhone very long. You picked it up again, and did what you'd avoided all day. You searched for news of the protest. You wanted to see it in black and white, the death of your fantasy, the real Jeff Brennan taking his identity back. When you saw that he'd cancelled his appearance, you went straight to his blog to find out why. And there you saw the blog post that explained Marie's happiness. She was mentioned, by name, three times in one short post. Jeff Brennan had realised that he should not have taken such a big step without consulting the love of his life, Marie. There would be other protests, but there would never be another Marie. He would only appear in public when he had discussed it with Marie.

You were confused, and then murderously jealous. Marie must have been seeing the real Jeff Brennan behind your back. It was the only way to explain her sudden appearance on his blog. But then why the loving text message to you? Why, in fact, would she bother with you at all, if she had found the real thing? Perhaps the text was intended for him, this other Jeff, this new rival. You looked at the loving words with a sudden hatred, finished your coffee and went straight to your car to drive home.

At this point in the story, we were interrupted by a sudden shout from the living room. My heart leapt. We had been away too long, and something had happened. It was my recurring nightmare come true. I had abandoned Daisy, and she had died alone. I started for the living room, but you put a hand on my arm. 'It's alright, Granddad.' You opened the door, and called out, 'Everything okay?'

'I was just asking the same thing. You've been gone ages.'

My heart slowly returned to its normal rhythm, and I was able to breathe without effort. 'I'll take the biscuits,' I said. 'You can manage the tea, can't you? There's a good lad.' We went back to the living room, back to Daisy and Marie, but separated from them by our shared secret. Again I was grateful for Marie's chattering. I could barely digest what you had told me in the kitchen, and yet I knew there was more to come. You would find a way to separate us again, and again I would be drawn into your confusing world of mistakes and misunderstandings, identities fluid like streams, merging and separating for reasons I couldn't fathom. I wanted no part of it, regretted I had even shown an interest in that infernal machine in the dining room. I should have left it under the brown tablecloth, and remained content with the simplicity of waking up, preparing meals, helping Daisy in and out of her wheelchair, walking to the High Street with her and doing the shopping, stopping at the baker's on the way back for a cup of tea and a bath bun. At my age, your world was too much for me to grasp. I had wanted to understand you, but it was too much. I wished I had shown no interest, and you had continued to feed me platitudes about how fine everything was.

I wonder if Marie knew what was going on. Perhaps that's why she talked on and on so nervously. Perhaps she knew, or half-knew, but didn't want to admit it. Certainly your tactics were not very subtle. After half an hour of almost uninterrupted monologue by Marie, you suggested to her that she might want to give Daisy one of her pedicures. She could stay in the living room, while you and I went on the computer. Marie looked at both of us a little uncertainly, but then shrugged and said, 'Sure.' So easy, so trusting. Then, to me: 'If you don't mind, that is. I can put a towel down to protect the carpet.'

'Of course,' I said feebly, and soon I was in the dining room with the door shut and the computer on and no escape from the whirring confusion. You told me how Jon had saved you, somehow breaking into the blog and taking it over, so that he could write whatever he wanted on it and the original owner was shut out. I didn't like that part at all. Having a fantasy was bad, but harmless. Breaking into someone else's website and taking it over sounded a lot like common theft. I didn't want a burglar for a grandson. But I kept quiet and let you continue, thinking perhaps that there were different rules on the internet. Perhaps if nothing is real, then property and theft are outdated terms. Still, it seemed to me that this chap had put a lot of work into his site, and it was rather unfair on him to lose it.

As the story went on, though, it got worse. You were now in charge of this website, and didn't know what to do. Writing blog posts was not as easy as you'd thought.

'Of course not,' I said. 'You said it's like a newspaper. Well, it took me years to learn to write good articles. I started at the *Camden Chronicle*, then went to the *Evening News*, then the *Daily Sketch*...'

'Yes, alright, Granddad.'

'My point is that it was only at *The Times* that I started writing anything half-decent. There's so much to learn, not just about finding a story but about structuring it, assembling the facts, choosing the angle, finding the right quotes to support your point of view...'

'Look, the point is, I've written blog posts before, it's just that there's more pressure now. I'm having trouble getting used to it. But I'll be alright. Marcus said he'll give me ideas.'

I expressed surprise, but you seemed to have forgotten that last weekend Marcus had been your blackmailer. This weekend everything was smoothed over, the loss of your job apparently convincing him that you'd tried your best, the threat of exposure retracted. Now, it seemed, he needed you. Possessing the keys to the highest pulpit in the land, you would be the means by which his message would be broadcast. And you needed him, because without his prompting there'd be nothing but a blank page and the slow blinking of an expectant cursor. On the basis of such mutual need, apparently, your friendship had been reformed. He would handle the publicity side of things, helping you to leverage your fame as the previous owner never had. I nodded as if I understood, and let you finish the story.

Your main worry, it seemed, was not the blog, but the loss of your job. Although you had spoken of it so glibly, it was still a source of concern. You didn't have the privilege that this other Jeff Brennan seemed to have, the ability to blog full-time without making money from it. You had bills to pay. You were thinking of 'monetising' the site – I didn't even want to ask what that meant – but it would take time. You couldn't just slap advertisements all over it, when for so long it had been ad-free. In short, you needed money. A loan. I felt disappointed and relieved. Disappointed because a small, sentimental part of me had believed that for once you wanted the benefit of your granddad's advice; relieved because I had no idea what advice to give, and was happy to be offered the shortcut of money.

'Of course,' I said. 'How much?'

You told me the figure, and I had to grip the edge of the table to steady myself. 'I'm not sure whether I'm able to find that much.'

'It's just to tide me over for a few months. Marcus says he has some ideas on how I can make money. He's planned some events for me. I'm famous now, after all.'

I felt dizzy again, whether from the thought of the unearned fame or the idea that this huge figure was just a few months of spending for you. I thought of those lessons I had tried to teach you when you were living with us: showing you the electric bill, counting out the money, explaining how much you could save by turning off the lights when you left a room. Taking you shopping, explaining the difference between the prices at the local greengrocer and M&S. You were surly and bored at the time, but I had hoped that something had seeped in, as it had with the cleaning of the clock. But there was nothing, no trace of me. I thought of the years I had spent saving pennies in a jar on the kitchen table, and I felt like a fool. You were not bothering with any of that. You had lost your job, and you still planned to spend in a few months a sum I thought fit to last me the rest of my days. I sacrificed my comfort, putting on an extra jumper and moving my chair closer to the radiator on cold days rather than turn up the heat a notch, while you just did what you felt like and then asked for loans.

'I'll see how much I can find,' I said. 'I don't think it will be as much as you want, but whatever I have is yours. No need to pay it back either, it'll be yours soon anyway.' You frowned and told me not to talk like that. 'Why not?' I asked. 'You can see from the state of this place that I'm not really attached to things any more.'

You looked around for the first time. 'There's nothing left, Granddad.'

You were right, of course. My cleaning and tidying had reached a slightly obsessive level. The feeling I had when I paid the Owen boys to take another bulging bin-bag down to the charity shop was irreplaceable. It was a sudden lightening after so many decades of increasing weight. I had accumulated things, and needed a big house to store them, and had worked for years of my life to pay not only for the things themselves but for the mortgage and the insurance in case they were lost or stolen. I had built a life around these things, and now I was throwing them in a bin bag and paying the Owen boys to take them to the charity shop. I had passed the charity shop a few times and not seen any of my beloved items on display, which meant either that I was paying the Owen boys to rob me or that the stuff had no value even to a charity shop. Still, I kept filling the bags and stacking them in the hall for collection. Where they went after that was of scant importance.

'I have everything I need,' I said. 'The dining room table's still here, and the computer on its trolley, and a chair for me to sit at. More than that is unnecessary. Daisy and I are unlikely to entertain very frequently.'

'You still have that old typewriter too. How's the memoir going?'

'See for yourself,' I said, gesturing to the two piles of paper. 'Fresh paper is on the right, used on the left.'

'You're close to the end,' you said incredulously. 'I never thought you'd keep going. I didn't realise you had so much to say.'

'I've lived for eight decades,' I said, a little hurt. 'You don't think I've seen enough in that time to fill a single stack of paper?'

You shrugged. 'I know you've seen a lot, but I didn't realise it was different from what anyone else saw. There are loads of books on the sixties and all that. How is yours any different?'

'Because it was written by me and no-one else,' I said huffily, and changed the subject back to the contents of the computer screen. 'I see Marie's status has changed back,' I said. 'It's no longer 'complicated'. She's 'in a relationship' again.'

You motioned to me to keep my voice down, a little unnecessarily I thought. 'Things with Marie are fine,' you whispered. 'She's happier than ever. You see, instead of waiting for me to fill you in, you could have gone on Facebook and found out what was happening.'

'Yes, I suppose so,' I said. Really you must understand that a lifetime's habits cannot be changed so easily. When I'm worried, I sit in my armchair in the living room, by the telephone, and wait for it to ring. That telephone brought me news of every major event in your mother's life, from exam results through to marriage, pregnancy and death. Whenever Daisy's in hospital, I wait doggedly by the telephone until it rings, knowing that if I leave even for a minute or two to make a cup of tea, I may miss the doctor's call. The gradual passing of my friends has been delivered by telephone, too. I can't imagine being expected to log onto Facebook to see their status change to 'Dead'. It doesn't matter that the phone has hardly rung in the last few years for anything except sales calls from call centres in India. In a crisis, I wait by the telephone. 'I'm glad she's happy, anyway,' I said.

Again you shushed me, before whispering: 'Now that I've acknowledged her on my blog, it's like she feels validated, like she's not being kept secret any more.'

'Validated?' I queried, deliberately using my normal tone of voice in response to your whisper. 'You make her sound like a credit card, Jeff.'

You sighed, and I could tell I'd said the wrong thing. Whenever I questioned something from your world, I was being old-fashioned and irrelevant. You, on the other hand, could disparage my clock or my typewriter with impunity. I seem to have been born at the wrong time. In my youth I had to respect my elders, and now that I'm old I must defer to the young.

'I'm going to write another post about her soon,' you said, trying to put my annoying interruption out of your head. 'Now that the blog's mine, I can keep mentioning her as often as I like.'

'It's not yours, Jeffrey,' I said sharply. Sharpness had never worked with you, but I couldn't help myself. This casual talk of taking another man's property was more than I could bear. I was overcome once again by a feeling of my own failure. Perhaps if I had persisted with the sharp tone when you were younger, instead of giving in all the time, you would have been different. Perhaps if I had done it with your mother, she would have done it with you. I had always given in, trusting you to make the right decision, to find your own path as my father had never allowed me to. And the result: your mother was dead, and you had turned into a common thief.

As I'd expected, the sharp tone only made you more defensive. 'What's done is done,' you said. 'There's no point in thinking about it, you just have to move on.'

I sighed. It was a poisonous formula I seemed to hear all the time on the radio, in the mouths of politicians, football managers and other cheap entertainers. Move on, look to the future, don't waste time thinking about the past. Centuries of consensus on the importance of accountability, blown away on the fickle breeze of talk-show psychology. I thought back on my years as a courts correspondent, when each case presented its own complications but offered the satisfaction of resolution: the past had been judged, however imperfectly, and punishment meted out. Things had been set right, a measure of balance restored. Nowadays murderers were probably allowed to plead not guilty on the grounds that their victims should just move on.

'Besides,' you said, 'I can do more with the blog than the

old guy did. I can use it to spread the word about climate change. It can have a real impact. For good, I mean, Granddad. For a good cause.'

'The end justifies the means.'

'Exactly!' you replied, and I silently despaired of your history teachers. Then again, maybe their task was hopeless. It's impossible to teach someone who thinks he already knows.

'You have to give it back, Jeff,' I said, more softly this time. 'It's the only way. Then all of these problems will go away. You won't have to worry about what to write, or how to make money from it. You can get a real job. I could have a word with a chap I still know at *The Times*. He's always talking about digital this and virtual that, even though I don't think he understands it any more than I do. He comes from the world of ink-stained fingers, glue and paste, the roar of the presses. He needs someone like you, someone who understands the new way and can help him let go of the old.'

You shook your head, but I could see you wavering. You always were easily led, and I knew that my only chance was to lead you more convincingly than your poisonous friends or the amoral platitudes you imbibed from TV. It had always been an uneven battle, and I had always lost before, but this time I sensed I had a chance. 'It'll be a regular salary,' I said. 'Probably a generous one, more than I'm sure you were getting at that provincial law firm.'

'You always said that was a good job.'

'It was, for starting out, but you can do better now. You can work in London, be at the centre of things, earn a good salary, have a nice flat. You can meet new people, travel. You can tell Marie everything and throw yourself on her mercy. She loves you. It may take a while, but she'll forgive you. You just can't live a lie, Jeff. Not all the time.'

You knew I was right, I could see it. You were still trying not to accept it, but inside you knew I was right. 'Jon said the same thing,' you said. 'Said he hacked into the blog to save me that one time, but he wasn't expecting me to keep it. He thought I should give it back, but still not tell the truth to Marie.'

'That's good advice too,' I said. 'One step at a time, you don't want to do everything at once. Be honest about the blog first, give it back to its rightful owner, and then you can talk to Marie later, when you're ready, if you're ready.'

You smiled a defeated smile. 'How come you're giving me advice all of a sudden? You never used to.'

'I always did,' I said. 'You just weren't listening. Now then, how do we get in touch with this chap? I can help you decide what to say.'

I felt excited as you fished in your pocket for your iPhone. 'Jon gave me his email address,' you said. 'He got it from the blog. Here: sinon1977@gmail.com.'

I watched in amazement as you logged on to your email account and typed in the address. You really were going to do it. You were going to take my advice for the first time in your life. Maybe I was not so old-fashioned and irrelevant after all. You were going to do it. That's what I remind myself. It really doesn't matter that Marie opened the door at the wrong moment, that you closed down the email window in a flash, that I had to go off and find a towel for Daisy's feet, and that by the time I got back, you were reading some article about healthcare reforms in America. It doesn't matter that, when I asked you about the email, you said that admitting to a criminal act in writing was perhaps not the best idea, and you needed to think about it a little more. I knew what that meant, of course, but really it doesn't matter. It doesn't matter that you'll never send that email now. What matters is that, if Marie hadn't burst in with her talk of towels, you would have done it. You really would have taken my advice and, after all the years of irrelevance, that small fact was enough to warm an old man's heart.

An hour later, after you'd climbed into your jeep and I'd waved you safely off, I went back into the dining room, took the brown tablecloth off the computer and started up the machine. 'Won't be long, love,' I said to Daisy, who was still in her wheelchair, which I know she doesn't like to stay in for longer than necessary. It was true, though. What I had to do would only take a moment, but it was important to do it right away, before I forgot. I logged onto my email account and composed a new message, typing out first of all the email address I had been so anxious not to forget: sinon1977@gmail.com.

Chapter 28

The flash blinded me, but I held my gaze steady. Marcus had taught us that. All famous people live with the temporary blindness. They stare at the camera, hold their eyes open and accept the few seconds of blindness as a hazard of the job. Better to be blind than to look bad on the cover of *Heat*. He'd trained us, day by day, putting his camera right in front of our faces and taking picture after picture with the flash on. Only when he'd gotten a good shot would he stop. A good shot meant one with the eyes open – not half-open, mind you, but fully, lusciously, sparklingly open. At first it was impossible, but after enough practice it became a habit. So now I stood smiling a perfect smile for the camera, seeing red spots floating in the darkness where the photographer had just been. I knew that, next to me, you were doing the same thing, staring bright-eyed into the darkness, smiling as if you knew what was in front of you. It would be a great photo.

After a few more shots, we were released. The red dots swam as I shook the hand of an unseen stranger and said how lovely it was to see her. Then, as always happens, reality returned. Your vision must have come back at the same time, because we both turned to look at each other simultaneously, and smiled for a reason no-one else would understand. I reached for your hand, and you grasped it eagerly, wrapping it in a film of sweat.

'You're nervous,' I whispered in your ear.

'Yeah, a bit.'

I squeezed your hand. 'You'll be fine, love.'

For a few seconds we felt so close, and the crowds in that large, dark room were irrelevant. The whole night could be a disaster and it wouldn't matter, because I'd still have your hand in mine, I'd still feel the softness of your palm, I'd still smell your aftershave, as familiar now as my own perfume, and I'd still be able to snuggle close to you, even in an empty, abandoned room, and feel that nothing else was important.

Then Marcus touched your elbow, and the spell was broken. He led us up onto a wide, empty stage with just a microphone and two chairs sitting slightly askance in the centre. I sat in one and you sat in the other. I wanted to touch you one last time before it started, but you were just out of reach. I smiled at you instead, and tried to wink, but you were just staring pale-faced at the microphone, crumpling your speech in your fingers. I don't think you even saw me.

Your publisher stepped up to the microphone, quieted the crowd, and launched into an extravagant paean to your blog. He praised its relevance, its panache, the power of the writing matching the power of the ideas. You, he said, were a modern-day Dickens, full of great thoughts and a fiery commitment to social justice, but able to condense all this into an immensely readable form and serialise it for a mass audience. All this from a man who openly admitted at our first meeting that he'd never read the blog, before offering an advance twice as large as his competitor's. Marcus practically ripped the cheque out of his hands, even though the condition of the large advance was that the book hit the shops in three months. Celebrity was short-lived, the publisher explained. Your sudden appearance after years of anonymity had put you in the public eye: now you had to capitalise on your brand equity. 'You have all the material on your blog. Just rehash it, slap an introduction on the front and send it to me by the end of the month.' Marcus willingly took the cheque, reassuring you on the way out that he would handle the whole thing.

So now we were sitting on a stage in a trendy venue of literary London, listening to praise from a man who'd never read your blog and probably never even read the book he was holding up for the cameras. And you were sitting behind him, ready to step out into the spotlight and read from a book of your old articles, selected by Marcus and with an introduction ghost-written by Marcus. You hadn't even cashed the cheque. Marcus had handled that, presumably removing his fifteen percent first. Your only involvement, in fact, had been to select the title: *The World We Live In* by Jeff Brennan. It was a decent title, but I was surprised to hear it from you. You'd always made it clear in your blog that you made no pretence to higher knowledge or understanding. You analysed individual parts of the world, but made no attempt to fit them together into a coherent world view. You were always suspicious of ideologies, preferring to stick to the small, the concrete, the knowable. *The World We Live In* sounded unexpectedly grandiose for you, as if you were promising something you didn't really believe existed.

Soon the publisher had finished gushing and you stepped up to the microphone, your speech fluttering in your hand like a white flag in the wind. You walked unsteadily, as if your legs might buckle. I couldn't bear to watch. I looked out into the cavernous darkness. The spotlight in my face turned the people beyond into a dark, threatening mass, their faces indistinguishable. I looked up at the ceiling and admired the ornate decorations, angelic faces peeping out from behind fake curtains. Their paint and gilding were long faded but that was part of the charm. This used to be a music hall, Marcus said. George 'Champagne Charlie' Leybourne once stood on these scuffed wooden boards and performed *The Daring Young Man on the Flying Trapeze* to wildly enthusiastic audiences. And now you stood there clutching a speech in one shaking hand and a book in the other, clearing your throat and making the old boards squeak and whine beneath your nervously shifting feet. You stopped, composed yourself. The anonymous faces out there in the darkness faced you, waiting. For a few awkward seconds, the silence was complete.

Then, into the silence, a voice broke. It was not your voice, not the soft voice I knew from a thousand murmured bedtime conversations. It was a strident voice, confident of the views it was conveying in a way that you never were. Maybe it was just the microphone, converting your voice into electronic signals to be sent to speakers in all corners of the hall. Maybe in that process of conversion, something of you was lost. In any case, the voice sounded so foreign that I looked up sharply, struggling to keep surprise from dislodging the benign, camera-friendly smile on my face.

It was you. The slope of the shoulders, the slight rounding of the back, the way you always stood with more weight on one foot than the other, all of this was as familiar as my reflection. The voice was rising out of that familiar body, but still it rang strange and foreign in my ears. The words, certainly, were Marcus's: he had written your speech for you, and trained you in its correct delivery. So probably it was Marcus's voice I was hearing in discordant echoes around the old, dark hall. In being trained by him, you had adopted his speech patterns, his rhythm and pronunciation. You were speaking his words in his voice, and holding his book in your hand. What were you, then, but a device for amplifying Marcus's voice? You were no different from the microphone you gripped with sweaty fingers.

The speech went well, though, as you'd expect. A book launch is a celebratory occasion and the crowds, buoyed up by free wine, will clap at almost anything. The applause did sound genuinely enthusiastic, though, and a satisfied hum spread briefly across the darkness before people settled down for the reading. I was relieved. The words that rang hollow and false in my ears evidently sounded different to everyone else. They didn't know you like I did. They were like the tourists who flock to a hot new destination, ignorant of the pristine beauty whose loss the locals mourn.

I thought the reading would sound better than the speech, but it didn't. I thought that, because they were your words, chopped up and reheated from an old blog post, they would sound more genuine. You'd chosen to read one of my favourites, a perceptive analysis of the 'Transition Towns' movement from a couple of years earlier, back when I was just an infatuated reader. I remember how much I loved that post when I first read it, I even have a gushing post on my own blog to prove it. I loved the care you'd taken to speak to real people in Totnes and Kinsale, the faithfulness with which you'd conveyed their views, and the fearlessness with which you'd confronted them. It was a typical Jeff Brennan article: fair to all, partial to none.

The version you were reading, though, was barely recognisable. Marcus had edited out all the balance. Gone were the questions of race and class that had so animated your original. Gone was the acute observation that, around the world, indigenous people were being driven off their land to support the same system of privilege that allowed affluent white villagers to 'transition' back to nature. Anything that challenged the self-congratulatory tone of organic orthodoxy was struck out. All that remained was a limp propaganda piece. As you read the article, it was as if you realised it wasn't really yours any more. You stumbled over words, and read some of the sentences with completely the wrong emphasis. It was so painfully different from the voice I'd heard in my head as I read the piece for the first time in my flat in London.

I couldn't allow any of this to show on my face, of course. Marcus had trained us in facial control, too. So as I turned away from you to look once again at the ornate music-hall ceiling, I was careful to ensure that a thoughtful smile played on my lips, as if I was looking to the ceiling simply to contemplate better the beauty and truth of your words.

When I saw the face up there, though, I had to struggle not to let the smile slip. It was that same, strangely familiar face as I'd seen in my dreams, both sleeping and waking, ever since the day of the protest, the day when I made my speech and the cameras clicked and I took the first step towards becoming famous. It was the man in the crowd, that strange, lost man who thought he was you. His bewildered face appears to me at the strangest moments, and whenever it appears I feel a mysterious pang of guilt. It's like I'm cheating on you. His face always appears out of nowhere, but I'm left with this weird feeling that it was me who sought him out. And I ask myself *why* I sought him out, and I never know. There was just something innocent about him, the way he just kept repeating 'I'm Jeff Brennan, I'm Jeff Brennan,' and then receded helplessly into the crowd.

There he was again, on the biggest night of your life, hiding up in the ceiling, another carved face peeping out from behind fake curtains. I resented him, left him up in the darkness and instead looked back at you, the man I love. A camera flashed, and my heart lurched. Was I smiling? Was a trace of my anger at the unwanted face in the ceiling betrayed in my expression as I looked at you? Was this his revenge, this strange man in the crowd? I tried to pick out the photographer who'd taken the shot, but beyond the spotlight there was only darkness. There was nothing I could do, except make sure I didn't let you down again. I put a smile on my lips and love in my eyes, and listened to you butchering the rest of the article.

When it was over and you were bathing in the applause, I got up from my chair and walked over to you. I slipped my arm around yours and kissed you lightly on the cheek, just as we'd rehearsed. I pretended to whisper something in your ear, and you laughed a little and pretended to whisper something back. Then we turned, triumphant, to face the crowd, arm in arm, like politicians on election night, whipping up a few cheers from the faithful and flashes from the photographers' cameras. The moment was preserved forever, Jeff & Marie together on stage, the happy couple.

I was silent in the taxi. I knew I shouldn't have been, but I was. I knew you needed me to praise you, but I couldn't. I stared out of the window at the London streets I no longer recognised. Luckily you were on a high, no matter what I said or didn't say. You hadn't eaten all day, so nervous were you about the event, and now you were running on pure adrenalin, euphoric about your success, needing only the occasional grunt or nod or smile from me. Later it would be different, later you would start to question and worry, but perhaps later I would be in the mood to reassure. For now I just let you talk. You talked about all the books you'd signed, how your hand got cramp and your signature became lazier. You talked about the fans, loyal readers of your blog for years, who'd lined up to buy your book. As I sat there half-listening, I wondered why they would buy for £17.99 in hardback the articles they'd already read for free on your blog. I wondered if they'd notice the differences I noticed, the bias Marcus had introduced, not only in the article you'd read out but in all of them. Probably not. They were happy to own a piece of you. If you tried to charge a £1 monthly subscription on your blog, they'd lead the outcry about the spirit of the web, but a hardback book was something worth paying for.

Soon the taxi stopped, and we were checking into a swanky London hotel, the kind where someone carries your bags up to your room and then spends ten minutes showing you all the 'features'.

'This room needs an instruction manual,' I said when he'd finally left us alone.

I was joking, of course, but you soon found a little booklet on the desk entitled 'Getting the Most From Your Superior Executive Suite', and began to read out with delight each new feature. The voice-activated music system entranced you for a while, as did the galactic minibar, but your clear favourite was the WiFi-enabled toilet, with its ingenious touchscreen display that swung out on an arm from the side of the toilet and allowed you to check email as you sat there. I felt tired as you talked, and needed a frozen vodka from the minibar to give me the strength to show enthusiasm. This was, after all, our big celebration. Your book launch, all that attention, all those books sold and signed. With all the free wine we could never drive back up the M1, so rather than depress ourselves with the slow night train we'd decided to splurge on a hotel. Well, you'd decided, and as it was your night I'd happily gone along with it. And now, after all the money we'd spent, I owed you some appreciation, a laugh or two as you shouted 'Hendrix' to the invisible music player, a gasp of awe as you blogged from the toilet, a shared smile as you discovered that the seat was not only heated but scented.

The strange thing was that your enthusiasm seemed a little fake, too. I think we both just wanted to go to sleep, but this was a room too special to waste time sleeping in. So we ordered room service, and twenty minutes later a waiter appeared with a trolley bearing silver platters and champagne in a bucket.

'I thought you might like our turning down service, now, sir?' the waiter inquired. 'As we are disturbing you anyway.'

You nodded vaguely, and an army of maids marched into the room, turning down our bedsheets, placing chocolates and rose petals on the pillows, diligently tidying away the shoes and coats that we had dropped on the floor when we arrived. From the bathroom came the sound of running water and the waiter, anticipating my question, explained, 'Many of our guests like an aromatherapy bath at this time. Our house blend of spices and essential oils has received the very top mark from the British Aromatherapy Guild for its calming and restorative properties. All a complementary part of our renowned turning down service, madam.'

I watched as the waiter carefully laid the plates of food

out on the table, while the maids scurried around tidying, turning down, plumping up, freshening, spraying, and mixing a renowned blend of spices and essential oils. You and I stood barefoot and useless in the middle of the room, clinging to each other as if marooned. You seemed as delighted by the whirlwind of service as you had been by the WiFi toilet, while all I felt was horror that so many people were putting so much effort into serving the two of us. The waiter's intricate preparations, his careful inspection and polishing of every fork, the way that after setting down each plate he rotated it to a precise angle for the food's optimal presentation, all smacked of ceremonial subservience. I pictured him smoking in an alleyway with one of the maids later on, complaining about the tossers in the Superior Executive Suite. I wanted to speed things up, to dump all the food down on the table myself, pop open the champagne, light the candle, thank him and send him on his way. I knew, though, that in your eyes I would be ruining things, so I let it continue, clinging tighter to you for protection. In response you squeezed my shoulder, kissed the top of my head and whispered, 'Great, isn't it? All this for us.'

After the ceremony ended and the waiter and maids departed with their tip, we sat down to our tepid food. 'Cheers,' I said, lifting my glass towards you. 'Congratulations.' I gestured around the room, at the down-turned bed, the sofa, the flat-screen TV, the bathroom from which aromatic steam was billowing. 'You've really made it, big-time.'

You smiled and we clinked glasses, looking out of the window at the dark streets of London. A gaggle of drunks passed by far below, but no off-key singing or smashes of shattered glass reached us. We were in London but not in London. At least it was not the London I knew. This was an insulated London, a London of cool sophistication, a London with all the shouts and smells and beggars and stabbers carefully edited out. Another London, that felt foreign and cold.

I puffed out my cheeks in a long sigh. 'We're not in Kansas any more, Toto.'

You frowned a little. 'I thought your folks were from California.'

I smiled and ate my dinner, which I have to admit was excellent. For a few minutes, as I felt the perfectly-cooked vegetables crunch between my teeth and the sauce explode subtle flavours on my tongue, I thought perhaps I could get used to this London. I could sip champagne behind toughened, tinted glass, inhaling specially formulated restorative steam from the freshly-run bath and looking out over the pretty sparkling lights of Bloomsbury. We could murmur softly in the candlelight, clink glasses and enjoy the fruits of our success.

It only lasted a few minutes, but for those few minutes I really thought I could live like that. Perhaps it was the soothing music, or the calming aroma of award-winning herbs and spices. In any case, it only lasted a few minutes, and then I saw our reflection in the glass, you red-faced and eager as you bit into a bloody steak, me straight-backed and sipping champagne beside you. It was like a caricature of the very people me and my parents and my grandparents had always laughed at. I thought of our flat in Milton Keynes and the simple meals we'd cooked together, and I wanted to sweep the champagne and the plates and the rich sauces off the table. I longed for the simplicity in which I'd been raised, the simplicity I'd had for a while with you too. The routine of work and home, the shared meals, the talking, the cuddling. I even longed for the clock, the familiarity of its regular mechanical beat. I wanted the world of you and I in a room together and no-one else, no armies of maids rearranging everything, no obsequious waiters, no remote-controlled curtains. I wanted to get away from this place where everything was uncertain, and back to a place I recognised.

It wasn't only the place I wanted to recognise, but the

person. I felt like I didn't know this person who laughed at voice-activated music and was wowed by WiFi-enabled toilets. He seemed so different from the man I'd fallen in love with, the one who was content to stay in the shadows, shunning fame and fortune, interested only in telling the truth. That man seemed to be fading in the glare of the photographers' flashes, while a more eager, thrusting version emerged, a man happy to exploit, to maximise, to capitalise. A more contemporary man, a more successful man, but a less lovable one. And as you embraced the spotlight, you gained not just money and fame but insecurities. Even at home, when Marcus wasn't around and the cameras weren't rolling and it was just the two of us, something had changed. You seemed to resent me, as if you were carrying some burden that I had given you. After all, it was me who kept telling you to go public. It wasn't fame and success I wanted, of course, I just wanted you to draw more attention to the issues we both cared about. But still, it was like I'd created this new you, and now I didn't like it and wanted to send it back. And I was beginning to think that maybe you did too.

In the old days, I was always amazed at how easily you forgot your blog as soon as you got home. I had to drag information out of you, otherwise you'd just talk about friends or tidbits of news. Lately, though, you'd been coming home with the exhausted, haggard look of a man who's truly suffered. And you talked about your blog incessantly. It's funny, for a long time that was exactly what I wanted, but now that you were doing it, I just wished you would shut up. I didn't want to hear an analysis of every comment, a justification of every position you'd taken, an endless search for reassurance. It felt tiring. It was like you were sucking something out of me, something I didn't want to give. I told you again and again that you were good, that your blog was good, that the people who criticised you were wrong, and on and on, and it was never enough. It was too much for me and never enough for you.

'Come on, eat up,' you said. In your mouth I glimpsed a grey, half-chewed lump of steak, while the cracks between your teeth were stained red. For a weird moment I wanted to run away from this man I didn't know any more, and I thought once again of the confused man in the crowd who could say nothing but 'I'm Jeff Brennan.'

You poured more champagne for us, and I forced some of it down, along with a few of the vegetables, now cold. 'Do you ever wish you could go back?' I asked.

The way you looked at me, I could tell the answer was yes. For a second there was real fear there, as if I had discovered your secret, but then you quickly covered it up. 'Back to what?'

'Life as it was before we got famous, before all this.'

You followed my arm as I swept it around the room, and then laughed dryly. '*This* is hardly a way of life. It's a one-off, a celebration. We're not that famous, despite what Marcus thinks. I'm just a blogger, a big name to people who follow me but a nobody in the big scheme of things. We don't get recognised and mobbed in the streets of Milton Keynes, do we?'

I looked down at the remainder of my vegetables and pushed them around in the sauce, watching the congealed butter sticking to my fork and imagining what it was doing to my arteries. 'But things have still changed, Jeff, haven't they?'

'Have they?'

You took my hand, and looked at me with such sincerity that I began to doubt myself. It seemed so clear to me that things had changed, and yet, when I tried to pinpoint exactly what, it slipped away like a half-remembered dream. 'You resisted it for so long,' I said finally. 'Then you met me, and because of me you went public.'

Now it was your turn to look down and play with your food. 'Not entirely because of you. I mean, you said some things, but so did Marcus, and I thought about it myself as well. It was a lot of factors.'

'You're sweet,' I said.

'Besides, I don't regret it. Things are still the same, just the occasional interview or speech, that's all.'

I knew it was more than that, but I didn't say anything. I knew that you were more insecure about the blog now because you were no longer just a screenname. People knew your face, and faces are important. Even in the blogging world, the physical still matters, as the long line for your £17.99 hardback proved. Anonymity had protected you. Now that people knew your face, it was more real somehow, and you fretted about every sentence far more than ever before. The quality had suffered, too, although I could never tell you that. I could never tell you any of it, which is why I said nothing. I knew you'd deny it, not wanting to hurt me, not wanting to make me feel guilty for a decision I'd helped you make. The decision was a success. That was your line and you would stick to it. All I could do was what I did: raise a glass of champagne and toast 'To Success.'

You smiled, relieved, and clinked back. 'To Success.' We drank our champagne and looked out over the sparkling lights of London, pretty and harmless like a Christmas tree. Soft jazz played in the background, and soothing aromas wafted from the bathroom. I let my mind become cloudy, chasing away the doubts. 'Things are good, aren't they?' you said, your voice hovering uncertainly between statement and question.

'Yes Jeff,' I said quietly. 'We've got everything we wanted. Things are good.'

Chapter 29

It feels quiet in the house today. When I talk to Daisy, my voice echoes off the bare walls. The Owen boys removed another few bags of stuff this morning. Gone are the last photos of your mother. I have no need for them. As long as I can still remember myself, I'll remember her. Every thought is filtered through her thoughts, every memory a shared memory. Even when I think of the times before she was born, I remember not the times themselves but the stories I told your mother. Four decades of life with her have become layered on top of everything else. She is as much a part of me as Daisy is. I have no need for photos to jog my memory.

The computer's gone, too. I felt rather guilty as I disposed of it, since after all it was a gift from you. But you did always insist it was old and worthless, and now that I am more aware of new developments I see that you were telling the truth. Compared to an iPad, it looks as archaic as my old typewriter. I still don't understand why all those people queued up overnight to be the very first to hand over hundreds of pounds for a high-tech slate. But I suppose it's not about the object itself, but about being first. They'll junk their iPads in a couple of years and queue up overnight for the next new thing. It's the way things are these days.

Still, as much as I tell myself that it's merely an acceleration of the perpetual deterioration of all things human, I do find it difficult to accept that something so new could so quickly become worthless. So rather than bagging the computer up with the rest of the rubbish, I left it in the dining room and let the Owen boys do the dirty deed. I even checked my email before I shut down for the final time, as if trying to reassure the machine that I still cared. I had a friend request from a young man in Australia who was interested in beekeeping. I followed the link to Facebook, hit 'Confirm' and typed mechanically: 'Thanks for the add. Love yr profile pic.' Then I swiftly shut down the computer, listening to the fan whirring loudly for the last time before falling silent. I picked up the brown tablecloth from the floor, unfolded it, shook it and spread it carefully over the machine, covering it completely. Some time later, I let the Owen boys come tramping through the house, and pretended to busy myself with watering a plant while they clattered and clunked back through, a trailing plug banging on the skirting board as they removed the machine from my life.

When you ask why, I'll tell you I received some upsetting messages. It's true, in a way. I did receive some hatemail on account of my profile picture. A certain Randy Williams from Maryland took great offence at the cigarette dangling from my fingers, sending me a message in which, among many unnecessary expletives, he expressed the wish that I got lung cancer and died. Then in another message, three minutes later, he added that before I got lung cancer and died, he hoped I had to watch my children get lung cancer and die first. 'WLD U STIL THINK SMOKEING WAS GLAMEROUS THEN????' It was upsetting, I have to admit. In eighty years on the planet I had never encountered such vitriol, even working on Fleet Street. But if you know me at all, you'll know that I would never allow myself to be chased off the internet by the likes of Randy Williams. The technology may be unfamiliar to me, but the principle is not. 'Run away once and you'll be running the rest of your life,' my father used to say. So, if the computer had held any interest for me, I would have gritted my teeth and stood my ground, giving Randy Williams a good deal more than he had bargained for.

But I did not. My interest was always feigned, and although

Marie was a better teacher than you, she never convinced me that using a computer would improve my life in any substantial way. I learnt it purely to understand you. It was something I should have done long ago, and I'm sorry. When you came to us, a confused little orphan playing the part of a tough, full-grown man, I tried everything to drag you away from that computer and make you talk to us. I thought it was for the best. It never occurred to me that, instead of dragging you into our world, I could have entered yours. I could have learnt what interested you, and started to communicate with you in your own language. Instead I retreated to my living room and the things I knew – tea, chats with Daisy, newspapers and the ticking of the clock – and you retreated to your bedroom and lived in imaginary worlds. A space grew between us, which at some point became impassable.

So now the only way I can access you is through your friends. I added them all on Facebook, and started sending them messages. I wanted to know you, and since you view identity as what you choose to show the world, I knew that I had to see you through the eyes of others. It was surprisingly easy. Fleet Street was a long time ago now – the newsrooms in which I spent so much time are now branches of Ryman's – but what Fleet Street taught me is still alive. The cynical advice of those ancient beer-steeped editors lodged somewhere deep inside me, and was immediately accessible as I friended Marcus, Dex and the rest of them and began to tease their stories out of them. The advice worked just as well for Facebook chat sessions as for the steps of the Old Bailey. Human beings are like houses, all with elaborate security measures to keep out intruders, but all with a weakness somewhere. Find the weakness and you've found the key. With Jon the key was friendship. I think he's not very keen on the new Jeff Brennan, and wants the old one back. With Annie it was guilt for the way she kept threatening to expose you. Dex was simpler: a small cash payment and he told me everything. With Marie it was love. The poor girl still thinks this is a romance, girl meets boy and they live happily ever after. I still feel a little ashamed at deceiving her, but I learned long ago on Fleet Street that sometimes you have to lie to get at the truth.

So one by one they shared their versions of you, and I wove them together into my best approximation of the truth. I think it helped that I am so old. Everyone assumes I am harmless, and has no interest in trying to impress me, so the usual guards come down. I had to prod and steer them a little, of course, to get them to give me what I needed. People talk in generalities, but journalism deals in specifics. You have to coax the details out of them. Still, with time and patience I managed to sculpt stories out of the misshapen clay they handed me. Things became a little awkward, of course, when they were forced to speak about my own involvement in the story. But I insisted on absolute candour and, although I'm sure they held back certain things to spare my feelings, I hope I got close to the truth. Like a good, diligent courts correspondent, I wrote it all down in my notebook, organised it, and then typed it up on my trusty old Olivetti. I left out the parts that seemed particularly self-serving and fixed some of the more offensive uses of English, but otherwise I tried to let them speak. The more friends I contacted and the more stories I gathered, the higher grew the pile of used paper on my dining room table. Only Marcus held out, understandably. Appealing to his vanity almost worked, but he's got enough sense to realise that his little gravy train could be derailed by something as dangerous as the truth. So all I could do was reproduce a few relevant extracts from his Twitter feed.

It started as something for me, Jeff, but at some point it became something for you. I want you to find it one day, after I'm gone, to remove the red rubber bands and sit down at the dining room table and read it from start to finish. Now that you're launching books and even making occasional appearances on satellite television, I am worried that you might come to believe the lie so strongly that it becomes, for you, truth. Well, now I have spoken with the real owner of your blog, and therefore of your book and your fame. I have set down his version of events, in writing, on solid bond paper, so that you can never truly escape from it.

His weakness, incidentally, was for truth. Like me, he wanted the truth to be set down in black and white somewhere. Even though he will never visit my dining room or unwrap the manuscript from its rubber bands, just knowing of its existence gives him solace. He was the most enthusiastic contributor of all, in fact, sending me far more material than I could use. Pages and pages of reminiscences about his Brugnetti espresso machine and the sunlight on the canal ended up in the bin, unfortunately. But I hope I've left in enough of his words to satisfy him, and also to leave you in no doubt about the real source of everything you now call yours.

As I write this I am sitting on a log in the back garden. It used to be the apple tree, but now it's a log. I can reach down and trace the cracks in the trunk and see, through them, the dark hollow inside. It must have been dead and hollow for years, so it's a wonder it stood up so long. There's no smell of rot or decay, only the freshness of spring. Already in this dead, desiccated log I can see new lives forming. There's an indentation in the trunk where rain will collect, attracting thirsty birds; its hollow core will be perfect for nests or spiders' webs; squirrels will stow acorns in its nooks; woodlice will inhabit its dark underbelly; weeds will wind around it, binding it to the undergrowth. Life goes on, even in death. One day death will fell me, too, but my words will remain. You will find them in a neat pile on the dining room table, bound with two red rubber bands. You will read the words and something of me will live again. Something, too, of my father, my mother, Fleet Street, the old house in Tunbridge Wells, porridge bubbling on the stove and my father setting the world in motion with the turning of a key. The clock bears these memories, too. If you listen long enough, you can sometimes hear, in its mechanical ticking, a glimpse or shadow of another world. Marie, perhaps, will discover these subtleties, but I fear you will never have the time. So I had to write it down for you, and trust that one day you will read it and rescue a part of me from the oblivion that comes to us all.

Death feels a long way off, though, on a spring afternoon like this. The sun has renewed its strength now after the long winter months, and pricks my skin with a sweet warmth. I wanted Daisy to feel it, too, so with much effort I lifted her into her wheelchair and manoeuvred her through the hall, the kitchen, out of the back door and into the spring sunshine. She's sitting across from me now, in one of the old sun-loungers that you thought were too rusty to be used any more. She has soft cushions underneath her, a blanket over her legs and sunshine bathing her face and arms. She looks happier than I've seen her in a long time.

At this time of year, of course, the warmth is still short-lived. Already I can feel the sun weakening. Soon I shall go back inside, get Daisy comfortable in the living room and return to my typewriter. I'll type up the last of my notes, feed the last sheet of bond paper into the typewriter, hear for the last time the comforting clatter of keys on platen, type the final full-stop, and lay the last sheet face-down on top of the pile. I'll make sure the corners of each page are neatly aligned, and then secure the whole thing with the two large red rubber bands, one lengthwise, one crosswise. If I close my eyes I can see it now, the completed manuscript lying on the dining room table, waiting for you. I can run my fingers over it, feeling the light, Braille-like indentations left by the typewriter's clattering metal keys. I can see myself drawing the curtains for the last time, turning off the radiator and closing the door, never again to be opened by my hands.

For now, though, I still sit outside, revelling in the last warmth of the sun's rays. Randy Williams seems a long way away now, confined to a computer somewhere in the charity shop or the Owen boys' bedroom. So do you, frankly, and Marie, and Jon, and Dex, and Annie, and your namesake embarking on his new life. Even the clock, whose steady ticks measured out so much of my life, now seems irrelevant. All I've ever wanted is in this garden. For the rest of my life I will measure the passing of time not by the ticking of a clock but by events in Daisy's life. If she is ready for her sandwich, it's one o'clock. If she wants a cup of tea, it's either eleven or three. If I am ironing her best blue dress, it must be Sunday morning and I will soon need to apply foundation over her wrinkles and carefully redraw the beautiful curve of her eyebrows. I will still talk to Daisy even though she'll never answer me, I'll still get down on my knees and pull the weeds from the cracks in the path even though I know they'll grow back again, I'll still clean the house on the first Sunday of the month even though the dust will spread faster than I can remove it, and I'll still face the toughest tasks first even though life will never be child's play. I may not sell any books or appear on satellite television, but I can feel each breath of wind as it coasts across the garden. I can hear the chatter of blackbirds in the oak trees, tell the time by the length and direction of my shadow, smell in the air the sausages being fried at number 37 and the sweet blossom from the plum tree at number 41. These are things that you, strapped into headphones and entranced by glowing screens, will never experience. You will rage against the passing of time, even as you squander it in meaningless communication. You will miss something without knowing what it is, and so I fear you will always be dissatisfied, always wanting more.

As for me, I may not have many years left, but I have thousands of moments. I can stretch out each moment, savouring it like a fine wine on the tongue, sharing it with Daisy, the woman with whom I have always shared everything and hidden nothing. To you this back garden was always small and boring; to me the possibilities are limitless. Even if I die this afternoon, sitting on this log, pen and paper falling into the undergrowth to be eaten up by weeds, it will not matter. There are so many things to see, smell, touch, so much to share with Daisy, sitting on her sun-lounger with the blanket over her legs. However much time I have, I think it will be enough.